RiftWorlds Online:
Book 1: Space Opera

A LitRPG Novel by
Brian D Howard

No part of this work may be reproduced in any way without the express written consent of the author, except for small samples quoted in reviews. For permissions and other requests visit briandhowardauthor.wordpress.com. This is a made-up story—fiction. Any similarities to actual people/places/events are coincidental and unintended.

Copyright 2018 Brian D Howard
Cover by GermanCreative
All rights reserved.

ISBN: 9781720294788

Join my email list to stay up-to-date and get announcements and sometimes free goodies at my website:
www.BrianDHowardAuthor.wordpress.com/preferred

RiftWorlds Online:
Book 1: Space Opera

Chapter 1

April 23rd, 2028, started out ordinary, like every other day for the past nine hundred sixteen days.

Lights on at 6:00.

Stand in your cell until everyone's counted.

Breakfast at 6:15.

Sick call starts at 7:15.

Work call at 7:30.

Your day gets scheduled to the minute. It's a routine you get used to quickly. I doubt FCI Otisville is too different from any other federal prison.

That day, at 6:35 we sat around the chow hall at tables with hard, round, attached stools, grown-up versions of the tables I remembered from first grade. Few of us bothered talking as we shoveled watery gray eggs, and stale toast into our mouths. The new guy complained, just like every other morning this week, about the lack of coffee. It's prison, what did he expect?

But ordinary wasn't destined to last long that day.

"Danberg, git up. You got a visitor," Bruce hollered. Not that Bruce is his name. To everyone else he's Officer Hofstetter. "Don't see them as people," a more experienced inmate warned me early on. But this C/O—Corrections Officer—was nicer than the rest, so I gave him a name. Bruce isn't a bad guy for a prison guard. I bet he's a friendly guy on the outside, but with us he's quiet. No fraternizing and all that. But he'll loiter and watch the card games and sometimes chuckle at a dramatic win or loss. He's a poker guy. I'm more a blackjack guy, but poker has grown on me. Blackjack is a little easier to count cards and know when not to push your luck. Poker feels a little more dangerous. Sometimes I kinda like that.

In prison you're either a number or a last name. Behave and you get to be a last name. I'd done a good job of not getting into trouble—as long as you don't count those first few weeks. But I was only nineteen when I was arrested. At almost twenty-two I knew better. Two and a half years out of nine. That was how long it had been since anyone called me Rick. If someone did, would I even realize they were calling me?

But his announcement told everyone something unusual was going on. Visiting hours didn't start until ten, and today wasn't even a visiting day. That meant either lawyer or cops. I would've bet hard and long against lawyer. Mine was about as useful as a marked deuce.

So, I followed Bruce, leaving half of my "breakfast" behind. "Huh, wonder what that's about," someone grumbled as I walked away. His curiosity wasn't genuine.

"Um . . . ?" I asked as Bruce led me through a doorway I hadn't been through for two-and-a-half years. He didn't say anything as other guards buzzed us through two more doors until only one more stood between me and the outside world.

I'd assumed by that point I was being brought for some unannounced court thing, but the woman in that final checkpoint space was no lawyer and no court bailiff. She stood like a soldier, more so than the prison guards. No, they stood with an overt authority. She stood with a disciplined confidence in a casual black suit. Silver-rimmed black sunglasses poked out the top of a breast pocket.

"Agent Wald, I hereby remand custody of inmate 55169B, Danberg, Richard to the Secret Service."

Now for one, I'd never heard Bruce sound so formal. For another, Secret Service? How could that possibly not end badly? I sighed and stuck my hands out for standard-procedure cuffing.

"Am I going to need them?" she asked with distaste dripping off her tongue. Gulping and saying no really is the only reasonable reaction in a situation like that, right? Because that's exactly what I did.

She stood aside, clearing the way to the exit. The buzz of the door being unlocked did not ring of freedom. "Walk," she ordered.

The East Coast morning sun was bright and warm against the chill morning air and exquisite. Yet I still turned and looked back at the door closing behind us. Things in there were predictable and understandable. Everything worked on a system, on a schedule. You could rely on that. By contrast, I had no idea what was going on or what to expect. She put her sunglasses on with a one-handed style that broadcast confident cool. I bet she swaggered when she walked, but she stayed behind me on the walk to the tiltrotor helicraft. I climbed in at her prodding and she secured the hatch behind us.

"Strap in." She conserved words like she'd only been issued a fixed ration of them that morning.

Engines fired up with a whine as rotors came to speed.

"Um, can you tell me what's going on?" I had to try.

"You'll be briefed on arrival," was all she gave me before putting heavy earphones over her ears against the growing noise. I followed her lead with a pair hanging next to me. Mine didn't have the microphone hers did. My stomach lagged as the pilot lifted off.

Briefed, that didn't sound good. That had a distinct military sound to it. I'm not very military. Well, okay, I'm not at all military. I'm a computer gamer. A great one, at that, but when it really came down to it, computer games had been the main thing I excelled at. And math, sure, but math is boring. Some coding, which I'd never be allowed to use again. Most of the other classes were just boring.

Gaming had always been a focal point in my life. I can find patterns like nobody's business, learning how to game the systems. When the first VR games hit big I was ready. I was a star. I could always figure out the tricks to maximize results without as much of the tedious grinding. Some of it was math: minimize this and maximize that, compare the damage-per-second of one weapon to another. Some of it was noticing patterns and finding loopholes to exploit.

Then SecondScape came out, a VR game which overlapped game aspects with the real world. Part virtual reality and part augmented reality, it was genius from a marketing perspective. Real-world obstacles became challenges to navigate, and visual overlays could transform mundane objects into more interesting treasures or tools or weapons. It was huge. Hundreds of thousands of people played. Then it was millions. The more bleak daily life got for people and the more stomach-turning the news, the more people escaped into a world they felt they had more control over.

SecondScape had a truly slick way of taking everyday objects and turning them into dual-purpose things. You could buy and sell real-life objects for what they did in-game. Money connected in multiple ways, several of which were designed to turn in-game purchases into revenue streams for the game company; but, that didn't go the way they expected.

People logged in from around the world as it replaced the old-fashioned social media networks. Language translation and currency conversion happened in the background, so a woman selling ceramic cats in China could tell me a price in yuan and I'd hear it translated in real time into dollars in English. It was supposed to make language barriers a thing of the past, and I guess it accomplished that. It was also supposed to globalize markets by taking currency exchange hassles out of the way.

There was this odd thing where you could ask that Chinese woman what those cats cost in Euros, or Philippine Pesos. Now automatic translations are cool, don't get me wrong, but sometimes you take a paragraph in English, translate it to Russian, then translate that to Japanese, and then from there back to English. Then you laugh at the results. Sometimes they're kind of strange.

As it happened, something similar happened with currency conversions. Translate something through enough countries quickly enough and the amount you got back could be greater or lesser than the amount you started with. It was a fun little cheat. Finding the patterns took math and patience and some clever coding and some time to kill. What can I say, I was in college and I had those.

Attention to detail matters, too. It was probably just one stupid missed comma. After my arrest I never got to look at my code again. I guess it looped somewhere I hadn't expected. I thought it was an amusing thing to play around with, find an extra percent here or there. And then there was the morning I woke up to see that accounts had been replicating for each transaction. That wasn't supposed to happen. Honest.

Buying currency of other countries to mess with exchange rates is currency manipulation. That gets you a prison sentence. Don't do it. Public service announcement complete.

Agent Wald's greatest talent, on the other hand, seemed to be sitting in silence. But she breathed, so she wasn't some science fiction android. Nobody makes them that realistic.

She just sat there, opposite me but offset a little, looking through a window further ahead. She blinked. She swallowed. Her eyes shifted from place to place now and then. Her hands shifted on her lap. But her expression, reflected in the glass, never changed. It got creepy as the flight went on.

I'd say it was about forty-five minutes of that before we landed. Not like I had a watch. We had to wait more while rotors slowed before the hatch hinged open.

We landed on the roof of an office building. I didn't recognize the surrounding buildings. It wasn't a New York skyline, I could figure that much out. Two more agents stood by a door labeled, "STAIRS." I didn't need Agent Wald's prodding to know where to go, but that didn't stop her from providing it. "Let's go," she said in a voice that was anything but encouraging. A cold wind offered additional incentive.

The two agents bookended us down three flights of stairs, where another door opened onto what could have been any corporate cubicle farm. People scurried out of the way, creating a clear path to a conference room.

"Wait here," Agent Wald warned before she closed the door and left me alone in the room. Eighteen words total. Come on, the math isn't hard, and it isn't like I didn't have time to keep count.

So I had a conference room to myself. A plastic pitcher of water sat next to a short stack of recyclable cups. I tried the communications panel at the center of the table. Disabled. As if I were some criminal they couldn't trust. Yeah, I didn't blame them.

They left me waiting a while, so I helped myself to water. They wouldn't have brought me here just to poison me. I sat back in one of the cushy chairs and propped my all-white prison sneakers up on another. If they were going to make me wait I'd make myself comfortable. And man, those chairs were pretty kick. Sure, maybe I was biased because the only padded surface I'd had for the last two-and-a-half years was a thin matt, hardly even something you'd call a mattress, but still. Kick chairs.

When the suit-and-tie parade began I made a point not to sit up straight. They'd let me wait. What were they going to do, arrest me for being disrespectful? They all sat down along the other side of the table. I turned a little, laced my fingers, and gave them my very best, 'wazzup' nod. I think I was supposed to feel intimidated, but if so it wasn't working. It was feeling good. They should have kept Agent McSternface.

"Richard Danberg," one of them began.

"I prefer Mr. Danberg or Rick," I explained, not sure where the cockiness was coming from or how long until it ran out. They wanted something from me. Something they needed me for. And McSternface—her new name as long as she didn't come into the room—didn't like me being involved. That right there made me determined to play this up. Plus, I couldn't help but screw with the guy. He looked every bit the formal type, who would go for Mr. Danberg and not Rick. The full name route would be tedious for him. First point to me. Take that, G-Man.

"I am Secret Service Director William Thomas," he continued, nonplussed. I might have scored that one too early. "A situation has arisen that we need your assistance with."

"Oh?" Okay, he was better at the nonplussed thing. But I tried anyway.

"Agent Smith, fill him in."

Agent Smith? Really? This guy couldn't have been more than a few years older than I was. His hair screamed company man and his skin was paler than mine. And that's saying something. At least I wasn't the scrawniest looking guy at the table. For the first time in a while.

"Are you familiar with RiftWorlds Online?" Agent Smith had a nasal voice, that annoying kind of voice where you want to tell the kid to speak from the diaphragm.

"Um, no. I haven't had anything to do with anything 'Online' in a couple years."

"Well, things have advanced since SecondScape. RiftWorlds Online took it to the next level with a direct brain interface. This, you can't run bots on. . . ."

"I heard those were coming."

"Not coming," he corrected. "Here. RiftWorlds launched a week ago. The biggest game launch in history. The first few days everything went well, and good reviews made it even more popular. Four days ago they started a tournament. Also the biggest. As of two days ago people are unable to log out. The first few times people tried disconnecting players physically? Those players died. There are approximately 120 million people, globally, trapped in the game and unable to get out."

Well, damn. That was the first thought in my head. I said it a couple seconds later.

"And how is this my problem?"

The door opened and McSternface ushered in a woman in a blue-gray suit with an American flag lapel pin. President Hearn. Everyone at the table stood. That was enough to get me to sit up properly. I probably should have stood; I voted for her.

Men shifted positions and she sat across from me. Things had just gotten a lot more real.

"Agent Smith was just explaining the situation," Director Thomas said. "Mr. Danberg was just asking how it was his problem."

Hah. I'd made him say my name the way I wanted after all. I'll admit I felt smug about it, but also confused and a little intimidated by the President's presence. But come on, she was the President. I think that's fair.

"They told you about the people trapped in the game, right?" she asked with the same majestic voice she'd campaigned with. I'm sure she's given a lot of speeches since her inauguration, but I've missed most of them.

"Yes . . . , Madam President." Hey, I can be polite and respectful, aside from the not standing up part.

"And that people are dying?"

"Yes."

"We think they're dying because their . . . avatars are dying."

Now that's taking realism too far. I didn't want to be that immersed in a game.

"That is where you come in, Mr. Danberg."

"Umm, hey, I had nothing to do with this!" If prison wasn't a good enough alibi what was?

"Nobody is blaming you, Mr. Danberg. Far from it. Right now we're not sure who to blame, but we have a lot of people working on that, and we're not the only ones. No, this is about something more . . . close to home."

I raised an eyebrow, still not understanding the connection.

"My daughter is inside the game," she said with a resignation out of character for the woman I'd voted for.

"I'm sorry." I know, kind of lame. I didn't know what else to say.

"So that is why you are here. I have a deal to offer you, Mr. Danberg."

She already had my attention, but that really brought it to focus.

"Our best resources are working on fixing the problem. In the meantime, I need a way to keep her safe. If you go into the game, find her and keep her safe until we can get everyone out, then I will officially pardon you. You'll be a free man with no felony conviction on your record."

It was a lot to take in. For a moment I just sat there like an idiot, trying to think what to say.

"Why me?" was the best I ended up coming up with. "I've never played the game."

"Because they tell me you're the best. Because she's my daughter, and I need her kept safe. You've never had a child, but if you did, you would understand. And I want the best. So that's you."

Appeal to my ego, that was low. "Hook me up with a leveled-up avatar with good gear?" It couldn't hurt to find out more.

"The game doesn't work that way," Smith explained. "Each player can have only one avatar. Nobody else can log in to another person's. They're genetically tagged. You'll have to go in at level one."

"So people have been leveling up for a week, and for the last couple of days people haven't been able to get out so they've probably been leveling up even faster. I go in at level one and if I die in game, I die for real. And if I can find her, and keep her safe, and not get killed myself, for however long it takes for you to fix things from the outside, I get let out about five years early and don't have to tell future employers I'm a felon? Is that what you're saying?"

"There will still be restrictions to your computer access afterwards," Thomas added.

"You know you're really not selling this well. No computer restrictions afterwards. I'm not going to mess up like that again. Saying no computer access is saying second-class citizen."

"She's my daughter, Mr. Danberg. And you're supposed to be the best. If that's not the case, if you're not good enough, give us the name of someone who can do it and I'll have you flown back to Otisville."

Oh, that was not fair. Come on.

I took my time running over pros and cons. If I refused, I'd go back to prison, and someone would probably make sure parole hearings went poorly. Once I got out I'd have a hard time getting any kind of tolerable or worthwhile job. If I did it, I'd either die or come out a hero, with the President and her daughter both owing me, plus a pardon, albeit only a partial one if they forced the computer access restrictions. That meant three possibilities, two of which kind of sucked.

I'd seen this movie. Wasn't the guy's name Snake something? The hero gets betrayed in the end, right?

Hero. There's a word nobody ever used for me before. I could be the President's daughter's hero. Maybe she could keep me from getting screwed over.

Risk my life against bad odds to be a hero? Me? Who was I kidding?

"Okay," I said anyway, to my own surprise.

"We'll see about the computer restrictions when you're both back out of the game alive."

Everyone stood, and I followed suit this time. Agent Smith led the way.

"Tell me more about this game, and anything you have that might help me find her," I said from a reclining chair as they hooked up monitors and an IV. Not far away an eighteen-year-old girl lay in an identical setup.

"It's comprised of seven different virtual environments called Worlds," Agent Smith lectured. "Each world reflects a different game genre. The worlds are connected by portals called Riftways. A central hub connects all the worlds, but there are Riftways from world to world scattered all throughout the game. There's a fantasy world, a post-apocalypse world, a space opera world, steampunk, cyberpunk, superheroes, and Western."

I could understand the appeal right away. Seven radically different settings to play in. And probably the idea to take things from one genre and play them in another. Steampunk adventurers in space, or Old West wizards. Cool concept.

"The President's daughter's avatar is Elven. She's a cleric, a healer that—"

"I know what a cleric is."

"Sorry, I had to explain it to Director Thomas. Anyway, her name in-game is Silleste. Before being locked in she had left the fantasy world, we know that. She dislikes westerns and superheroes, so that narrows down a couple."

"Leaving four complete game environments to search?" And I thought the odds were bad before. This was not helping.

"I don't think she's into punk genres. I think that makes space and post-apocalypse the best places to start," Smith suggested.

Fifty-fifty was better, at least.

Leads and IVs ran all over me. They asked me if I was ready. I lied and said I was. They put a blindfold/visor-like thing around my head that covered my eyes and ears. It did a fantastic job of blocking out all outside sound. I could barely hear my own voice when I asked, "How long will it take to get started?"

Nobody answered. Instead every sense went dark, or silent, or whatever you'd call them getting no sensation whatsoever.

9

Chapter 2

I couldn't tell you how long the utter lack of brain input lasted. Visual came first, a swirling gray fog I perceived around me even though I couldn't see myself. Figures surrounded me, too mist-shrouded to make out more than their presence. I could tell they were different, and that there were seven of them. One for each World, I saw where this was going. I'd seen similar enough in other character selection screens.

A woman's voice came next, friendly and welcoming.

"You are about to enter RiftWorlds Online, a gaming experience like none other. You are approaching a universe that spans space and time in an entirely unique experience both shared with others and tailored to your individual personality. Be ready for the ultimate adventure. You will never be the same again.

"First you must create your alternate self. RiftWorlds Online takes things beyond characters or avatars. Your brain is being mapped to customize your experience with information from both your conscious and subconscious minds."

How's that for creepy and invasive? But it was too late to do anything about it now. There wasn't even a user agreement, no privacy statement about how that information would be used. There must have been something in the packaging about all that. Leave it to the government to not bother telling me about any of this.

"The first step along your journey will be to select the World you will enter. There are seven, connected by a central Hub, and connected to each other in many different places. Review the seven Worlds and step towards the one you choose."

The mist thinned some as if dispersed by a gentle breeze I couldn't feel. I still couldn't see the figures any clearer, but a box of text floated in front of each. Looking for an elf cleric from fantasy-land I figured I should read that first.

Fantasa'an, Fantasy world
The high fantasy world of Fantasa'an is a diverse world of humans and elves and dwarves, of magic and heroes. Explore the depths of magic or wage war against armies of legend. Travel magical lands and see new wonders beyond imagining. Race Options: Human, Dark Elf, Dwarf, Elf, Halfling, High Elf

A step closer and the mists parted before your classic ragged-edged, parchment fantasy world map with what looked like one huge continent ripped in half diagonally.

"You do not have to be human in Fantasa'an, which offers one of the widest selections of playable races." The disembodied voice didn't seem to be kidding. I perused the list:

Human
The most diverse RiftWorlds race, humans are the only race that can start in any world. They easily learn to get along with other races and can become any class. Arms or magic or diplomacy, if you want the least restrictions, step forward to be Human. +5 Primary Attribute of Choice, +2 Charisma +25 Health, +25 Stamina, +25 Mana, +25 Focus Most races can choose between different customization packages or backgrounds. Humans can have twice as many.
Dark Elf
Subterranean dark elves revel in secrets and worship evil gods. Prowl the darkness and own the night. Step forward and begin your quest for power. +5 Agility, -2 Strength, +2 Intellect, +3 Magic, -2 Charisma +40 Mana, +25 Resistance +10 Sneak Nightvision 40m Dark elves choose a Background (Clergy, Nobility, Scholar, Warrior).

Dwarf

Mountain dwellers, dwarves are at home above ground or below. Steel and stone and the blood in your veins are all you need. Step forward and forge your path.

-2 Agility, +5 Constitution, -2 Charisma, +5 Strength
+50 Health, +50 Stamina
Night vision 40m

Dwarves choose a Background (Clergy, Crafter, Nobility, Warrior).

Elf

Elves are graceful and quick and beautiful, but not as strong or tough. They excel at magic but can learn to become good at almost anything. Step forward, the forest awaits you.

-2 Strength, +5 Agility, -3 Constitution, +2 Appearance
+100 Mana, +25 Resistance
+10 Sneak, +10 Speed
Terrain movement penalty reduced 50%
Nightvision 20m

Elves choose a Background (Crafter, Monastery, Nobility, Wanderer, Warrior).

Halfling

Halflings are small in stature but well-liked by almost everyone. Leave your worries behind and step forward to chase your joy.

+5 Charisma, -5 Strength,
+25 Focus
+50 Evasion, +25 Resistance
+10 Sneak

Halflings choose a Background (Clergy, Crafter, Rural, Scholar, Urban).

High Elf
High elves come from a tall, mountain range home and are well adapted to cold, to mountains, and to seclusion. Their ice wine is well known. If you prefer your challenges more intellectual, step forward. -2 Strength, +2 Agility, +5 Intellect, +3 Magic, -2 Charisma +40 Mana, +25 Resistance +10 Meditate Nightvision 20m Cold and Altitude Adaptation High elves choose a Background (Crafter, Monastery, Nobility, Wanderer, Warrior).

Elf seemed a decent choice for a cleric, although dwarves looked tough. Fragile clerics brought a lot less to a party, in my experience. Hopefully she was putting the rest to good use to make up for disadvantages. Like lowered Constitution, which usually affects Hit Points and general abilities to stay alive. Dead clerics are one of the most useless things. Right there with bards, depending on the game mechanics.

I wasn't willing to move any further forward. Who knew where some point of no return was? I pulled back and scanned the other worlds.

Next I gave post-apocalypse a look.

Wastelands, Post-Apocalypse World
Society has collapsed. Will you struggle just to survive, or will you carve out your own little empire among the wreckage? Will you roam the wastes as scavenger or predator, or perhaps band other survivors together and create pockets of civilization among the wastelands? Come see what you are really made of. . . . Race options: Human

Not the most encouraging place to start, all things considered. I scanned the others to find the Space Opera description, which I found much more promising.

> ### Futura, The Space Opera World
>
> The World of Futura has many planets to explore, where military conflict can be anything from small-scale skirmishes to sweeping space armadas, and rebels struggle for independence from Federalist forces. Futura offers a wide range of available races. As for adventure, your options are as wide as the sky. High technology, alien mystics, heroic military officers, roguish pirates and smugglers, ancient lost civilizations. . . . New wonders await.
>
> Will you live by your wits and your laser blaster? Will you command a starship exploring the frontiers? Will you battle alien invaders with your comrades as ground infantry or a glamorous fighter pilot? Step forward and embrace your destiny.
>
> Race options: Human, Android, Cyborg, Dwarf, Elf, Fenurian

I already knew I'd start in either Space Opera or Wastelands. Hopefully she'd be one of those. But I had to consider the possibility she wasn't. With that in mind, I needed to figure out what I'd need to find and protect her. She was a cleric, so focusing on healing abilities would be redundant. But I'd be starting alone, so I'd need to be something that could work alone. I figured a space character would give me access to communications, travel, and scanning stuff I could use. Struggling to survive in a wasteland? Not so much.

I wasn't sure about embracing destiny, but I stepped towards it.

The mist shifted, a whirling galaxy of stars in an ocean of blackness. The view zoomed in—or it rushed at me—bringing one spiral arm closer and closer, sweeping past nebulas and stars until I saw a map of dozens of star systems connected by dashed and dotted trade-route lines. Wastelands seemed a much smaller place to search.

"You do not have to remain human if you do not want to," the woman's voice suggested. "The options are yours. Step forward to claim your race."

Figures stepped out of nebulae and galactic gasses, encircling me. Familiar text boxes floated before each. As I looked at each the figure stepped forward, giving me a clearer idea what to expect.

Human

The most diverse RiftWorlds race, humans are the only race that can start in any World. They easily learn to get along with other races and can become any class. If you want the least restrictions among the stars, step forward to be Human.

+5 Primary Attribute of Choice, +2 Charisma
+25 Health, +25 Stamina, +25 Focus
+5 starting skills at +5 each

Most races can choose between different customization packages or backgrounds. Humans can have twice as many.

Android

Androids have the most restrictions but come with several unique advantages. They can never use Spells or Prayers, have reduced Charisma, and are immune to poisons, toxins, and mind control. Androids cannot be magically healed, but instead are repaired. They have the slowest Health regeneration of all the races. Interested in immortality? Step forward and never age.

+5 Strength, No Magic, +10 Will, -5 Charisma
+100 Focus
Nightvision 30m

Androids can be built for many specialties, and android players will choose from a model (Explorer, Specialist, Soldier) to customize with multiple Packages (Armored, Assault, Built-in Equipment/Weaponry, Durability, Mobility, Quickness, Tactical).

Cyborg

Cyborgs mix human and machine parts to create a range of different capabilities. Cyborgs learn any magic at a slower rate than most other races, but they can learn it. Want the best of both flesh and machine? Step forward and see what you become.

+5 Strength, +5 Constitution, -10 Magic, -2 Charisma
+100 Stamina, +50 Health
Nightvision 20m,
Slower health regeneration, can be healed with magic and repaired.

Cyborg players will choose from customization Packages (Armored, Assault, Built-in Equipment/Weaponry, Durability, Mobility, Quickness, Retractable Claws, Tactical).

Elf

Elves are graceful and quick and beautiful, but not as strong or tough. The most mystical race among the stars, they can learn to excel at almost anything. Step forward and become the master of your future.

-2 Strength, +5 Agility, -3 Constitution, +2 Appearance
+100 Mana, +25 Resistance
+10 Sneak, +10 Speed
Terrain movement penalty reduced 50%
Nightvision 20m

Elves choose a Background (Crafter, Monastery, Nobility, Scholar, Wanderer, Warrior).

Fenurian
Fenurians are a feline spacefaring race from the forest planet Fennur. While they are new to space exploration, their influence is expanding. Whether scouting a newly discovered planet, or dogfighting in their sleek fighters, or negotiating trade deals, Fenurians are natural explorers. If your curiosity drives you to be the first to see new sights, step forward. +5 Agility, -3 Willpower, -2 Constitution +50 Stamina, +20 Speed +10 Balance, +10 Engineering terrain movement penalty reduced 50% Fenurians choose a Background (Engineering, Exploration, Military, Social).
Mordian
Mordians are a fierce and proud warrior race. Strong and tough they live for the pursuit of greatness. Whether you're a Samurai-like warrior, or a mystic leaving your monastery home, or blazing your trail across the stars, you will be the master of your own destiny. Step forward and grab it. Make your people proud! +5 STR, +5 Constitution, -5 CHA +50 Health, +10 Mitigation Speed +10 Mordians choose a Background (Exploration, Military, Monastic).

Some of them were easy to rule out. Android would be too limiting, especially alone. I had no interest in being a cat-man. The Mordian was . . . ugly, with exaggerated, harsh features that suggested angry as the default state. Space-Elf was intriguing, but when it came down to it, cyborg struck me as being a good mix of flexibility and customizability. Best of flesh and machine, indeed.

And when it came down to it, this wasn't a game for me. I had a mission. As much as Space-Elf sounded more fun, fun wasn't the goal. Cyborg struck me as the right combination of searching and protecting. I stared at the half-human, half-robot, gulped and stepped forward. The figure nodded approvingly before fading into dust along with the others.

"There are eight Primary Attributes, four physical and four mental. They range from one to one hundred.

"**Strength** affects carrying capacity, armor that can be worn, chance to hit with some melee weapons, and melee damage.

"**Agility** affects Speed, Evasion, Dodge chance, and chance to hit with ranged weapons and some melee weapons.

"**Constitution** affects Health and Stamina, ability to resist poisons and some spell effects.

"**Appearance** affects social interactions and can be more or less effective with other races.

"**Intellect** affects chance to hit with magic, vision range, and likelihood to detect concealment.

"**Magic** affects Magic Damage and Mana.

"**Willpower** affects ability to resist mental magic effects and increases Mana and Stamina.

"**Charisma** affects social interactions."

A table showed me what I had so far.

Attribute	Base	Cyborg
Strength	10	5
Agility	10	
Constitution	10	5
Appearance	10	
Intellect	10	
Magic	10	-10
Willpower	10	
Charisma	10	-2

"You may add five points to any two Primary Attributes. Which two would you like to increase?"

That one took a little mulling over. Agility and Constitution both seemed like they'd be important for survival. So one of those was probably going to happen. But Intellect seemed important, too. In the end I settled on Agility and Intellect. I've always been the type to go for getting hit less than just toughing it out.

"You are almost there," my disembodied companion said. The mists surrounding me coalesced into a humanoid form. Nothing else existed. "Will you be male or female?"

Binary gender, huh? I've played both plenty of times. I thought about it. There was too much I did not know about this game. This wasn't the time to experiment more than necessary.

"Male," I said, since it hadn't given me anything to step towards this time.

The misty figure solidified to become me standing in basic white briefs. As if I hadn't worn enough basic white in prison.

"Now we can customize your appearance. You can look as different as you like."

From there she ran me through a list of questions. Did I want to be taller? I decided on slightly shorter, thinking it would make blending in easier. I went for a little more muscular looking. Hey, a little wish-fulfillment wasn't going to hurt the mission. They had weights in prison, but all I'd managed to do in a couple of years was get leaner. Apparently, my body wouldn't bulk up nicely. So, I put on some muscle for my new me. Not over-the-top, but some.

I kept my hair pretty much the way it is, with an easy to manage undercut at the back, but I tried darker than my normal light brown. I darkened it in stages to a fairly dark brown, not quite black. A gentle red highlight made a nice finishing touch. I changed my mind and picked a rich, dark red. I could have had any color, or even combinations of colors. Blue would have stood out too much, but dark red looked wicked cool.

She wasn't kidding when she said I could appear different. I experimented with different facial features, sharpening them up some, to look a little more fierce and rugged, but keeping the overall look similar. I could adjust any measurement, and I probably could have resized individual muscles if I wanted to. Pretty darn impressive.

Then I was presented with customization options. Each had a point cost, and I was given a 120 point budget. Most of them also had some kind of visual component, and I could preview what they would look like. Armored and Durability packages looked like they had a lot of defensive beefiness but cost the entire budget. I skipped over that one.

Armored Package (120)
+5 Con +100 Toughness, -2 Appearance/Charisma, +10 Mitigation

Durability Package (120)
+5 Con +100 health, -2 appearance/charisma, +10 Mitigation

I considered a package with built-in, upgradable weapons. Knowing I couldn't be disarmed definitely had its appeal. In this case, a laser blaster bolted to my forearm. Another one I'd have to blow the whole budget on. Handy as it might be, it just wasn't cost-effective.

Built-In Weaponry (120)
One arm receives an implanted ranged weapon appropriate for your World, which can be upgraded later. Sometimes obvious and difficult to conceal.

I took a Mobility package with thruster-assisted jumping that quadrupled jump distance because that sounded useful. It came with a recovery time after each use, but also offered the biggest gain.

Mobility Package (25)
Choose one: - Booster-Assisted Leaping: quadruples jump distance but takes a short time to recover before they can be used again. - Jumping Legs: longer legs with extra joints double jump distance with no cooldown between use - Increased Running: running speed increased 50%

A Tactical package cost quite a bit but included a lot. It turned my right arm into a gleaming steel, obviously robotic one, and replaced my right eye with a goggle-like lens that stuck out a little and wrapped around the side. I liked that better than an Assault package more focused on offense.

Assault Package (65)
+2 Strength, +5 Crit Chance +15 Ranged Attack +20 Speed

Tactical Package (65)
+2 Intellect, +2 Willpower, +5 Crit Chance
+5 Evasion, +5 Ranged Attack
Double nightvision range (40m)

Ninety down, thirty more. That left me enough for either Quickness or retractable claws in one hand adding 50% to melee damage.

Quickness Package (30)
+2 Agility, +5 Evasion
+50% movement speed

Retractable Claws (25)
+50% melee damage

That was another tough one, but in the end I went with claws in my left hand. It had the obvious "I always have a weapon" appeal, and I figured I already had boosted jumping mobility, and +2 to Agility didn't seem like that big a deal. On top of that, a damage bonus that would probably scale with level overshadowed flat attribute gains.

"Only one step remains: your name. You should never use your outside name in RiftWorlds Online, and do not reveal personally identifying information about yourself. Take time to think carefully, and then speak your new name."

Oh, yeah. I hadn't thought about that part. Names were always the hardest for me. For a lot of players they weren't that big a deal. But I refused to be Cyborg215, or something like that. For me, they always mattered. Names are part of an identity. When you become famous, or infamous, in the online community, you learn to pay attention to things like that.

It could have been a head scratcher, if I had a head. I didn't seem to. Not yet, anyway. I like my name. Rick Danberg. It's got a ring to it, you know? I tried to think of a name that sounded like a hero that would come to the rescue. Jack and John were too obvious. Non-human names come easier for me, but just didn't feel right for a cyborg commando.

I looked at the appearance I'd selected. I wanted something part action hero and part bad boy, since I looked like a combination of both. A first name came to me, but the last name took more. The cybernetic arm and eyepiece led me to Steele, which I discarded immediately. But from there my brain made one of its characteristic leaps, and I spoke with confidence.

"Max. Max McAlloy." Hey, never take life 100% seriously.

"You are now ready to enter your new life in RiftWorlds Online, Max McAlloy." She sounded proud, an interesting touch. "Brace yourself!"

Chapter 3

The sudden existence of reality came with the same abruptness as tripping over a bump in the sidewalk. I blinked my eyes at the bright light high in a cloudless blue sky, shielding myself with a shiny hand made of who knows what metal alloy.

That jarred me into focus. Oh, yeah. The game. This was more real than I expected. A mix of earthy scents drifted on a chilling breeze. A gray jumpsuit and black, sneaker-like shoes were far too familiar, which was disappointing. At least the shoes weren't the white of prison sneakers, and gray was a change from khaki. The fingers of my left, flesh hand ran over smooth fabric.

Rough canyon walls sloped gently up away from me. Blue-green grass lined a canyon floor dotted with purple-leafed low shrubs. I squatted down, checking out the grass. This was no rendered field; these were individual blades of grass. They moved independently. I plucked one. It broke with a smooth edge, the first hint it wasn't real, but it even had a scent. Something herbal. It reminded me of one of the spices in Mom's kitchen, but I couldn't place it. I considered tasting it, but decided to just drop it. It fell realistically, drifting several inches in the breeze.

"You are in the Keldor Mountain Range, not far from Outcrop, a small spaceport town, on the planet Relkit III," my helpful narrator explained. "Relkit is one of many worlds within the galactic Federation of races. Take some time to explore, get a feel for your mobility. Let's start by heading west, directly ahead." At least there was a tutorial, then.

I walked forward, which felt no different from walking normally. A smooth dirt trail wandered through the canyon, easy to follow. I ran forward, and a blue bar came into view towards the upper left wherever I looked.

"This is your Stamina Bar. Strenuous activities deplete it. Things that raise your Constitution will give you more Stamina. Penalties apply to most actions below 25%." Okay, pretty straight-forward.

The canyon curved while the stamina bar slowly decreased. I stopped before a cluster of large boulders, and the bar replenished very quickly.

"You recover Stamina whenever you aren't exerting yourself, and especially when resting. Cyborgs recover Stamina very quickly. Those boulders are taller than people can jump up to the top of, but you have thruster assisted leaping. Try it."

If that didn't sound like oversimplifying I wasn't sure what would. They were about the height of a two-story house. Sure, just trot over there and jump, right? Fine, leap of faith. I ran. I jumped.

Ports opened at the back of my shoulders and hips and, sure enough, I sailed up to the top of a boulder, landing neatly on my feet. The ports closed. I reached around, and the jumpsuit didn't seem any worse for wear. That was handy. A cool-down timer started, counting down from five seconds.

> **+100 XP (100 total)**

Once the timer reached zero I hopped down, and similar ports at the bottom of my feet let me land lightly. Okay, that was cool. A couple stories up and down I could do. Good to know. It also reassured me that yes, things would be pretty much as simple as just do it. That would speed up the learning curve.

The patch of boulders here looked like they had tumbled down one side of the canyon. It would make a good ambush point. That would've been a fun welcome to the game. Good to see they were nicer than that. I trotted along the continuing path to see what would happen next.

Something hit me from behind and knocked me down. So much for nice and not ambushing me! I got to my hands and knees to face a red and blue six-legged lizard, looking me in the eye. Or lens, since it seemed to be looking at my right eye. What, a lizard that ate bionic parts? That's not creepy at all, right?

"You have been attacked by an alien creature." So helpful, stating the obvious. "Get up and punch it while it decides what to do. Your likelihood of hitting depends in part on the ratio of your Melee Attack attribute to your opponent's Evasion."

Who was I to argue? I hopped up to my feet, more agile than real-world me, and I slugged it good. Metal fists, it turns out, are decent to punch with. Didn't hurt my hand at all. A red bar showed up over the lizard-thing and shortened about an eighth or so.

"Enemies you fight have a red Health bar. You do, as well. Penalties occur below 50%, and if it runs out completely, you die. You will need to kill this lizard before it kills you. It will probably eat you if you do not defeat it."

It lunged at me, hissing and snapping like some twisted chihuahua-crocodile crossbreed. Scales around its neck flared out. I managed to avoid it and I punched at it again, but missed. We went back and forth, and it scored a bite on my leg. It hurt. Not mind-wracking agony, but it was still real, genuine pain. My health bar showed up, except it was red on top and silver on the bottom, then it got marginally shorter.

"Cyborgs are part human and part machine. The red part of your Health bar represents damage that can be healed magically or will heal over time. The silver part represents damage that must be repaired."

The critter lunged again, but this time I was ready. I hadn't been distracted by hearing about the Health bar because, honestly, I'd already figured that part out. So instead of catching me off guard like it might have, I bopped it good on the nose.

Unarmed Combat Skill +1 (1)

"You have gained a point in a skill. The more you use a skill, the better at it you will become. You have also scored a critical hit, doing bonus damage. The higher your Crit Chance is, the more likely a critical hit is. Critical hits add your Crit Power to the damage you inflict." Yep, she was a master of the obvious. The critter's Health bar dropped by about double what it had before. About two-thirds remained. "Try using your claws," she suggested.

I looked at my fleshy left hand. The critter was either dazed or waiting patiently. That would be pretty stupid, but this was the tutorial, after all. I wouldn't expect them to do that later. I clenched and unclenched my hand, expecting some kind of mental command, and, sure enough, claws popped into place. One sprouted out each knuckle, nasty serrated blades about as long as my outstretched hand and fingers. Blades coming from between the knuckles would have made more sense, but they worked. At least they didn't hurt or seem to cause any damage coming out.

I punched at the lizard-thing with them, jabbing them deep into it. The thing screeched a sound somewhere between a hiss and a squawk, about as pleasant as a screaming baby. The health bar dropped much more dramatically this time, losing about half what was left. Okay, I could handle this. I took a couple more swipes, during which it made more feeble biting attempts, before I caught it with a good slash that finished it off. The claws retracted automatically, retreating away without leaving a mark behind. I don't think they were actually stored anywhere in side my hand.

> **Unarmed Combat Skill +1 (2)**

> **+300 XP (400 total)**

I half expected a selection ring around it and another oh-so-helpful suggestion I check it for loot. Nope. Nothing but a corpse. But, after a little looking around, I found a dead body a couple of meters away.

It looked human, face down, with blue hair and a gray jumpsuit suspiciously similar to my own. Either that was just the local fashion, or someone actually failed the tutorial. As uninteresting as the jumpsuit was, I couldn't help but hope it was just a local fashion. I wasn't ready to lose that much faith in humanity.

I rolled it over and spotted a pistol. Ah, reward for checking, I guess. The body had what looked much more like a gunshot wound in its chest than any kind of lizard wound.

"You now have your first weapon. Notice the counter displaying the number of shots remaining."

	**Item acquired: Basic Laser Pistol** This simple laser pistol doesn't look like much, but it's functional.
Range	50m
Accuracy	+1
Damage	25
Shots	20
Durability	15/50

The weapon itself wasn't terribly interesting or unique looking. Rounded edges, but still basic pistol. A counter on the back under the rear sight read 20. And here I'd been hoping for one of those games with unlimited ammo. Oh, well.

"Weapons will generally come with basic, automatic holsters. Simply put it where it feels right to assign that holster location for that weapon."

If it hadn't been for the jumping experience, I might've been confused at that point. But sometimes you just have to roll with it. I holstered it on my right hip and, boom, a holster and belt took place to hold it. Basic black, just what I expected.

I tend to pick up these games quick. If not, I probably wouldn't have ended up in jail and then been recruited to rescue the President's daughter. I could be sipping beer on a ratty sofa blowing off class coming up on graduation. Just then I'd settle for the cold beer.

Lacking cold beer, I figured it was time to move on. The trail wound up to a set of switch backs along one canyon wall. This was prime ambush territory, so I kept the pistol out and ready. Reaching the top of a ridge would have been anticlimactic if it weren't for the view.

A broad valley sprawled away into an expanse of blue forest. A red-and-brown raptor circled casually at about my altitude over the trees. The mountains curved outwards in both directions, a mix of rounded edges and jagged peaks, the taller ones capped in white. Off to the north, thanks to a pop-up map that showed what I'd explored and bits of what I could see from here, a small spaceport perched on a plateau jutting out from the range.

A ship angled in from over the forest and lowered itself to land, too far away to see details. Magnification wasn't part of my packages. I'd watch for that in upgrade options down the road.

The trail followed the ridge before dipping down into the range again. It looked like a solid day's hike to the spaceport, which seemed a likely destination. A transport and communications hub seemed a good place to start my search for Silleste. I trotted off, alternating between faster and slower to maintain my Stamina bar. I didn't feel any exhaustion from it, which was nice. Track days in high school had sucked, but no stomach cramps in this life, it seemed.

I came into a valley, too gentle to call a canyon, but still clearly defined not just by the path snaking through it. Scraggly trees scattered up the slopes and huge boulders sat here and there along the trail. More ambush territory.

I told myself I was getting paranoid, but I figured as soon as I stopped expecting an ambush the game would throw one at me. I had plenty of experience learning there was only one good side of an ambush to be on. I ran towards one of the boulders and leapt to the top, landing in a crouch behind the tallest part of it.

A soldier in gray combat gear toting a rifle walked along, his head scanning side to side. I flattened myself down, pistol out.

"You are about to encounter your first dangerous opponent. How you choose to act will determine your first character class. Will you hide behind a rock and attack from behind after he passes? Will you fire from cover? Will you charge and take the fight up close? Or will you observe and then let him pass? Choose your destiny." A text box appeared with more.

Quest: Intro to Tactics
Defeat your first armed opponent to select your starting Class.

Interesting way to pick a class. Nicer than scrolling through a list, but this time I would have preferred a table of bonuses. I needed to play this right if I was going to accomplish my mission. And live, let's not forget that part.

The guy kept coming. A decision would be made for me if I didn't make one. If I let him get close we'd be fighting in tight quarters, which would minimize the range benefit of his rifle. Plus I had claws, which seemed like an advantage. But here I had cover and he did not. If he got close, I would still have that option, but from a maximum-benefit-minimum-risk standpoint, sniping from here won out.

I took aim and fired.

Chapter 4

Somebody once said, "The most unfair fight is a sniper ambushing someone." Somebody else said, "Never fight fair if you want to win." I gotta say, I agree with both. I kind of felt sorry for this guy. Here he was, just hiking down the trail, minding his own business, on some patrol he probably thought was boring as all get out. He probably walked this route at least every day.

Kind of like the perimeter guards at the prison. Except those were real people. This guy had to be a computer-generated non-player character instead of a real person. Because if I logged into a game like this, which had to be on the pricey side, and my role was to just patrol a mountain trail waiting to be ambushed by newbies . . . I'd want my money back.

I figured he was about fifty meters out, my pistol's maximum range. The shot zipped right over his head. And with it went the element of surprise.

Pistol Skill +1 (1)

I got off another shot while he was scrambling for the limited cover his position could provide, catching him in the side. His Health bar showed up and dropped down by about a quarter. Three more hits like that; that sounded doable.

He found a large rock to kneel behind, but more of him was exposed than I was. We both aimed, both using solid rock to steady our weapons. His was almost certainly more accurate and more powerful than mine.

We both fired. Both shots hit rock, mine doing nothing and his throwing a shower of dust and debris. Yep, his was definitely more heavy-duty. After that we both fired away, trying to stay as much in cover as possible.

I managed a hit on him, taking him down to about half, and he hit me in the shoulder. It hurt more than the lizard thing had, and my Health bar dropped about a quarter. I slid backwards and let myself drop off behind my boulder. His weapon hit harder, but I was tougher, all things considered.

> **Pistol Skill +1 (2)**

I sprinted across to another rock and crouched down. It was his move now. I aimed at the open space he would have to come through to get to me.

It was nine deep breaths before I saw him. I can't tell you why they were deep breaths. I wasn't winded at all, wasn't shaking from adrenaline. But I had my target again. Naturally, I missed, and he ducked back. Things were feeling stalemated.

"This is your last chance to surrender," the man announced.

Really? I shoot at him out of the blue and he'd be willing to accept my surrender? Either he was far more forgiving than I was, or he was ballsy.

Two clunk sounds preceded a round object bouncing to land pretty much at my feet. A grenade? Seriously?

It was a good thing this game worked through a neural connection instead of any other interface. Sure, in many games a grenade isn't fatal. But instinct kicked in and I jumped. Hard. I'd forgotten in that moment I had boosted jumping, which took me even higher. And a little forward. By the time the blast happened the boulder was between me and most of the blast.

As it was, it took me down to about 20% left. And I was coming down on the other side of the boulder. The same side as a guard about to step around and finish me off. He hadn't caught me leaping to . . . safety?

I turned down and came down behind him. I wish I could say I came down claws ready. Or I shot him in the back on the way down. Either of those would have sounded cooler than what actually happened.

I landed behind him a bit like an idiot. I tried to turn in mid-air, but it seems the game had more physics than I was prepared for. Or there was some Aerial Acrobatics skill I needed to level up first. So we both spun around to face each other. The remainder of my health bar pulsed at me, warning me, without any pop-ups telling me what penalties I was under.

Normally, this is where I might point out that pistols work better in close quarters than rifles. Which on paper is true. The guy was better than I gave him credit for. He full-on butt smacked with his rifle and knocked the pistol out of my hand, then brought it back around and up to his shoulder.

Any gun wins in a fist fight. So I knew this was going to end badly if I didn't do something. You know when a rifle is at its least advantageous? In a wrestling match. I dove and tackled him.

We rolled on the ground, at first trying to get control of the rifle. We rolled right, we rolled left. Stirred-up dust caught in my throat.

He was bigger, and knew what he was doing, but I had one edge he did not. Actually, it was four edges. Serrated ones. I snicked them out and punched him in the gut over and over in classic "button mashing" glory until he stopped moving. And then a couple more times, well past the point where his red Health bar ran out

I rolled off him and got up to my knees, noticing the decrease in my blue Stamina bar. It was down about 10%, if that. I'd expected more. That +100 from being a cyborg helped.

Overlapping transparent windows popped up when the guy died. I checked over them in order, dismissing as I went.

Quest completed: Intro to Tactics
Quest Rewards:
Level gain
Class gain

Level 2 gained!
+15 Health
+15 Stamina
+6 Mana
+12 Focus
+5 Primary Characteristic Points
+10 Skill Points

Class gained: Hunter
+3 Agility, +3 Con
+100 Stamina
+10 Evasion, +10 Speed
+5 Sneak, +5 Dodge, +10 Track
Choose one:
+5 Melee Attack, +5 Ranged Attack
+10 Melee Attack
+10 Ranged Attack

Not bad.

The man's body lay in a pool of blood. Now I had the time to notice details I had been too busy before. I suspected he was designed with some randomness around a basic template. Who knew how many I'd see before I found duplicated faces. Or would I? He was not wearing the ever-fashionable plain jumpsuit, but pants, boots, a shirt and jacket. The shirt and jacket were a mess, especially on the shredded side with all the claw damage. It was a detailed game.

I took things that looked valuable. He had two small rectangular things that looked like ammunition cartridges on his belt. I took those and put them on my belt, yielding a pop-up confirming them as:

Basic E-Rifle Magazines (50) x2

The small communicator on his left shoulder I debated with myself about. On one hand, it was bound to be valuable. But would it make me trackable? I left it. If they were standard issue I could get one later if I needed one.

The rifle rounded out my gains for this encounter.

Item acquired: Basic Laser Rifle	
Range	75m
Accuracy	+5
Damage	50
Shots	50
Durability	35/50

That definitely looked like an upgrade. I kept the holstered pistol, though, seeing no reason to discard a usable weapon with three shots left.

I had another weapon, and a class. Hunter sounded about right. Hunt a woman down and then protect her. Hunter was a good start. Certainly better than Dead Soldier.

I waited around while my Health bar inched its way back to full. So far, I only seemed to be taking damage to the red bar that recovered naturally. Did it take a specific kind of damage to hit the silver bar? Or did that start later in the tutorial or after? Newbs die easy in a lot of games, and I wasn't convinced this was one of the more forgiving ones. In the process I confirmed I healed faster when resting, so there was that. When I was fully recovered and ready, I hopped up and trotted down the path, toting my new rifle and prepared for more. I was especially on the lookout for anything that looked like a potential ambush.

Generally, a tutorial will tell you when you've finished it. Given the lack of such an announcement, it was safe to assume I was not done. Or it was not done with me. Tutorials exist to teach new players valuable lessons. I kind of figured "avoid ambushes" was one the developers wanted to teach the newbies. Learning quick is an important element of survival in new games. I was determined to be a quick learner. Especially considering the potential consequences for not.

"It is time to learn about your character sheet. It will display whenever you want it to."

More tables popped up in front of me. I stopped, not wanting to trip—or get caught off guard by another patrolling sentry—while studying new information.

The sheet had four main sections: Primary Attributes, Secondary Attributes, Tertiary Attributes, and a short skill list. I started with Primary Attributes:

Primary Attributes	
Strength	15
Agility	18
Constitution	18
Appearance	10
Intellect	17
Magic	0
Willpower	12
Charisma	8

All in all, not bad, I supposed. Charisma was lower than I would have liked, especially if I was going to have to ask around to find Silleste. The game wasn't going to just offer me a quest with NPCs (Non-Player Characters) leading me from place to place until I found her. If it did, I was going to be really creeped out about what that meant for the game reading my brain and acting accordingly. I had five points to spend on these, so I popped them into Constitution. Sometimes, survival is about being tough.

Secondary attributes started at 100, modified by Primary Attributes and class and race modifiers. Cyborg and Hunter did good things to Stamina, considering these all maxed out at 1000 and I was already 20% there.

Secondary Attributes	
Health (CON)	175
Stamina (CON/STR)	225
Mana (WIL/Mag)	16
Focus (Will)	122

Tertiary Attributes were the longest section, and had important numbers. Attack bonuses, Evasion to take less damage, chances for critical hits and how hard those crits would be . . . all good things adding to survival, which had to be the primary mission, no matter what the suits outside said. Can't rescue anybody when you're dead, right? As for Ranged vs Melee Attack, I decided five each was better than dumping it all in one spot.

Tertiary Attributes	
Ranged Attack	121
Melee Attack	116
Evasion	126
Toughness	0
Resistance	0
Melee Damage (STR)	15
Magic Damage (MAG)	0
Crit Chance	17
Crit Power	12
Mitigation	0
Speed	28

The skills list looked like it needed work. But I was just starting, after all. Presumably it only listed the skills I had. No way those were all the skills the game had.

Skills
Unarmed Combat 2
Dodge 5
Pistol 2
Track 10

I had ten skill points to spend. I put three into Unarmed Combat, three into Pistol, and four into Dodge. Early on, fighting skills would probably play large roles in survival.

An inventory tab listed what gear I had, with basic stats for everything. Most likely anything could have some possible use or stat modifier. Except for the jumpsuit, which only sported Durability.

The sun crept across the sky and shadows changed accordingly. Clouds trekked from horizon to horizon. I passed through valleys and over ridges. A sweet scent wafted from a patch of orange flowers. Dust stirred up, smells, the level of detail impressed me. Had someone programmed this terrain, or had some algorithm generated it?

About half the day passed before I came to another wide, shallow valley. Burning wreckage bookended the valley, with a line of what I thought was the demise of a vehicle convoy at one end and the smoking corpse of a larger air vehicle of some kind at the other. A group of soldiers and a more ragtag group skirmished among rocks and shrubs and tall grasses in between.

"Welcome to the end of the RiftWorlds Online tutorial," my ever-present narrator said. "One last thing to discover is that in most lands you will encounter rival groups or factions. Choose carefully which side you help, for your friends and enemies can have a direct impact on your game experience."

Game experience. There was a euphemism if I've ever heard one. Life or death. Pick your friends and enemies carefully. Got it.

"Federal troops and rebel Separatists struggle for control of this system. Will Relkit remain a part of the galactic Federation? Will their fight for independence lead to freedom or civil war? What part will you play in a drama that spans countless systems and planets? It is time for you to choose your destiny. Welcome to RiftWorlds Online. Good luck."

Quest: Choose a Side

Federalists and Separatists are clashing nearby. Choose which side to help. Defeat all opponents.

Chapter 5

Figuring out which side was which was not too hard. Black uniforms on one side, multiple colors on the other. Ten on six. Rebels are always the underdogs, right? Now and then I'd like to see the "Brave imperialists holding out against insurmountable odds by the brutal rebellion."

Was it the easy decision it presented itself as? Was this Federation the source of law and order in the galaxy, or were they tyrants? Were the Separatists noble freedom fighters, or ruthless terrorists? The truth might have been anything. No, my choice was about more pragmatic issues. On one hand, side with the winners. On the other, side with whoever could help me more. Federal troops already had the numbers advantage. Me joining in would only go so far to win favor. No, when you need their help, the underdogs will always appreciate you more.

With that covering the strategic decision, the next question was more tactical. What did I need to do? I was near the centerline of the field. I got down in what grasses I had available and crawled forward. It was time to put some of those Sneak points to use, and maybe get some more while I was at it.

The outnumbered six mostly held ground, crouched down low or just plain lay belly-down. The Federals crept forward, crouching low. Some would fire while the others rushed to a cover spot. Classic leapfrogging.

The Federals would move past my position. Crossfire it was. I crept forward more until I found a vantage point I liked, gaining another handy point of Sneak. The rifle display showed forty-six shots before reloading. It looked like the range would be fine. I steadied the rifle and aimed. The Federals moved in a disciplined manner: fire, move, switch. Fire, move, switch. There was always enough firing to keep the Separatists from getting good shots off. Since nobody was firing at me yet, I didn't have that disadvantage.

Three raised up to fire, and I started with the one on the right. I was rewarded with a floating, "Critical Hit! 62 damage!" and his Health bar suffered accordingly. Yep, Rifle damage plus my Crit Power. Simple math so far. He and the guy in the middle turned as I missed the middle one, despite a brief notification of "+1 Rifle (1)."

Laser fire lanced across the valley in all directions as the rebels took full advantage of the distraction to fire on running federalist soldiers. Federalists fired back on the run, but their health bars showed more abuse than the rebels.

I took a "grazing hit" to my right arm, for 25 HP, so either they had wimpier rifles—which I doubted—or a graze was a half damage shot. If there was some random element to damage, I hadn't seen it yet. What I'd seen so far suggested fixed damage rather than randomized. Not that I was thinking that during the actual fighting.

I got off more shots, missing more than hitting, as soldiers tried to find the compromise between ducking behind cover and staying in formation. Each group of three seemed to stick together, leaving their leader identifiable. Whether killing him would affect the rest or not I didn't know, but he certainly had to be worth more XP.

But before I could even start on him I had to deal with the group of three whose attention I'd drawn. You know, by shooting one of them in the back pretty hard. All were hurt more than I was, but one of them only barely. That still seemed like solid three-to-one odds, which did not thrill me. Oh, for a grenade, right?

They advanced gradually, although still at longer range. I had some time before they were on top of me, but only so much. Maybe if I had started in Superhero World I'd have more powerful claws, in both hands, and some kind of nifty area-effect attack with swooshing visual effects. Then I'd leap at them, probably covering the distance in one jump.

Jump! That had to give me some tactical advantage. I took another aimed shot, hoping for a headshot on the grounds that it ought to do some kind of extra damage, and got him . . . in the gut. He stumbled a step and dropped about half the health he had left. I ducked my head down against their counter shots and snuck quick peeks in both directions.

No boulders in sight. Low brush, tall grasses, and the occasional tree. Some trees were big enough to cower behind. A couple looked big enough to get up into. Would that give me a high-ground advantage, or just leave me trapped in a place I couldn't dodge without falling?

More shooting to do before figuring that out.

One rose from his crouch and must have pulled the trigger. Mostly he shook his gun in frustration. Out of ammo or . . . jammed? Could a laser rifle jam? Malfunction, I suppose. Not the most reassuring thought either. If his could, mine probably could, too. Pistol and claws against three—two?—rifles wasn't any better odds.

But his delay gave me a valuable opportunity. I lined up careful aim and fired like mad. Good old-fashioned button-mashing where you just hit a button over and over until something dies. Several shots missed, but he never fired back before he fell, dead.

> **+200 XP (1200 total)**

His two buddies weren't stupid, and they took full advantage of my distraction. By the time I caught on they had separated and gotten a lot closer. The more I focused on one, the more his partner would have an easier time gunning for me.

Maybe the game wanted me to pick the easier fight. There was probably an important lesson in there somewhere, but first there was some more important learning about killing paired hunters.

Hunter. That's what I was supposed to be. If they were going to fight like the soldiers they were, I needed to fight like a hunter. That meant smarter. I had the high ground, and I had a jumping boost they didn't know about. I fired shots off a little wild to distract them while I scoped out the terrain again. There, a low dip. From above, nothing noteworthy. But it would give me cover from downhill. That was an improvement already.

I took another graze, and a pack of misses, on my way before I dove into it, hitting soft ground hard. Not hard enough to take damage, but it still hurt. I rolled over to the edge, glad to have more Agility than I could claim in real life, and took my first aimed shot. That got me another critical hit notification, along with "+1 Rifle (2)," and finished that one off for another 200 XP. I was glad I picked the more injured one first.

The other one fired but less of me was exposed now. He was closer, about thirty meters. More virtual button mashing commenced as bits of dirt exploded to rays of super-hot laser light. Or whatever it was. All I knew was the rifles shot red rays of burny pain.

Most of my shots went wild. Some of them hit him as he advanced, and I got him low on health before the gun stopped firing.

Zero, the display under the sight taunted. Crud. I ducked down and back out of his sight, and I drew my pistol. His head would come over the ridge, and I'd plug it. Or put a hole in it, anyway. I had everything lined up, so ready, so proud of myself. I was hurt below half, but I was pretty sure one more hit and he was mine.

What I saw was not a crew-cut, helmetless head. What I saw was a smaller thing, about fist-sized, that bounced on the ground and bumped off my forehead.

Grenades in this game, at least the explosive ones I'd seen so far in Space Opera World—yeah, yeah, the one, but still—were gray spheres with one black stripe. This one sat in the grass inches from my nose.

Military people probably have some special things they're trained to do in situations like these. Pick it up and throw it, maybe. Or pray. As a proper Manly-Man-Hero-Guy™ I grabbed it up, rolling up to my feet in an impressive display of ground gymnastics. I threw it just past him and let his own body shield me from the blast.

Okay, no. That's not what I did. What I did was far less manly. You ever seen someone startled when a fly or a bee landed on their nose? And they did this spastic thing where they're all, "Ah! Ah! Git it away"? Yeah. It was kind of like that. I flailed away with both hands, batting it away and over the ridge. But it did get over the ridge before it blew.

The ridge sheltered me from some of it. After the noise and concussion battered me and might have stripped off my face from the feel of it, I was left with four hit points, and a flashing, scary-short Health indicator. I also couldn't see anything that wasn't part of the game interface, and my ears were ringing.

I waited for the end. What else could I do? I couldn't hear footsteps over the stupid tinnitus, or see anything. I still felt around for the pistol, which I found. For all the good it would do me.

My Health bar ticked up. Black turned to gray. The Health bar ticked up again, and the gray became different shades of gray. And then I could see, and the hissing static in my ears faded away. I poked my head up over the ridge and into the valley.

+200 XP (1600 total)

Chapter 6

The action had wound down; bodies lay strewn about like scattered litter. Two rebels remained, one kneeling and tending to the other. Victory. Cool. But ow. In most games, being hurt doesn't affect you until you run out of Health. Just then I could have done with less realism. My silver health bar, representing the cybernetic parts of me, didn't move. I'd taken damage there, finally. No natural healing for that part. I really hoped leveling up included automatic healing. It often did, and I was so close to level.

Quest completed: Choose a Side
Quest Rewards: +300XP (Total 1900)

The almost-forgotten narrator voice came back one last time:
"Congratulations. You have completed the tutorial. You have learned the basic of how to navigate and survive RiftWorlds Online. A vast amount of content awaits or you to explore. More than any one person can experience. Your next step should be to find and talk to a class trainer. Perhaps the people below can help you with that...."

Quest: Find the Hunter Trainer
Seek out and talk to the Hunter Trainer in nearby Outcrop.

Things were bound to get harder from here. Tutorials are usually more forgiving than the rest of a game. That did not bode well for the rest of my time here. I was going to need better gear.

GrenadeDude had been close to the ridge, counting on the blast being on my side. The whole back of him was... gross. Let's just leave it at that. I doubted I'd find anything lootable, and even if there was I didn't really want to touch . . . that. I shuddered instead and headed down the slope to the other two.

These were in much better shape. You know, for people who had been laser-burnt to death. No jumpsuits for these guys. Black uniforms with jackets and pants. I considered taking a jacket, just so I wouldn't look like a newb toon. But I also didn't want to be mistaken for one of the Federalists. I wasn't sure I wanted to take sides just yet, and if I did, looking like my chosen enemy would probably not win me friends. And that's what I needed.

Their rifles looked better than mine, so I grabbed one.

Item acquired: Federalist Laser Rifle	
In most ways just a basic rifle, but more accurate and with slightly better range.	
Range	85m
Accuracy	+10
Damage	50
Shots	50
Durability	45/50

Yep, a little better than mine. Any upgrade is good. I kept it, shouldering it with a sling that appeared when I tried, and worked my way down the slope.

The hurt one kept an eye on me as I approached until he tapped the woman wrapping bandages around his abdomen. The game didn't offer up exact hit point numbers, but he was down to a short stub of Health. Bandages covered four separate wounds.

She stood up, drawing a pistol. The move would have looked better had she not winced while standing and nearly fallen over. HurtGuy—no name floated over his head, so I gave him one—raised his rifle and both gave me skeptical looks.

"Hey, if I was gonna kill you wouldn't I have done that from further away?" I held up my flesh hand and my alloy hand, wondering if racism was a thing here.

"True," the woman conceded. "Who are you?"

"Max," I said, puffing up my chest and trying out the whole heroic main character thing. "Max McAlloy." I felt a little heroic. I had taken on more than my share and come out . . . well, battered, but winning. These two had survived against seven. Three more would have tipped the scales, which meant I saved their lives. Of course, they were NPCs and might not even care.

"I'm Reck," the man said, setting down his rifle with a groan. I'd guess he was in his thirties, but his eyes looked older, with extra creases reaching across his temples.

"You look like a wreck," I joked.

"Have you seen your . . . face?" the woman asked. "I'm Dara. Thank you for helping out. Things weren't looking good there for a while. We were already a bit messed up when we ran into these guys." A smear of grease darkened her left cheek; a bruise highlighted the other.

I didn't have a mirror, obviously, and I couldn't pan a camera around to see myself. I padded my face with my fingers—the flesh ones. On about half my face I found metal skull. Wonderful. I didn't look Terminator enough already, huh? I half expected a further Charisma reduction, so I checked. No change there, although Appearance had taken a hit from 10 to 6. Wonderful. Their Health bars were recovering about twice as fast as mine. Was it going to take magical healing to make me appear normal again? Or some tissue-regeneration bath? All the more motivation to find that elf cleric, huh?

"So, what happened?" I asked. Dara wasn't bad looking, with a decent figure under worn and torn improvised fatigues, but unless she liked her men shiny I suspected flirting wouldn't go far.

"We were out scouting. We ran into some trouble and were on our way back to report it when we ran into these lovely individuals."

Reck stood up with another groan. About half his health was back. "We should get moving."

"Where are you headed?" I was pretty sure I knew, but it never hurts to ask.

"Outcrop. The starport," she explained, packing up her medical supplies into a bag she slung over her shoulder. She hesitated, looking back and forth between Reck and me.

"You're with the rebellion, right?" Hello there, elephant in the room.

"Yes. You're at least no friend of the Federation?"

"No, I guess not."

"Well, then here's the thing," she said, standing, "We have a hideout in the city. I can't tell you where just yet. You can come with us to the gate. After that, if you want to be part of us, we'll arrange a meet."

"Well, are we going?" Reck asked over his shoulder as he set off.

It was still going to be quite a hike on foot, but the vehicles were toast. So off we hiked. Reck set the pace, limping along, and we had no problems catching up. I felt more comfortable once I'd healed up—the organic parts, anyway. My face was still about half missing. It had to have been a nasty sight. The missing chrome Health still gnawed at me, a lingering vulnerability.

"So, what's the story here, anyway?" I asked when I got bored with the quiet and had seen enough mountain views to stop being impressed by them.

"With?"

"The Rebellion. How come?"

Dara squinted one eye and raised the other eyebrow as if they had to balance each other out.

"I'm new here."

"The Federation kept things peaceful and good for a good hundred years or so. Now there are new rules all the time, each one more oppressive than the last. They've rotten from within with corruption. They want to control all interplanetary commerce. They board ships at random for inspections, and confiscate cargos with new, trumped-up charges. Licensing fees for all kinds of things. Increased taxes, increased surveillance and scrutiny. We stand for freedom and independence."

I could understand that. I'd heard the story plenty of times in other settings, and not just games. My time in prison might have biased me a little. Still, not my mission.

"Head down," Dara barked after about three hours of hiking. We all took cover where we could, glad we were off the sheer rock face with its barely-wide-enough-to-walk-on trail.

Some kind of hover Jeep cruised over, well within rifle range, with four soldiers on top and a laser machine gun on the bottom. The soldiers faced forward, talking about something. They passed by at a good running pace, not showing any signs of noticing us.

"There's a mining operation not far from here," Dara explained. "They arrest anyone who gets close."

That sounded like a source of quests, something to keep in mind for later. I marked the current position on the map as "Mining Base Quests nearby."

"Well, they say it's a mining operation. But they have a lot of guards around it for something as simple as mining. No, there's something there they don't want anybody seeing. Classic Federation. Anywhere they don't want you to go is off limits, trespassing."

"Don't get arrested," Reck warned, coming out of a moping silence he'd been nursing, the hangover of grief, I suspected.

"Let me guess, no right to a trial?"

"Oh, that's not it, you get a trial. Not even a show trial, at that. But they happen at far away planets. So they can have an 'impartial' jury, they claim. Usually they're on planets either nobody would want to live on or nobody can afford to live on. So there you are, halfway across the Federation, with nothing. Even if you're found not guilty, you're still stranded somewhere you either hate or can't afford, and by this point you've got no job, so no income. Then they get you for vagrancy, or you end up in indentured servitude. Vagrants tend to become fuel miners. Do you want to guess the life expectancy of fuel miners?"

'No, not really," I admitted. They were really playing the recruitment angle. If I were here just to play, I'd have gone for it. "But I'm sorry, it's not my mission. I'm here looking for someone. An elf, a healer. Her name's Silleste."

"Maybe she can fix your face," Reck taunted.

"When we get in I'll ask around. Maybe we can help you find her," Dara offered, much more helpfully.

"I'd appreciate it."

+100 XP (2000 total)

By the time it got dark we still weren't there. A cluster of flashing lights passed overhead, a ship coming in.

"We should be there about noon tomorrow." Dara shrugged out of her pack. We all picked smoother patches of ground to rest on as twilight began. Dara passed out Ration Bars, which came with a Stamina buff I didn't really need. Clearly what had been rationed to stretch as far as possible was flavor.

We all rested quietly as the darkness deepened faster than I expected. Stars came out brilliant diamonds against black velvet. One moved straight across the sky. It came across the same route once more before I fell asleep. Something in orbit. I couldn't help but wonder if there was an actual ship or station up there, or if it was just a cosmetic feature. A bird called in the distance. Something chirped like a cricket.

The last thought I was aware of having before drifting off was, 'Do we dream in the game?'

Chapter 7

I couldn't sleep on the cruddy prison mattress. My android cellmate sat up, his eyes glowing a faint orange in the subdued lighting. I rubbed my flesh eye with my flesh hand. A sheet would have been nice.

I ignored the stupid white sneakers waiting on the floor. My bionic feet didn't care if the floor was hard or cold. I brushed the backs of my alloy fingers against the bars. I didn't want to wake anyone else, but I needed sound. My cellmate certainly never made any.

"Just walk out," the dwarf across the hall suggested, running thick, pale fingers through his impressive blond beard.

"Huh?"

"You heard me, boy." He brushed at the sleeve of his shirt, too long for him and all he seemed to wear. If his leg hair were any thicker, he could braid it. "You know this isn't real. Walk out."

The bars felt real enough. Cool to my flesh hand and hard to both. I pulled, hard. Nothing happened. As expected.

"Not like that, boy," the dwarf grumbled. "Turn around. Shut your eyes. And just step backwards."

Stupid and pointless as it sounded, there didn't seem to be any harm in it. So I did.

And backed into a huge Mordian biker.

"Oh, sorry." I meant it.

"Meh, don' worry about it, mon," he said in a Jamaican accent that matched with exactly nothing else about him.

I looked around the bar. I was supposed to meet someone, right? I was pretty sure I was, but I couldn't remember who. Hopefully I'd know when I saw them, or they'd recognize me. Smoke hid most of the ceiling and wafted around the lights, casting a yellowish hue over everything. Sultry music guided a cat woman dancing on a small stage.

"Your shot," the man in camouflage overalls and the mother of all black cowboy hats said as he handed me the cue stick. The guy was such a showoff, and he was probably sharking me.

I lined up the only shot available to me, the solid-green six. Any other shot would hit one of the rolled-up hedgehogs. The shot itself was clear, so maybe I had a chance after all.

I felt the cue as it slid over my knuckles. It tickled. I hit the ball perfectly, just above center and not too hard. It collapsed as powdery white dust.

"Ooh, that's gonna cost you," a cigar-smoking elf leaning against a tree pointed out.

"Okay, now you have to take your shirt off," gloated a woman in tight jeans and a blue lace bra the same color as her hair. She laughed, a musical laugh that pulled her head back, lengthening her neck.

What else could I do? I took off the khaki shirt, adding it to a waist-high pile of discards. Was I always this muscled?

She took me by the hand and led me to the door. A sweet, honey scent followed her.

We stepped out onto a tropical beach where green water lapped against white sands and toucans wheeled in the air. The warm, salty breeze mixed well with the warmth of the suns on my skin. I breathed in the clean air, welcoming its freshness after the dank bar.

"Gretzl," a burly android said in welcome. Two of his hands held a large tray of drinks. Text floated above it labeling it, "A tray of drinks." At least it wasn't *"The* tray of drinks." That would have been creepy. One of his other arms pointed out a sign.

"NO FENURIANS"

"Huh?" I asked

"It's the fur," she said, still holding my hand in hers. "It clogs up the plumbing."

We walked through the sand, my metallic toes sinking into the super-fine sand deeper than her stiletto heels. The sand we kicked up drifted in the breeze like fine ash.

She led me to the edge of the water. It lapped over our feet, but I didn't feel it. She laughed as her jeans got wet. A taller wave splashed over, getting both of us to the waist. Her jeans clung even tighter, which I wouldn't have thought possible. The fabric was so thin it may as well have been painted on.

With a laugh she stepped in front of me and turned around. Her lips were also the same blue as her hair and her nails, vibrant and rich, police officer blue.

She kissed me. It was a slow, long kiss that grew and grew in intensity. I stood speechless when she let me go.

"Stay right there," she purred. "Whatever happens, don't move."

I turned to watch as she strutted up the sand, kicking off her blue stilettos.

And she danced, slow and lithe, with her hands up over her head. Her body was all curves and sinuous movement. A crowd gathered behind her to watch.

With just her thumbs she slipped her jeans down, teasing. One hip exposed and then covered for the other to be revealed. She turned in slow circles, edging the jeans a little lower with each seductive turn.

Faces in the crowd changed. Concerned frowning replaced lustful leering. Then widened eyes changed the frowns into quivering, slack-jawed terror.

"What, is this not allowed here?" I asked. We probably should have been in a room somewhere.

Her response was either a shrug incorporated into her dance or part of a shoulder roll that led her whole body in a slithery spiral. She looked right at me and smiled. And laughed.

People ran away, heading further up the beach, away from us. Panicked screams drowned out tropical songbirds and a cooing dragon nuzzling the sand.

I turned to the side to peer out to sea, expecting a monstrous head or invading armada. At first all I saw was ocean. Until perspective helped, and I realized the ocean was not a field of rippling waves, but one colossal wave easily ten stories tall. And charging fast.

"We have to run!" I'm good at pointing out the obvious. How could she possibly have not noticed that?

She turned, but instead of running wriggled her butt, lowering her pants down below full, round cheeks. She left them there just long enough for me to notice the lack of underwear.

"Whyever would we do that?" she asked, now with a Texas accent.

I couldn't move. My feet were stuck. The ground was not sand, it was cement. Dry cement encased my feet fully; I was stuck facing sideways. I could look at the coming wave, or I could look at her. She unhooked the front of her bra and teased with it, never actually uncovering too much but each time suggesting she was about to

Roaring warned of the coming wave, now faster and bigger. An aircraft carrier halfway up tipped over, spilling airplanes into the sea.

"You know it's not real, right?" the pale, Nordic dwarf said. He drew a flaming sword and struck a heroic pose in his glistening chain mail.

"Is she real?" he asked, looking more serious. "Are you? I think the only thing real here is me."

Chapter 8

I woke on hard ground beneath a blue sky. Lines of clouds took different colors from the rising sun, yellows and oranges bright and dramatic. The dwarf's words hung in my mind like a fog. I hadn't expected to dream in game. Sleep really only ever seemed to happen in single-player games, and then it was just . . . poof, it's morning now.

The tutorial had mentioned the game mapping my brain to tailor the game experience. How far did that go?

The realism in the game gave me a shudder. I was hungry, which corresponded to a shortened Stamina bar. Was the dream something out of my subconscious, or had the game server created it? My flesh muscles were even stiff when I moved. Did Android players get that? My clothes weren't getting dirty, although they did deteriorate from damage.

Reck and Dara were both awake, and looking better. Both had full Health bars and looked ready to go. Dara tossed me another ration bar, which threw my Stamina back to normal and removed the hunger. Better than prison breakfast? Let's just say eating under an open sky was a solid improvement.

We hiked through the morning, ducking behind bushes for another hover Jeep patrol. When we came into view of Outcrop I paused to take in my first settlement on an alien planet.

The name made sense. It struck me more as a town that a city, but it perched at the end of a stone outcropping jutting out from the mountain range. A wall encircled the entire thing, while landing pads fanned out from the wall along the far edges. Towers rose, castle-like along the walls, but topped with altogether different turrets than any castle I'd ever seen. The trail joined a road passing through the only gate. Not somewhere I'd want to attack.

Dara pulled two beige ponchos out of her pack and handed one to Reck. They both pulled them over their heads. The material resembled plastic and hung to their knees.

"You'll be fine dressed as you are, but let me carry that rifle through for you." She took it and vanished it under her poncho.

It still took an hour to reach the gate.

"Things are pretty peaceful here. As long as you don't start any trouble, you shouldn't run into much. We used to have our own police, but the Federals replaced all that. They don't look like they're on high alert, so we should be able to just walk though. Still, try to avoid eye contact if you can."

The open gate had room for four lanes of traffic, although none flowed through it. A pair of soldiers stood guard. Two hover Jeeps sat on one side, opposite an armored personnel carrier with a rear assault ramp lowered.

I tried to stride casually, as Reck and Dara did, but it felt false. A pistol still hung on my hip. I wanted to flex my claws to reassure myself they were really there but knew better than do that in view of the soldiers.

Now, in most games, guards at city gates are overpowered like you wouldn't believe. These didn't appear any different from the soldiers I'd fought meeting my new friends. I found myself holding my breath as we walked through. The code for this game had to be boggling, unless it was letting my brain fill in details like that for me.

Within the walls, foot and ground vehicle traffic limited ground-level views. Pod-like cars and enclosed motorcycles zipped along amid people on hovering disks or walking. Colors splashed over the place, except for the utilitarian buildings displaying quite the array of . . . beige. Most weren't tall, from what I could see from here, increasing the "town" versus "city" impression.

"So," Reck said, "watch yourself on the streets. You probably won't run into trouble, but make sure you don't start any. Federal patrols are pretty commonplace, and they're not likely to stop and ask questions."

"Got it."

Dara glanced around before handing me back my rifle. I expected to feel eyes on me with it slung on my shoulder. "Now, the first place you should probably head is down that street towards that dome. About four blocks down watch for a greenish door with black trim down one of the side streets. I forget which side. After that, there's a large market about six blocks north. Meet me there at noon in three days. I'm doing to do some asking around and see if I can find out anything about this Silleste you're looking for. I'll let you know then if I was able to find anything out."

"Thanks," I said, meaning it. "I appreciate it. You guys take care."

"Nah, laying low never makes enough difference," Reck replied with a grin. If I didn't already have a mission, helping these guys out would have been a good one.

Dara checked over her shoulder more than once as they walked off; whether she was checking for me or anyone else following I couldn't have guessed. A block away a hover truck passed between them and me, and when it was gone, they were as well.

I suspected the green door place was the trainer I was supposed to find. In any other game, I wouldn't have worried about toting around a rifle looted from a dead soldier. But his troop-mates occupied the town. Sure, maybe the game wouldn't include the soldiers noticing and asking me where I got it. The consequences of being wrong, however, I was not too keen on. I weighed the risks of a soldier asking me versus a merchant asking me, and I chose selling it as the lesser risk. I looked around, working out in my head where everything should be, and set off.

The diversity of the town suited a starport. It still seemed about half human, but I saw furry Fenurians, hulking Mordians, and all the other listed races. An elf in a pristine, skin-tight, white jumpsuit toting a boxy toolkit jogged along, and I wondered if that was the first player character I was seeing. Nobody else I saw ran, and that struck me as a sure sign, as it was in pretty much every other game. I watched him go, not sure where to even begin speculating what the crafting system might be like.

At each intersection, vehicles and people and... other things I didn't have a name for crossed through without incident. Still, I crossed carefully. Exceptions happen. But it seemed an ordered place where people knew which side of the road to be on. People mostly ignored or avoided each other.

About two blocks from the market I encountered the first exception.

Chapter 9

So far, I liked the town; I wasn't sure if I was willing to call it a city or not. In most games, a city could either be something a dozen blocks across you could explore fully, or it could be several zones, each containing just the area needed for its quests. This, so far at least, seemed to be an entire town. For all I knew, every building contained people with potential quests to offer. What had that narrator said in the beginning? More content than one person could explore? If it generated content dynamically as someone explored it, that would do it.

Few buildings included any signage, and not all signs were in English. Different languages by race, I figured. One blocky building stood out as a strip club, although the silhouette dancing on their sign wasn't entirely humanoid. Too many arms. A hovering robot ranged from building to building collecting scrap, or recyclables, loading its finds into a compartment at the top. Litter sat along the edges of buildings. Details, right?

I was about two blocks from the market on a narrower, more shadowed street between buildings four stories tall on the right and five on the left. The shadowing wasn't intense and didn't seem to affect me at all, thanks to cyborg nightvision, although I could make out where its forty-meter range ran out.

I don't know what made me look up. I hadn't seen any birds, or any wildlife at all really, in town so far. So I couldn't tell you what I expected to see, except a robed figure falling towards me I did not.

I dove forward, rolling out of the way and coming up to my feet as quickly as I could. As it was, I barely avoided a spinning kick I hadn't risen enough to be hit by yet. He must have thought I'd be faster.

The blue-skinned figure with short, purple horns and purple ridges and stripes was my first Mordian. Between the metal staff and the whirling mass of blue, gray, and black robes I guessed a Monk class. That meant close-in, melee fighting, leaping and tumbling to move in and out of close quarters. Whether it wore armor under the robes, or what protection they might grant him, I couldn't say. He'd hit fast, but not as hard as others.

He wasn't a spellcaster, or he would have opened up with magic.

Opposite ends of the staff came at me one after the other. The first one whacked me in the left arm just above the elbow for a hefty 30 damage. The second I was ready for; I brought my cyborg arm up, blocking with that and getting a pop-up I dismissed in a rush to get it out of the way:

Race Ability unlocked: Cyborg Arm Block
You can block melee attacks with your cybernetic arm, protecting softer body parts. Agility scores are compared to determine whether to apply double any natural Toughness (minimum +10) to reduce damage. Reduced damage is done directly to cybernetic Health which cannot be healed magically. Use with caution. Stamina cost 5, no Cooldown.

I dodged the next several blows, scooting back with each. Was he herding me? If so, it was back towards the last street I'd crossed. Close-quarters fighting wasn't going to work in my favor.

He leapt forwards and right; I ducked low and avoided a hard swing. He kept his balance with the swing, and circled me.

Ah, old-school PVP combat—me against another player. Strafing, the tactic he used trying to keep me spinning while he circled me, was definitely old-school. It hadn't worked as well since VR games made keyboard and hand controllers obsolete. I kept turning and avoiding, letting him think I couldn't turn fast enough to get him. But I knew how to counter this, and I had just the thing for it.

I stopped, throwing some of my weight the other way, and let my claws extend as my arm snapped into place. I hit him hard, slashing him across the chest.

Race Ability unlocked: Power Attack
Make an extra strong melee attack. Doubles melee damage. Stamina cost equal to base melee damage, Cooldown 10 seconds

I traded 15 Stamina to do 45 Health in one hit. Not bad. That knocked him down by something like a third. He stepped back, surprised.

"PVP the noob, huh?" I taunted him while he glared at me. I wasn't the easy fresh meat he expected. He jumped forward, not replying. I slashed at him, but he blocked it with his staff. A sparking flare of silver light flashed at the hit, like with my arm block. So, we each had some special defense move.

We traded back-and-forth blows, both missing more than hitting. Our Health bars seemed to suffer relatively evenly. We were both at about one third left, both coming up on penalties for being under a quarter, when his hand flashed up to his face, drinking a healing potion with his staff in just one hand for that short moment. His Health bar doubled. That was not good. Cheater. I didn't have any of those!

But it also delayed him a moment, which meant time to change tactics. I jumped up and back and drew my pistol mid-air. By the time I was back on the street I had already fired four times, emptying the pistol.

Only one of them hit, but that was another 25 HP chipped off of him.

He charged forward, clearly wanting to negate the pistol's range advantage, but again I was ready for him. I jumped forward—a regular jump since my booster's cooldown timer hadn't run out—and threw everything I had into a claw slash. The jump lifted me enough, with his staff off to the side winding up for his own power attack, I raked him across the face.

Power Attack Critical Hit! 57 damage!

+500 XP (2500 total)

He went down sprawled on his back. I landed, barely, on my feet. Since no box had popped up saying anything about bonus damage for the face slash, the crit had done enough damage to finish him off.

"Hah! Who's the noob now?"

That was when it hit me, looking down at the dead body. This guy was a player. He started it, but I killed him. That meant somewhere in the real world, hooked up to a game system, a real person had just died. I had killed a real person. With friends and a family.

Should I have tried to talk him down? He might not have listened, he never even said anything. But I knew. This had not been some NPC spawned randomly. He was a player out to kill other players for their loot. Murdering prick or not, I had killed him. The blood on my claws looked real. I retracted the jagged blades knowing the blood would be gone the next time I needed them.

I had also leveled up.

Level 3 gained!
+23 Health
+19 Stamina
+6 Mana
+12 Focus
+5 Primary Characteristic Points
+10 Skill Points

On impulse I checked my face, all healed up and properly skin-covered. Much better.

The characteristic points I put into Charisma for 2 to get that to at least not-penalty status, in case less than the default ten brought any penalties, and Willpower for 3. The skill points I split between Dodge and Unarmed Combat. I considered one of the weapon skills, but I'd come back to my claws a lot.

Then I turned my attention to the dead Mordian. The robes were monk-only, of course, but I took them to sell. The staff didn't seem like something I'd be as likely to use, but still wasn't something to leave behind. He also had a communicator, which I figured this time I'd keep, plus 14 gold chips and 7 silver ones.

Item acquired: Acolyte's Robes of the Focused Mind	
These robes allow fluid movement, with padding where it is needed the most. Monk only.	
Toughness	+5
Resistance	+5
Focus	+10
Durability	32/50

Item acquired: Defender's Combat Staff	
This metal staff is well balanced, with non-slip grips. Two-handed.	
Damage	+100%
Evasion	+10
Durability	41/75

I dragged the body—heavier than it looked—off to the side to be less obvious before I continued my way to the commotion of the market. One glance back at the dead body. Would the purple-on-blue face haunt me later? What did he look like in reality? He could've been—no, I didn't want to go there.

The market was a square about three blocks to each side, pretty sizeable. Buildings around the edges sported shops at ground level and three to five stories of apartments with balconies above that. Holographic signs projected out above the doors for each shop. Names on larger signs rotated through different languages. One cycled through eight before returning to English.

The flea market of a fanboy's dreams filled the center space, like the vendor room of a convention. Tables in rows sported a bizarre assortment of goods. I suspected quite a bit was player-crafted, but you never know. Who knew whether the vendors were players or not, but I doubted it. Sure, working a market stall ought to be pretty safe, but not something I'd want to do in a game I'd spent good money on. But, bunches of players grinding crafting skills up and selling their goods to these guys? That I believed.

I spent a fair amount of time looking things over before I made any decisions. I stuck to the shops around the edges. Those seemed more certainly NPC merchants, and I thought my luck might be better with them than with other players. So far my first interaction with another player left me reluctant to seek out more.

"You might want to be careful toting that rifle around like that," one shopkeeper suggested, pointing at the Federalist rifle slung across my back. "Could find yourself getting into trouble." Perhaps that, as much as the jumpsuit, had signaled newbie to the monk. Tutorial gear: dead giveaway.

I sold the rifle, the staff, and the robes for 8 gold chips and 5 silver. In the process I confirmed the expected standard exchange rate: 10 copper per silver, 10 silver per gold, 10 gold per platinum. That brought my total wealth to 23 gold, 2 silver. I also gained a point of Haggle. Eventually I was going to want to upgrade from the starting pistol, but I was willing to wait until after finding the trainer. Odds were there would be a better weapon merchant there.

What I did want was a better outfit. I spent some time looking at the market crowd, getting an idea for local fashion. Nondescript was the goal. I paired a red shirt and brown jacket with black pants and boots. The ensemble gave me a whopping 4 Toughness, one from each item, and 5 Resistance, from the jacket. All for 63 copper. I got quite a look when I asked if I could sell or exchange the jumpsuit I was wearing.

I passed up armor vests and jackets out of my budget, along with helmet sensor packages. Nothing military grade, but any of it would have been nice upgrades.

Now I felt more relaxed trekking the streets to the trainer. I found the black-framed, green door with no further issues. No sign marked the door. If Dara hadn't told me to look for it I don't know how I would have found the place.

Weird was about the best word I could think of for what I saw once I stepped inside. People and beings in a range of sizes and colors lounged on chairs and couches surrounded by a freak-show zoo of trophy heads mounted along the walls below a tall ceiling. A red-skinned lizard-thing stood behind a bar serving a smoking drink to a tall elf with a green cape thrown over one shoulder. The hunting lodge of the future. Now if only one of them had "Hunter Trainer" floating over their head.

When in doubt, ask a bartender. Hopefully the couple of points into Charisma had been a smart move. I strode up to the bar and slid onto a stool, leaving one empty between myself and the wiry elf. Lean muscles and a circled-crosshair tattoo adorned his bare right arm.

"Hi, I'm new around here, but I was told this was a place hunters hang out. From the looks of it, I'm thinking the guy wasn't lying."

The bartender laughed, a staccato croaking sound I could have lived without hearing. The elf turned, giving me a long, weighing look. He looked along the walls, from trophy head to trophy head, with a proud gleam. "You've come to the right place, kid." His voice was soft, deeper and throatier than I expected. No high-fantasy melodic voice for this guy. Maybe it was a Space Elf thing.

Quest completed: Find the Hunter Trainer
Quest Rewards: +250XP (Total 2750)

"You look like you've got the eye for it, I'll give you that. I guess we'll have to see what you're made of." He finished his drink and slid off his stool. "Come on." He led the way to a door at the back, and from there down a stairway to a shooting range. Rifles of all description lined the back wall. He led me past them, through the room to another.

This room was smaller, about the size of a decent living room. Couch seating circled the room leaving an empty space five or six meters across. He sat sideways on the couch and patted it in front of him. I sat, seeing a nicer and larger pistol on his thigh than mine.

"Why don't you tell me why you're really here?"

So much for a simple prompt asking me if I wanted to increase skills. His right hand rested atop his thigh, much too close to that pistol. No doubt this was a test, but this didn't strike me as a room you take someone to kill them. If it were my couch, I wouldn't want to kill someone on it.

"Look," he added at my hesitation, "people come here for training. To either become a Hunter or to become a better one. I don't have to ask to know you're looking for that, too. But why you want to be a Hunter, that interests me."

"Honestly, I have a mission." No point trying to talk around it. "There's someone I need to rescue. I can't do that as some brawler or staff-spinning monk or straight-up soldier type. I need to be able to find her, maybe track her. If she's in trouble—and I'm expecting her to be—I'll need to scout out the people who have her, and then slip in and rescue her. Can you honestly tell me Hunter isn't the perfect choice for that?"

There. Honest and flattering at the same time. Curry favor where you can, you know? I didn't think the guy would refuse me, but still. True, nothing yet suggested she'd be in trouble. Maybe I was just looking for problems where they didn't exist. But Murphy's Law can be a bitch sometimes, and I'd rather be prepared for the worst than not.

"I can respect that. Thanks for being honest with me. Not everyone is. Some are looking for revenge, some for worse. I'm Brellan."

I'd found my first class trainer. I introduced myself and we spent the rest of the day learning basics. Again, I was really hoping for just, 'poof, here's a bunch of skill points.' We spent about an hour of him criticizing my inability to move quietly enough for him. But after that came a sudden +10 Sneak notification.

We broke for dinner, which we ate upstairs at in a large dining hall attached to the lounge, decorated in similar fashion. More people had gathered, most in camouflage cloaks or other hunting gear. Four long tables of boisterous talkers made quite a din.

An odd couple the next table over caught my attention while squat robots served dinner. Although the food itself was quite good, it was less captivating than a man in one of those old British safari hats, complete with monocle, gesturing flamboyantly with a clockwork mechanical hand. "It had to be an instanced zone, I'm telling you."

"Yeah, so?" the pointy-eared elf across from him asked. A carved, recurved longbow ran across his back over a brown cloak. I listened to their story enough to catch the lack of Elven clerics. Mostly they compared which world's Hunter class was the better for soloing. They each had their merits, apparently. The fantasy Ranger was less for showmanship if nothing else.

I weighed introducing myself, possibly even making a case for laser weapons, although I was clearly nowhere close to their level range, whatever level they were. What this game needed was a Consider system to tell you how much more or less powerful a target was.

A little powerleveling or some twinking with high-end gear could do a lot for my odds. But what did I have to offer them?

"Those guys regulars?" I asked the woman beside me. She looked much more like I expected, garbed in green and brown armor with compact weaponry mounted to the forearms.

"The blowhard is," she nodded. "The archer I've never seen before." She went back to her meal, not offering more. I figured I'd leave it at that. If Captain Steampunk was a regular, I could come back and find out more about him later if I wanted.

The suggestion of instanced zones gave me pause. Content locked to one player or one group was nothing new. If the game were data-mining my brain, what else could it do?

For the evening, I had time to kill but no desire to go anywhere. I relaxed in the lounge with a datapad catalog of the animals found on the planet. The diversity was impressive. I made special note of the flying ones. Space Dragons were certainly something better avoided.

Training resumed in the morning and filled every minute up to dinner. We spent hours at the shooting range, which gained me +10 Rifle skill and unlocked a new Sniper Shot ability.

Class Ability unlocked: Trainee's Sniper Shot
Each second of aiming with an appropriate rifle adds +10 to Ranged Attack and to Crit Chance up to a maximum of +50. This stacks with the normal +50 Ranged Attack bonus for aimed shots.

Ah, numbers for aimed shot bonuses. Good to know. And +50 to 100 was a decent bonus. Not huge, but every bit, you know?

I also picked up three more pistol power packs.

The first part of the afternoon we spent wandering the streets, following people. Brellan pointed out body language to indicate which way they were likely to turn. He talked about how to stay out of sight and stay inconspicuous. That netted me +10 Track, which was also for tailing people.

After that I climbed on a hover bike behind him. It was basically a flying Harley. We zoomed along low to the ground downslope towards a patch of forest. I spotted a tusked mountain goat thing called a gusker I'd seen in the animal database. It's short, boxy head turned to watch us pass.

The rest of the afternoon we spent tracking things through the forest. Okay, most of that time I spent just looking for tracks. It was frustrating, but it was also relaxing and pleasant. A musty scent hung in the air and sunlight cast dappled light on the shrubs and ground cover.

"So, just to be clear," he said at one point when we stopped to rest under a sprawling tree with coarse reddish bark, "hunting animals and hunting people aren't the same thing. Both in methodology and . . . morality. Bounty hunters can be a dangerous sort. If that's where you think you're headed, I'll help you out for now, but there will be a point where I'll have to refer you elsewhere for training. You saw the people at dinner, right?"

"Yes. An interesting mix." My stomach tightened up, and it was not from hunger.

"People come from different planets, even through Rifts from other Worlds. There is some fantastic hunting around here, up and down the range. We track and stalk our prey. We study it and observe it and learn its behaviors and patterns. Then we set up the right approach and we take that animal, as cleanly as we can. It's a predator/prey relationship. We're never careless about it, and we respect the animal's place in the ecosystem. We live by rules. One of those rules is we don't hunt other people."

His face hardened, especially around the eyes. He was serious. Dead cold serious. Possibly as in I'd be left out here dead if I got this wrong.

"I understand where you're coming from, Brellan. The girl I'm looking for isn't a bounty. We already talked about this. I'm not trying to become an assassin. There's no revenge, no dark motive at all. She's . . . someone important. I have to find her and keep her safe. I . . . I made a promise. And I intend to keep it."

Was it technically true? Not really. I hadn't promised the President I'd succeed. But failure just didn't seem an option. Would they just pull the plug on me if I failed? I'd like to think not, but it would be an awfully convenient and easy option. The scarier worry was whether they'd back stab me even if I got her home alive. I mean, come on, you've seen the vids, how often does it end neatly for the hero?

"I just want to make sure we understand each other. Our hall has a reputation. Sully that reputation and I will find you."

I raised my hands in defense. "Whoa, yeah I got it." A long moment passed while he regarded me with that cold stare.

"All right. Good," he said, nodding approvingly and standing back up. "Let's get back to work." He was back to the more cheerful, if sometimes harshly judging, self. By the time we stopped to head back I'd scored another +10 Track

Before dinner he presented me with a new pair of boots. They were taller and sturdier, but also lightweight and more flexible. "You aren't going to get far trying to sneak around in what you're wearing."

Item acquired: Basic Hunter's Sturdy Boots	
Sturdy boots for any terrain	
Toughness	+1
Resistance	+1
Durability	35/35
+10 Sneak	
Provides -10 modifier to others' attempts to track you.	

Dinner was similar to the night before, except tonight's bragging—I mean storytelling—came from a slender Fenurian who rocked from foot to foot as she talked. I guess being covered in fur negated the need for clothing. Pants and a tail seemed like it could be an awkward thing. Harness straps crossed over much of her, with a range of gear and weapons attached. A dark green cape around her shoulders, the only piece of clothing per se, came to about her tail and seemed to shift between green and brown depending on the angle.

"So, you've got a pistol," Brellan said the next morning at breakfast. "Perfect. I wouldn't want you doing today's challenge from too far away. I'll drop you in the foothills. There's a bird called a grawk. When you have killed one you can signal me, and I'll pick you up."

"You want me to track a bird?" Really? As part of an epic quest, I could see. But at level three? This bird was not in the database I scrolled through, or if it was, it was in a section I didn't get to.

He laughed, and several others nearby joined in. If this was one of those initiation-type jokes I was going to be upset. Or it could be a string of go here, go there, go to this other place. I never liked those quests. Who does?

"Only partly. Grawks feed on little vermin that follow murse. Well, live on them, basically."

Murse I had read about. Huge, lumbering things somewhere between an elephant and a moose. The murse head on the wall was about as wide as my arm span.

"If you can't follow a murse, then you're hopeless. You'll find one, or its tracks. You get close enough, you shoot the grawk. Mind you, grawk are skittish, so you'll need to be quiet."

Quest: Stalk the Grawk
Brellan wants you to track, stalk, and kill one Grawk.

"And," one of the other guys added, "don't startle or anger the murse. You get trampled by one of those and you're . . . never coming back."

Brellan confirmed I had a communicator, paired them, and we zoomed along the mountains again. He banked through sharp turns and hopped over low ridges as if to test my stomach. It might've been metal, too, because I was fine with all of it.

Once he spotted one, and pointed it out, he took us down a good kilometer away and dropped me off. He started me in a clearing at the border between denser and thinner forest. The denser zone stood between me and my prey.

"Good luck, kid," he said with another laugh.

I glared at his back as he sped away, still sticking close to the terrain. I wanted one of those bike things. The game had mounts in it. Hopefully they didn't come with some stupid level requirement.

"Well . . . ," I said as I puffed up my chest and set out. First was finding a path through heavy underbrush. Several times I had to work my way around large patches with wicked looking thorns. A red tint on the thorns suggested they'd already found prey. Or they were poisoned. Hey, poison isn't always green.

It was warm work. I had to move quietly among places that weren't clear enough to pass. Brellan probably dropped me off at the worst starting place on purpose. Dank air hung, lifeless and breezeless. Decay was the perfect word for the scent that relentlessly pursued my nose.

A good three hours passed while I wormed my way through. My patience and diligence paid off with another +1 to Sneak, bringing it up to 17.

Eventually I broke through to a wide clearing. A shallow, broad valley crossed my path, sloping downward to my left. Yellow grasses, sparsely speckled with pink and blue flowers, waved in a welcome breeze. On the far side and downslope, some three hundred meters away, a murse munched away at low-lying growth. It followed the tree line, dawdling away before stopping to much again.

Pistol range was seriously inadequate for the distance. In some games I'd just slowly move forward and see if it reacted based on distance. In this case, I wasn't going to take that chance. For one thing, it deciding to aggro and stampede me out in the open would not end well. For another, there was a deadline here. Following it waiting for it to calm down was not going to be the best use of my time. So, getting close quietly was the only thing for it. I was supposed to be a Hunter after all. That should have involved me using a rifle. Who hunts with a pistol, anyway, right?

While I was debating with myself, a bird swooped down from the trees and dive-bombed the murse. It swooped back up and perched up in the branches somewhere. Yep, this was definitely the target for me. Stupid one-chance missions. . . .

I made my way up the valley, further away from the thing, before moving across. I still moved slow, and froze when the thing lifted its head. It ambled away to another clump of undergrowth. Once in the cover of the far tree line,

I crept through the trees after it. Time can be such a weird thing. Sometimes an hour goes by in a flash. Other times? Other times creeping through trees trying not to make a sound is the when time . . . slows . . . down. Agonizingly slow. I did end up gaining 2 points of Sneak, now 19, 29 with my boots.

The sun had passed its zenith by the time I got close enough to get a better view of the beast. Shaggy brown fur rippled in the breeze like grass. I could have walked under the thing as it stood on legs I could take cover from gunfire behind. Behemoth as the thing was, its head wasn't as big as the trophy one back at the space-safari lodge. Still, it took whole bushes in a single bite to gnaw on patiently like a cow chewing cud. Well, bull in this case. Yikes.

The birds, now they were distinctive. Bright, vivid blue, royal-looking birds the size of a hawk with a short beak and undersized talons. Its feathers shone in the sun as it swooped down for another attack run along the beast's back. Without a sound it rose back into the branches, with something the size of a mouse in one talon.

Again the murse moved, clomping its way to another bush to rip up in one chomp. I moved on ahead of it while it chewed ponderously. All I had to do was wait for it to come close enough. A bird struck again, lighting in branches closer to me but still too far for a good shot. Sure, +50 aim bonus was good, but closer would be better.

The huge head rose. Soccer balls with pupils scanned the ground in my direction. I didn't even breathe. More lumbering brought it closer before it pounced and bit a bush like a cat going after a fluffy toy. It was far more agile than I'd ever have expected from something that big. Don't piss off the murse!

That was when an extra complication showed its head. A complication in an oh-so-familiar jumpsuit. A complication with a rifle. They got a rifle but not me? The jerk just strolled out of the tree line across the shallow valley, which was narrower at this end.

Seriously? I hadn't seen anybody in dorky jumpsuits at the lodge, so he had to be out on some other class's training quest. Either way, the last thing I needed was some noob scaring this thing off. Kill stealers are the worst. Well, I'd put PVP spawn campers lower, but that didn't seem to be an issue in this game. You can't gank somebody at their spawn point over and over again when they only die once.

The wannabe hunter started across the grasses, rifle ready, moving slow. Not a complete idiot, just a partial one. The murse tromped closer. A bird swooped over it, coming up empty taloned, to land in a branch not ten meters from me. I held as still as I possibly could, drawing the pistol ever so slowly, hardly daring to breathe. I drew a bead on it, waiting for the next exhale.

I barely hit it. Winged it, in fact. Literally; I got it in the wing. But it went down. Which was enough to make me happy just then.

> **+100 XP (2850 total)**

Laser pistols in RiftWorlds Online don't make noise, which worked in my favor just then. There was the red beam of light momentarily connecting me to my target though. And those eyes, each the size of my head, swiveled up.

I'd swear the thing stared right at me, maybe sizing me up. Snow-shovel ears twitched and turned, though, and it shifted its attention back up the valley. That head turned, scanning for something. It was too much like scanning for predators for my liking. Whatever natural predators this thing could have was not something I wanted to encounter without serious, military-grade . . . military.

It ended up seeing the noob now almost halfway across the valley. It reared up and snarled a groan that shook my heart like a sick nightclub base rumble. Its front . . . feet came down hard with an earth-shaking whump. The newbie turned and ran, full-out, while the thing yanked its feet back out of the ground.

The mammoth turned and worked its way back up the valley. I fetched my azure prize and signaled Brellan for pickup. It was about ten minutes before he showed up with a much too happy smile.

Chapter 10

The slight whining hum of whatever powered Brellan's hover bike heralded his arrival up the valley. I waited in the shade, letting myself enjoy the smells on the breeze. A dusty scent blended with the musk of damp earth, a hint of blooming flowers. And something smelled like sourdough bread. I had no idea what that came from. The bike settled on retractable landing struts and lowered closer to the ground, settling into the grasses.

"Took you long enough," Brellan carped as he hopped off. Tightness in his face didn't match the smile he put on. "But you got it. Good work." I stuck the bird in his outstretched hand.

"Not the prettiest kill, but you could still mount it if you wanted. Just from the side a little. Not that grawk are really trophy birds." He plucked a long wing feather off, suggesting, "You should keep one of these, however. I'm sure you learned a couple of things today, kid. Keep the memento so you don't forget."

Quest completed: Stalk the Grawk
Quest Rewards:
Reputation increase with Outcrop Hunters' Hall
+500XP (Total 3350)

Level 4 gained!
+23 Health
+19 Stamina
+8 Mana
+15 Focus
+5 Primary Characteristic Points
+10 Skill Points

I tucked the feather into a pocket, glad to have an outfit that included them. Yet another upgrade from newbie jumpsuits. Then again, if weapons could fashion their own holsters dynamically, maybe pockets were more of a perception thing. Metagaming is all about remembering it's a game and working out how the game works. 'Gaming' the system, if you will.

"Come on, we should head back." The smile sagged away, letting an underlying glumness show. I climbed on behind him, and we rose away, climbing with the bikes droning whine.

We skimmed the treetops in silence. If he didn't want to talk about whatever was bothering him it didn't seem my place to push it. Instead, I took the time to review my stats and spend points. I put all 5 characteristic points into Agility, taking it up to 23. That bumped Ranged Attack and Evasion by 5 each to 123 and 128. The skill points I split between Sneak and Pistol. One to help me avoid trouble, and the other to give me more options when I couldn't avoid it.

A shuttle, marked in Federalist blue and white, descended towards the town, landing somewhere in the center of town. Not on one of the landing pads. Interesting.

"Troop ferry," Brellan grumbled. "Probably forty to fifty more in that, a whole platoon." A low growl rumbled in his throat I only heard because I was as close as I was. "Third one today."

"Something going on?" I had waited long enough to ask.

"Seems like it. Nobody's got good guesses about what. I'll tell you one thing, though. There's a lot of nervous people in town. Old fears getting stirred up. Some of our members with . . . past problems with the Feds . . . are talking about leaving. Some were packing things up when I left to come get you." While it all sounded like potential new quests, it also sounded like trouble. I wasn't looking for trouble.

Brellan brought us over the wall and dropped to street level, zipping over traffic and between rooftops faster than I would have. We set down behind the Hall. A pair of women in brown overalls ran out and took the bike in through a loading door.

"We've got a little more work to do, you and I. So, we're going to finish up what we can tonight. You're always welcome in our Hall as long as you don't bring trouble with you. But . . . , um, if you think you might have plans that involve going anywhere else? I'd seriously consider going there early tomorrow. I won't be at all surprised if this place is locked down by tomorrow night."

"I've gotta find someone," I reminded him, doubting he'd forgotten. "I'm supposed to meet someone at noon tomorrow I'm really hoping will have a lead for me. Wherever that points I'll try and head for right away. Thanks for the warning."

I had found good people, and I appreciated that; I enjoyed dinner a little more for it. Other hunters included me in conversation more. I was becoming one of them, starting to belong. I could see myself getting attached to these people, getting involved in their quests, probably tied to the resistance I would reconnect with tomorrow. What new quests might Dara offer me tomorrow? How many would just be tangents taking me away from my mission?

Nervous undertones rang in conversations in voices quieter than normal. No one boasted of their day's deeds. A slight hush dampened everything. It made dinner harder to enjoy, although we all tried to. Several shared final meals before departures. One woman mentioned boarding a shuttle right after dinner.

Some words were left out, avoided. Invasion. Occupation. While many seemed to have ideas of what to expect, none shared details. More than one said they hoped they were wrong, or they didn't want to be right. I was sure new quests were becoming available throughout the town based on what sides people had chosen. Some of those quests would be for players siding with the Imperials. Like I needed open season for PVP combat.

After dinner, Brellan took me downstairs again, through the shooting range to one of the rooms beyond. An elven technician with a toolbox on his lap sat on a couch next to a drab green bundle. The elf stood when they entered.

"First," Brellan said, "a quick upgrade."

"Have a seat," the elf said, indicating the spot he had vacated.

"Upgrade?" I asked as I sat.

The technician had me take my shirt and jacket off and fiddled with my arm. He opened a panel and brought tools to bear, even plugging a hand computer into it. I couldn't see what he did to the implant that included my right eye. I was, however, rewarded with a dialog box spelling out the upgrade. I certainly wasn't going to complain.

Tactical Package II
+4 Intellect, +4 Willpower, +10 Crit Chance
+10 Evasion, +10 Ranged Attacks
Triple nightvision range (60m)
X10 vision magnification

I liked the upgrade, all good stuff. Especially vision magnification. Increased Crit Chance, even if a small increase in the grand scheme of things, I welcomed. I've always been a fan of getting more critical hits. In some games they're showier, and that's always a fun touch.

"Now, get changed and come back out," Brellan instructed before leading the technician away. I checked the bundle next to me: green and brown pants and an olive colored jacket. Brown reinforced patches covers shoulders, elbows, and knees. Both were nice upgrades, as well.

Item acquired: Hunter's Basic Reinforced Pants	
These brown and green pants offer a small degree of padding and reinforcement.	
Toughness	+5
Resistance	+5
Durability	25/25

Item acquired: Hunter's Basic Reinforced Jacket	
This green jacket offers a small degree of padding and reinforcement. When combined with Basic Hunter's Pants provides +5 Sneak.	
Toughness	+6
Resistance	+6
Durability	35/35

I hung onto my prior outfit, which I rolled together neatly. You never know when more run-of-the-mill clothes might be a good idea. The new outfit looked more Hunter-y, and fit perfectly. Brellan nodded approvingly when I rejoined him in the firing range.

He had one more gift for me, a long, scoped rifle. A cord connected the scope to the weapon just above the handgrip. I couldn't find a safety mechanism.

Item acquired: Hunter's Training Laser Rifle	
The classic sporting rifle, accurate with good range but less capable of sustained rapid fire. A scope allows for Sniper Shots. Weapon Link compatible.	
Range	100m
Accuracy	+20
Damage	40
Shots	40
Durability	50/50

This was a nice weapon. The damage wasn't as high as the soldiers' rifles, and it didn't seem burst-capable. When I gripped it for firing, however, I learned more about it. For one thing, a "Safety Off" indicator came up in my view, along with an ammunition counter. On top of that, a crosshair in my vision showed where the rifle was pointed. I brought the rifle up to my shoulder and sighted through the scope. A dotted line showed me where it would shoot. Now, there was something the other rifles didn't do.

"The upgrade to your arm and visual implant will give you this ability with any weapon fitted out for it," Brennan explained. Now I understood what Weapon Link compatible meant. I liked it.

We spent another couple of hours shooting, going through quite a few energy packs, picking up another +5 to my Rifle skill. He supplied me with two additional rifle power packs and two pistol ones. His final gift was another ten gold chips to buy additional gear with.

"You're as ready as I can make you right now. Good hunting, and stay out of trouble."

I thanked him and headed to bed. Tomorrow I had shopping to do, which would conveniently put me in the market by noon. Sleep was fitful but dreamless.

Chapter 11

I got to breakfast a little late, greeted by quiet, subdued conversational murmur and long faces. I ate in silence, alone. People spoke in short sentences. "When's your shuttle leave?" "An hour." They conserved words as though rationed or competing with Agent McSternface. Nobody used the word evacuation. But it certainly felt like one. Disconcerting, to say the least.

Afterwards, I couldn't find Brellan to say goodbye, so I shrugged and left the Hall. Rain fell in gentle sheets outside, not a pounding storm, but enough to get me soaked by the time I reached the market. Air cars hovered a good half meter above the street, which at least meant no tires splashing in the puddles.

A much smaller crowd dawdled in the market than before, but still enough hide in if needed. Colorful ponchos and rain cloaks obscured most of the figures bustling from covered stall to covered stall, or in and out of buildings. Androids marched about, ignoring the rain. A pack of Mordians strode through the crowd, dripping water on anyone who didn't get out of the way in time. Very few Fenurians. Go figure, right?

The rain was not so pleasant. None of that "clean earth" scent with regular rains. This smelled somewhere between sulfur and wet dog. Not overpoweringly strong, but noticeable. Ten silver for a rain poncho became my first expenditure of the day. I could have done three for a disposable one, but it seemed like a good thing to have. A spindly blue-and-chrome android hawked them from a kiosk, its amplified voice carrying over the background. I browsed the near-endless variety on a screen and it printed the poncho on the spot. I picked a deep green, keeping with the theme so far.

The poncho helped a lot. Sure, I was saturated at that point already, but did I mention the rain came down cold? Better equipped for it, I was ready to wander. One discovery was there was no simple, "Common" language. Most of the other races seemed able to speak human, but many of them spoke their own languages among their own kind. Real-time translation didn't surprise me, especially for a game sending input directly to my brain.

A follow-up discovery was for 10 gold I could buy language skill chips to learn a language instantly. For 50 gold any cyborg or android could buy an upgrade package that would let them plug similar chips into their heads. The other option was to own, or rent, a computer with the appropriate neural electrode accessory. I was already hooked up to something like that in real life, it seemed rather meta to do that in here, too. Either way, it was out of budget for now.

I spent a little more time in a covered, U-shaped booth browsing bags. Shoulder bags, duffel bags, purses, backpacks, the works. Pockets only go so far after all. The booth was arranged by type and size, larger ones on shelves and counters, smaller ones on hooks. Head-sized robots hovered about overhead, dropping to make suggestions in feminine voices.

I picked up a pair of weatherproof cargo boxes for my belt at 10 silver each, and a backpack for 25 from a dwarf in a sleeveless gray tunic. I couldn't plan on getting all my gear from looting or from quests. That meant making money. Some I could get from quests, but looting was likely to be a big part. It usually is. That meant having places to put stuff.

Item acquired: Basic Belt Box	
This hard-sided box with hinged top is a convenient, weatherproof container for small items.	
Durability	20/20
A single compartment can hold up to 2kg of small items.	

Item acquired: Basic Backpack	
Utilitarian backpack with adjustable straps and extra external pockets	
Durability	30/30
Main compartment can hold up to 20kg. Each side pocket can hold an additional 5kg.	

I spent longer than I expected in a weapon shop with an impressive array of pistols. An orange-skinned Mordian with a deep husky voice perfect for radio waited behind a counter before a wall packed with guns like they were cell phones.

I learned more about the game's weapon hierarchy just by comparing what he had to offer. Laser weapons were the bottom tier, big surprise. Up from that were pulse weapons, which fired a concentrated pulse of laser instead of a beam. Plasma weapons did more damage in general, but less to armored or hardened targets. Particle beam weapons could be ionized to do extra damage to anything electronic. Like parts of me.

About a dozen laser pistols fell in my price range. Some were only cosmetically different from each other. The Mordian introduced himself as Gorranth and we compared different models. He didn't rush me, didn't pressure me, and answered questions without condescending. I held several in my hand comparing heft and balance and feel as if I knew what I was doing. Some sleeker, sportier ones had better accuracy but less damage. Some bigger, boxier ones did extra damage, but there was always a trade-off, either in accuracy or reliability.

"This one is one of our most popular in your price range," Gorranth offered, handing me a slightly heavier gun with rounded edges and black trim on a gray frame. It fit well in my hand. "The LaserTech E-100, one of the most reliable weapons you'll find at this price bracket. Take care of it, and it'll never go wrong."

Item acquired: LaserTech E-100 Laser Pistol	
A sleeker, well-balanced pistol, tough and reliable. Weapon Link compatible.	
Range	55m
Accuracy	+5
Damage	35
Shots	20
Durability	65/65

One of my favorite features? It was Weapon Link compatible. Just like the rifle, it became an extension of me. It could even accept a scope, although at 50 silver, the scope was out of budget. For now. Gorranth took my old one in for trade, for all of 10 silver chips. I left his shop with 24 silver remaining, but 1 point of Haggle higher.

I all but lusted after the range of cybernetic upgrades. Attribute boosts, improved jump jets, armor plating I could snap on, and more. Most came in tiers, no doubt tied to level ranges. Even the cheapest ones ran 100 gold and up, far out of budget.

The rain ended by the time I got outside, although sun only fell on select spots. The rain poncho refused to absorb water, which meant a quick flap and it was dry enough to fold and tuck into one of the backpack pockets. I stood a little taller walking back out into the market. Without any kind of ceremony, I had graduated myself out of newbiedom.

A squad of eight soldiers in heavier armor than I'd seen before marched through the market. Humans and aliens scattered to make way for them. The troopers' blue-and-white helmets only turned a little. Not scanning the crowd, not looking for anyone. Just making their presence known. I got the unspoken message: don't cause trouble.

About half an hour of people watching later I found Dara leaning against the corner of a more permanent looking booth, her arms crossed. I weaved through traffic, pausing for someone in colorful armor on an even beefier version of Brellan's hover bike. Others moved out of its way, too, as it zoomed through. Player, for sure.

"Hey, Dara. You're looking less battered."

"Your face is looking less battered."

"Touché." And then the awkward kicked in. It would have been rude to jump straight into, "So, were you able to find anything out," but I wasn't sure what else to say. "How's the rebellion going," didn't feel any better.

"I see you've done some shopping," she said, breaking the silence. "That's a nice rifle to start with. I've used one of those before."

"It does seem like an upgrade, all in all," I agreed.

"So, we did some asking around about that elf you're looking for. She's been here. Week ago, maybe two. But she showed up with a guy from Fantasa'an, chain mail and sword type. They were both kind of noticeable around here. We don't get a lot of Rifters through here. I'm not aware of there being any Rifts nearby, so they must have come by ship." She picked one foot up, propping it against the wall behind her with her knee sticking out.

"She seems to have dropped out of sight, but the guy is still around. He's been poking his nose into things a bit, chatting up a lot of people. Most nights he's at a bar across town. Felnin's, it's a . . . quirky place where people go to hire people to do whatever it is they don't want to do themselves. Don't cause trouble in there."

She uncrossed her arms and stepped away from the wall. "If you get tired of looking for her, or you find her and need something to do, my people could use someone like you." Her wink could have had a few different meanings. If I didn't have this mission, I might've spent time finding out.

"Thanks," I replied instead. "I appreciate it. I'll check the place out. Who knows, I might pass this way again. If I do, I'll look you up. Say hi to Reck for me."

"I'll do that. Take care of yourself. Try not to get your face blown off again. That was gross."

Figuring it was a bit soon for the bar, I filled the afternoon wandering. I found some of those little, grind quests for cash and XP. There were no huge rewards, but four 50XP quests added up a little. That and another 185 silver at least made it not a wasted afternoon.

A woman in a reinforced, dark gray technician's jumpsuit complained about a part she was missing for the cargo lifter she was repairing. Naturally, there was only one place to get it. Just as naturally, the man with the parts was her ex and refused to sell anything to her.

That man, hardly a catch in the looks department with a smooshed-looking broad nose that hardly stuck out from his boxy face, was frustrated about a recent shipment of parts that had been impounded "by mistake." He assured me that the clerk I'd need to talk to wasn't too loyal, but I might need to be creative.

So, I jogged over to a customs office. A pair of Federalist troopers stood nearby enough to come running to any trouble, while others supervised operations at landing pads and staging areas. One side was the customs office, the other was a traffic control tower two stories taller. I prepped myself to see what side quest this guy would have. Another squad of troopers in heavy armor marched by, tromping through what remained of this morning's rain puddles.

This guy turned out to be a woman. A stuffy looking space elf not as attractive as most I'd seen. Her stiff bureaucratic black tunic buttoned clear up to her neck. A row of rings ran up the side of her ear, connected by a delicate chain.

"Uh, hi," I started. Slick, I know. "I'm trying to check the status on a package. I've got the ID number here." I handed her the printed ticket number with a scannable hologram instead of a barcode. Her pained expression showed the true passion she held for her job.

Her counter surface doubled as a display, although polarization kept me from reading it from my side of the counter. She set the paper down in a marked spot and the display changed. A few quick taps finished the check. The initial result was a frown.

"It was held up," she explained. "Some of the permits weren't right."

"So, what do I need to do?" This time cut to the chase seemed the best route. At least until I knew more.

"Well," she said, drawing the word out, as she swiped part of the display. "It looks like everything has been corrected. All that's left is a ten-gold-chip fine. Do you have that?" Ten gold, 100 silver. About four times what I had. Wonderful. Not that I wanted to pay that much for an errand quest. There had to be another way.

"Um, no."

"Then I guess you'll have to figure something out."

This, I figured, could mean a couple of different things. One was I'd have to figure out a different way to replace the shipment. Another was a way to raise the money, which wasn't terribly appealing. The other possibility I saw I liked better; she could be suggesting I could find a way to manipulate the situation, or get her to want to help me. I took the hint, definitely more Charisma next level.

"Bureaucracy, it's everybody's favorite thing, right? I know when I had a clerk job once everybody acted like everything was my fault. Like I filled out their forms for them."

"That's the way, all right. What kind of desk did you run?"

"I helped out at a licensing office." True, real-world experience. It was just a seasonal job during college, and I'd hated it. "I think the thing that surprised me most was how easily things fell through cracks."

"And what are you getting at?"

Her frown and suspicious raised eyebrow were not encouraging. Yet the more I thought about it, the more it seemed I was on the right course. She reminded me of the women at the prison commissary. This woman probably worked for the Federation, probably hardly paid at all. Her job was boring, and people treated her like the enemy all day long.

"I know fees and fines aren't the same thing, for one. A fee, that's tied to a checklist somewhere. Those get checked. Fines? Fines are a little different." I loosened my posture, going for more casual and relaxed. Non-threatening. "If I had the money, I'd pay it and it would go on the books and go away. Would it achieve anything? Probably not. It's not like it's gonna teach the shipping guy to fill forms out right. Right?" I pulled out two round gold chips, almost all I had, and set them on the counter.

"You probably spend a lot of time watching money go past. I know sometimes I'd see application fees higher than my daily pay." I nudged the two chips closer across the counter. "But mistakes happen all the time. If you were to . . . say . . . accidentally delete the fine, I might be so relieved to find out everything was actually in order after all that I'd accidentally leave something behind." Another nudge closer. "On the counter."

Her eyes wavered between mine and the money. "That's true, mistakes do happen."

I pushed them to the edge of the counter off to her right. "Maybe you should check the file again, maybe the machine scanned the code wrong or something."

Her fingers tapped and swiped with well-practiced, efficient movements. One of those movements brought her hand near the two chips, which she swept off the counter. "Oh, my. It seems there was a mistake. There's no unpaid fine on this shipment at all."

She pushed a small data chip into a slot, dragged something towards it, then handed me the chip.

"Your package is in holding bay nine. Give that to the clerk there and he'll get you your package."

"Thank you. I'm glad you do better work than some of the others around here," I offered with a wink. She smiled back, this wasn't her first bribe.

Bribery skill +1 (1)

I got the box, which I exchanged for the lifter part. "Sorry about the fine, I remembered that just after you left. Here's a ten-gold chip to reimburse you," he said, handing me a slightly larger, octagonal gold chip. I took the part back to the mechanic, who thanked me with a bouncing smile and an offer that if I needed anything repaired she'd give me the friends' discount.

That and other boring errands filled time. Another troop shuttle came in slow over the town before landing. Finding this knight and getting out of town after Silleste felt more urgent.

Felnin's lived up to "quirky" before I'd even stepped inside. The exterior pretended to be a crashed silver rocket ship straight out of classic 1950s sci-fi. An opened ramp, complete with stairs, made a canopy over the ground-level entrance. Felnin's name was right on the side of the ship in big, red, vertical letters.

The inside didn't fit. Outside, the ship leaned at an angle. Inside, levels of ringed balconies ascended straight up. The inside was also larger than the outside. Game physics. Things would have been on the tight side otherwise.

Smoke lingered in the air from floor to—as far as I could see, at least eight balcony's worth.

The inner core of the place was some eight meters, empty except for two shafts of light a meter across forming whitish columns in the smoke. A Fenurian in an eye-poking orange cloak stepped into one and rode it upwards, stepping off three levels up. Around that was some ten meters to the walls. Each level had a long bar with plenty of seating plus tables and booths and open floor space.

A dance club this was not. Also, not somewhere I'd want to have a brawl. Especially not on the upper levels, where being pushed or thrown could have painful consequences. While glowing blue railings circled the center where the light elevators were, I couldn't be certain they were solid. The ground floor was the only space open enough for any real dancing, but nobody was.

The biggest Mordian I'd seen yet leaned against the wall plenty close with a menacing axe. Its blade glowed a shimmering orange. Dara's suggestion of not causing trouble sprang back to mind.

I was still a little early for eating dinner, so I played the proper tourist and checked the place out. Each level had a different space theme. While nothing quite broke any copyrights, I recognized each one. A holographic Rift hung in space on each level, shimmering black with uneven edges. People ignored the themed scenery, which could have been sports teams or animal motifs painted in parking garages to identify different levels.

The patrons themselves were less eclectic. More than half were human, which seemed about typical of the town so far. Others mixed together, but most segregated themselves.

A group of Mordians in studded black . . . fetish gear? . . . laughed and drank at a large booth, the only ones on that level. Space bikers. Of course. The shiny gold android waiter seemed appropriately uncomfortable as it hustled in and out of interaction distance. Two levels up seemed an okay place for me to hang out and eat.

A naked, black and white tiger-striped Fenurian brought me the day's special: a bowl of wriggling green worms and an opaque blue drink in a tall, narrow glass for 1 silver. A pack of six other Fenurians lounged at a booth with no table, passing around drinks they all seemed to share. I saw a cargo harness on one, a long poncho on another. One wore a slinky red glittery dress slit for her tail. The waitress was one of only a few I'd seen completely naked. Again, though, when you're covered it fur it's not really the same, is it?

The worms were moving, still alive, in varying shades of green, big like earthworms. Not very appealing, big surprise there, but at least I could call them worms. There'd been a few prison meals with lumpy mashes nobody could agree on how to identify. These weren't bad, but weren't good either, although they did come with an impressive Focus recovery boost.

Almost enough to offset the Focus recovery debuff from the drink. The drink had a pleasant fruitiness, even if it could've just been mouthwash flavored like fruit. Not something I'd order to go, that's for sure.

Music wafted about the place like the fog, although the fog did a better job of staying in the center.

After I ate I loitered, moving from level to level, still avoiding the Space Bikers, trying not to stay anywhere too long alone with nothing to do but watch people. I favored booths, less visible than tables.

When a big dude showed up in chain mail, he had to be the guy. He kind of stood out, not only for being about a head taller than me and burly to match. Light glittered off chain links from collar to about half down his thighs. A big, stereotypical shield hung with a rifle on his back over a white cloak fastened under a set of white, plastic-looking shoulder plates.

I stood up, watching him ride the light to one floor above me, one short from the top. I circled around to the light shaft elevators to ascend on a column of light myself. What can I say, it still amused me. The music, coming from a small band of space elves on six, was quieter on nine as I stepped off.

Banners of futuristic space trooper regiments lined the walls, one for each table. The one behind the knight was a gold gauntlet on blue. A waitress in a crisp navy-blue uniform with white piping took his order on a tablet.

"Mind if I join you, good sir knight?" I asked him, clueing him in I wasn't a local NPC, but another player aware we were in a game, albeit a deadly game we were trapped in.

"Have a seat," he offered as he leaned back in his chair. His voice matched the chiseled face that suggested someone overcompensating for not feeling "manly" enough. You know the face: squared jaw, sturdy chin, the fairy-tale price look, with the perfect clean-cut blond taper cut to match. I lowered myself into a chair, choosing one just off from straight across from him. I didn't want my back to the open core either.

"Do I know you?"

"No," I replied, "but I've heard of you." He perked right up at that one. Who doesn't want to be a little famous, right?

"Only good things, I hope," he said with a chuckle.

"Well, I need some help, and I was referred to you."

"Ah. Then you've come to the right place," he declared, louder than I would have preferred.

The waitress returned with a platter. From the menus I'd seen, his budget dwarfed mine as she presented him a big steak and something dark in a mug. He asked her to bring a mug for me, waving off my attempt to say he didn't need to. At least a little discrete, he waited for her to walk off before saying anything else.

"So, how do you like this game so far?" he asked. Filling in time until she came back with my drink, maybe. He cut a strip off the steak and cut that into individual bites.

"Well, I haven't died, so that's a good thing. The whole can't-log-off thing kinda bites, though."

"Yeah, they really left that out in the ads." His eyes lowered, as did the corners of his mouth. "That took some real adjusting to. I've heard that if we die in here we die out there, too."

"I'm pretty sure that one's true," I agreed, not willing to say I knew that when I came in. It was too early for him to start questioning my sanity. I'd already done enough of that myself. Those last whispered words from the Secret Service guy still hadn't left me: "If she dies in there, so do you."

"I have a wife and kids on the outside. So at least I'm pretty sure my meat body's being taken care of. There's a rumor going around though that if your body out there dies we continue in here and don't even know it happened."

"That's a creepy thought," I admitted. "But I'm sure people are working on fixing it. There's gotta be a million people in here."

The waitress came back with my mug, an interruption I was more than ready for. If Silleste died before I found her, would I even know?

"So, what kinda help are you looking for?" he asked once she had marched off with her crisp military precision.

"Looking for an RL friend of mine. In here her name's Silleste." I tried the drink. It smelled like coffee but tasted more like root beer with both caffeine and alcohol.

The guy tensed up at the name, and his right hand moved a little closer to where he'd be able to reach his sword.

"I heard you two came here together from Fantasy Land. Did something happen?"

"Who are you?" he demanded in a lowered voice. Sure, now he wanted to be discrete.

"Whoa," I tried with my hands out. Perfectly non-threatening as long as the claws stayed in. If he did make a move for his sword, I'd have the edge. Totally worth the points I'd spent on that in the beginning.

"We were attacked. Now tell me who you are." This was not going where I expected. Okay, fine.

"All on the table then, I'm Max," I started. "Did she tell you anything about her life outside?"

"Only a little bit. She lives with her parents, I know that much. There had been enough warnings not to talk about it. Where are you going with this?"

"Yes, she does live with them, her mom, anyway. Her mom is... a powerful person, with a lot of influence. And she's worried about her daughter being trapped in here. I came in to find her and keep her safe until they fix it so we can log off again."

"Bullshit."

"Really? You think I'd make that up?"

"You expect me to believe you came in here willingly, knowing you couldn't get out?"

"And knowing thousands of logged-in people have died, probably because their toon did. It's true. We die in here and we die in RL. It's also true that people are working outside to fix it. We just need to hang on until they do. And, yes, I came in here voluntarily."

"Why? If you're telling the truth, why would you do that?"

"You ever heard the expression, 'an offer I couldn't refuse'?"

"What, money?" The raised eyebrow lifted more into incredulity.

"Not quite." I took a deep breath. Was I ready to trust this guy? No. Did I have much choice? Also no. "Our bodies are in the same room. If she dies, I die. And I don't buy the idea we continue in here if our bodies die."

Time dragged as he stared at me, gauging. I took another deep breath and waited his response.

"I think I believe that," he concluded. "I'm Sir Altion Relwick."

"Thank you, and well met. Do you know where she is?" Well met may have been a little disingenuous, but I was dealing with somebody getting to be the knight of his own personal fantasy.

"Nope."

Great. Perfect. Big, shiny dead end. I had just put a lot of faith into someone I didn't know from Adam, for what?

"Not really, anyway. She's off planet, by about five days."

I kind of snarled at that. It fit my mood right, and I needed to express it somehow.

"We were attacked," he began, leaning forward for a long story. "Mercenaries or bounty—"

A glob of something green interrupted his story, missing him and hitting the wall behind him, splattering threads that hit his chair and the table and seemed to solidify almost immediately.

I whirled to a stand out of my chair, which clattered to the floor behind me. My new pistol was in hand without a thought. To the right was the long bar with a few people—mostly aliens—who hadn't yet turned to see what was going on. On the far side, before a line of empty booths, an elf with muscled arms and an obvious armor vest pointed the kind of oversized rifle perfect for the space marine theme of the level we were on. The elevator light shafts dominated the left side, with open space around them.

Altion wasn't far behind me pulling out a sword and slinging his shield. He destroyed the table getting it out of his way. Gotta love tanks and their high strength scores.

The guy got another shot off before I could, and it splatted against Altion's shield. Green threads shot out from the splatter, reaching out. They evaporated instead of hardening. So, they needed contact with something else. I dropped to one knee and fired a brace of shots that missed. But it drew the man's attention as Altion charged.

I dove out of the way of the next shot and returned several. One hit him, doing much less damage than I would have liked. I had a feeling Altion's sword would make a mess of the guy, especially since the fighter had been in the game longer and had to be higher level than me. So, me keeping the elf distracted seemed a solid plan. It would have been, if our attacker had been alone.

Two men in similar vests stepped forward a level above, aiming rifles. Helmets with partial visors no doubt gave them armor and stat boosts and who knew what other bonuses. Twin, sustained lines of red hatred lanced out, and they walked the lines into me, searing lines into the floor behind me before they carved into me. Together the two attacks knocked down a third of my health.

A lot can be said about the value of experience and training. Real soldiers train and practice constantly so that when it's needed, it's right there. Firefighters, police officers, race car drivers, whatever, the key is not having to stop and think to know what to do. My real-life combat experience amounted to little more than a six-week free trial of some karate classes and a friend inviting me to a gun range a few times.

But I've spent a lot of time with online computer games. Player-vs-Player, PVP combat does a lot to teach you how to react. There was a time I worried I spent too much time in games. You have a lot of time to think about things like that in prison. That's about all you get to do. Now, however, all that time was butt-saving. I didn't have to pause and think about what to do. Like any conditioned response, the stimulus happens and the response can be automatic. Their weapons would slice me up at range.

So, I jumped. I leapt right at them, pushing hard to get the most out of the jump boosters in my back and feet. Altion would have to deal with one on his own. If I took on two and left him one and he complained? That would be later, if I was still alive at that point.

Both stood close to the edge, so getting to them wasn't hard. I was still going up with some momentum on my side. I hoped it would count as some kind of charge attack. Claws came out on the way, and I hit the guy on the left with a power attack punch to the chest as I slammed into him. Fifteen Stamina to do 45 damage to the guy seemed a good trade. We both went down in a tumble. I tried to get to my feet first. The standing guy might or might not try shooting me at point-blank range, so I was going to roll up. If the guy missed me he'd gank his partner.

Or at least that was the plan.

The guy grabbed me from behind and threw me. I smashed into a table, knocking it over and ending up behind it. I think I would have taken damage from that if I hadn't picked up armor along the way. In any other World I'd probably have crashed through the table, but there didn't seem to be much wood furniture in space. I know, right? But I was behind a sturdy table and my gun was still in hand.

Twin beams drew lines up the table as I came up to aim. Being able to just walk the beam to their target gave them an edge in accuracy that made it hard to focus. A little Focus traded in aiming time netted a handy critical hit, taking the damage up, which added to the claw wound to take him to about two-thirds of his Health.

I got down behind the table just as the red beams sliced through where my head had just been. Oh, for a grenade. I needed a plan.

Motivation to come up with one came in the form of a green grenade. Jerks! My jump boost cooldown was over, so I grabbed the edge of the table and I leapt with all I could. I couldn't see their faces to find out what kind of reaction they had to that. Honestly, they should have seen it coming. I'd already shown I was a jumper. It didn't seem they had though. I slammed into both and knocked them down. The grenade exploded behind me, hurling sticky green fibers that hardened whenever they hit anything. None of them got me. Lucky.

The table moved under me as they both pushed at it. I wanted to see at least one of their rifles loose on the floor. Not that lucky. I rolled to the edge, whacking my leg on a table leg, but able to reach under the edge with my left arm. I heard the cry and felt resistance as serrated blades found something fleshy to bite into. The table flipped, dropping me to the floor before it tumbled over the edge to fall far enough to account for a breaking sound when it hit the floor.

The two rolled off their backs. I was already on my side and able to get up faster and come down hard with my claws right into one of their faces. The head hit finished that guy off.

+500 XP (4100 total)

His partner was the less hurt one, though, and that guy kicked me hard with a power kick to the gut that tossed me right to the edge of the round, open core with barely more than half my Health. His rifle came up. I tried to roll away, but he followed me, scorching my thigh. I kept rolling until I was face up and I shot at him, squeezing the trigger as fast as I could, but he did the same thing. His damage output was far higher. Not a workable plan!

I rolled more, further away from the opening, and up to my feet. He was still hosing me with his laser, so I charged him. He was more ready for that than I planned, and he even dodged to my right so I couldn't just slash at him.

"Look out!" Altion bellowed. A pulse blast I would have sworn had blue electricity swirling around it barely missed me and scarred the floor. Someone one floor up again. What was it with these people? Altion rode a column of white up and past me, going after the new attacker.

I whirled as the jerk I still had to deal with brought his rifle around. Above, a helmeted figure with breasts and hips fired now at Altion, confirming the whirling blue electric effect. An ionized weapon, which at least shouldn't have extra effects on the fleshy Fighter, who took it on his shield. There wasn't time to see how he was doing, other than his Health bar was not full. The man with the rifle, about a third of the distance from me to the edge, was already firing again.

Range was not an option. Pistol versus rifle was not an option. I needed something drastic. He'd dodge left—my right—if I charged him. Fine, that would work for me.

I didn't just charge, I leapt, going for all the momentum I could muster. I aimed right, anticipating his dodge. He did dodge to his left, enough to foil a claw attack. That wasn't my plan though. I bull-rushed him, full-on running back flying tackle with enough momentum to push both of us out into the open core.

His feet banged the floor right at the edge, stealing some of his momentum and setting him spinning. Enough jump thrust should push me further out than him. He fell away while I hurtled across the space, not fast enough.

I reached out with my free hand to grab a floor to catch myself, half expecting to feel my arm torn from my shoulder. No pain ripped through me, and I spun as the claws caught only enough to slow my fall and redirect myself. I tumbled, flopping across the floor below until I came to stop at a booth of people staring at me, slack-jawed.

+500 XP (4600 total)

"Excuse me, sorry about that," I said as I worked my way to my feet with full Health. I'd leveled up again, but that was something to deal with later. My pistol was still alive in my hand, with one shot left, after all that. Game physics are good. In the real world I'm pretty certain it would have gone skittering away at some point. I moved to the edge, knowing full well now the glowing railings were solid enough to feel but not enough to prevent falling. The sprawled figure on the floor so many levels below was not moving.

Several floors up, Altion traded blows with the helmeted woman, who now swung a baton that sparked dramatically when it stuck the fighter's shield. They circled each other. The woman was about half dead. Altion drank a potion with his shield hand, shooting his Health bar from the barest sliver to a little under the halfway mark. Good call, but cutting it a little close.

As quick as I could I holstered my pistol and unslung my rifle. I brought it up, letting the scope's physical image overlay with the one it fed me though my hand. I aimed on the inhale, again trading Focus for accuracy, lining up the dotted line projection only I could see as they circled.

The fighter swung his sword, and although she had cuts in several places, she dodged most of his swings. The woman jabbed or swung the baton, and Altion blocked with his shield. Every time it hit him sparks flooded across him and he staggered. I followed her as she circled and when she lunged forward to take advantage of him being dazed I fired.

Fifteen points of Crit damage added to the 40 from the rifle. Her armor's Resistance no doubt reduced that, so her Health bar dropped about a third of what she had left, putting her somewhere about a hundred, I estimated. Sheesh. I really needed Crit damage to be higher, or get a headshot bonus. A shot like that would be hard the way she was ducking and moving avoiding his sword. I had interrupted her attack, though, which I think saved Altion.

"Strength, be-yotch!" he yelled as he took full advantage of her minor distraction. He slammed into her with his shield, pushing her back just far enough to teeter at the edge. I aimed as she wheeled her arms for balance only to watch her fail and fall. I followed her down, watching her slam into the floor hard enough to crack it. She landed flat on her back and wasn't moving. Now I had a moment to check the level.

Level 5 gained!
+23 Health
+19 Stamina
+8 Mana
+15 Focus
+5 Primary Characteristic Points
+10 Skill Points

The +5 went straight into the Charisma I'd been yearning for. I figured that had to help. Skill Points took more thinking about. I upped Bribery by 4 and Unarmed Combat by 6, bringing them to 5 and 15. Bribery was certain to get used again, and if I kept getting into situations where my claws were all I could work with, I needed to be better with them. Both reasonable choices.

"Hey, you okay?" Altion asked me as he approached, having ridden the light elevator down.

"Yeah. It was close, but I leveled up. So all good now."

"Cool. That was fun."

"Fun...," I repeated skeptically. Okay, it kind of had been, but fights like that were always more fun when respawning was an option.

"Well, you leveled up and we've got bodies to loot," he pointed out. I couldn't argue with that, so I followed him up to the one who had started the whole thing. The guy's clothes were a mess. He took several sword cuts going down. Blood was a thing in the game. The final blow, to the side of his head, chopped the point off the top of an ear.

"No money on him at all," Altion pointed out. "Pretty sure that means hired mercenaries who didn't want to risk losing things if they got captured, and didn't want us getting money for killing him. A shame, but I can't say I'm surprised. Not the first I've seen, but we'll get back to that."

Altion claimed a pair of grenades and tossed me the bulky rifle.

Item acquired: G&R PR-10 Plasma Rifle	
This solidly built rifle is designed for battle. Rugged and reliable, it fires bolts of super-heated plasma. It includes an integrated Gelcaster in an under-barrel mount.	
Range	90m
Accuracy	+10
Damage	85
Shots	40
Durability	73/80

Plasma damage has greatly reduced penetration against hard armors, effectively tripling the Toughness those armors provide.

Generic Gelcaster	
Gelcasters fire a capsule filled with gel which can spread or splatter on impact. Uses five-round compact magazines.	
Range	30m
Accuracy	-10
Damage	By Ammunition
Shots	5
Durability	50/50

WebSplatter Gel
Limited area splatter Snare effect. Its duration depends on the target's Strength.

"Huh, so that's what that stuff was," I said. "I'm glad it didn't actually get either of us." The fighter just nodded. We moved down to the one I killed who had not fallen to his death. The face under his helmet was young, twenty if that. Like the rest, no money and only carrying the basics.

Most of these had been NPCs. The woman leading them? I wasn't sure. Again, they started it, they would've killed me. What's the sane approach in an insane situation? I wished I could put those thoughts out of my head. In here, worrying about who was real and who was code-generated was the new metagaming, right? But I'd been a fan of metagaming. I'm good at it. I was going to need therapy if I got out of this alive.

The laser carbine wasn't a bad weapon, but did not have a Weapon Link and couldn't mount a scope. Altion wasn't interested in it, so I took it as sellable loot. At his suggestion I also took the kid's vest and helmet, stashing both in my pack for now.

Item acquired: Polymer Armor Vest	
While not terribly discreet, this vest does help reduce damage from energy weapons.	
Toughness	+5
Resistance	+15
Durability	16/35

Item acquired: Polymer Armor Helmet	
This simple helmet is upgradable and offers some protection against Flash effects.	
Toughness	+10
Resistance	+20
Flash Resist	+20
Durability	36/40

"Did you get XP for the chick?" Altion asked as we rode the elevator light shaft down to the floor—a floor conspicuously devoid of dead bodies. A smear of blood ran from where one had fallen to the door. One had survived and dragged the other away.

"Just a little, but I barely helped on her." I'd missed the notification but picked up another 150.

"Okay, then. She got away. Damn. I wanted a look at her rifle." Disappointment rang in his voice. "Let's get outa here." Again, I had no argument with that, and followed him.

Chapter 12

We rounded a corner, nearly smacking into a group of four trotting Federation soldiers. "Watch it!" one of them hollered at us, but they kept going, tromping past.

"They watch for people running," Altion pointed out. We strolled a couple more blocks, keeping our pace casual, and stopped at a bench.

"As I was saying before we were attacked, Silleste and I were attacked by mercenaries or bounty hunters of some kind. Pattern, maybe? She said she thought they were after her. She used an illusion scroll to make it seem like she was still with me while I tried to hold them off. I told her to go, to get off world without telling me where she was headed. I held them long enough for her to get away before soldiers happened across us and broke up the fight. I saw her get onto a ship, and watched that ship leave. I've been waiting here, watching for any sign of anyone else asking about her."

"So when I mentioned her, your first thought was I was hunting her."

"To be fair, you do kinda look the part." Touché.

"So why did you two come here, anyway? Run out of quests in Fantasyland?"

Altion's face turned sheepish, and he even blushed. "Yeah, that. No . . . no shortage of quests. It's kinda my fault."

I turned on the bench. This ought to be good, right? I waited patiently, leaving an expectant expression on my face, for him to continue.

"So it's pretty standard that areas near starting points are safer, and get more dangerous with distance, right? Yeah, it seems to work that way here, but not all the time. Through one of those friend-of-a-friend things I heard about a hidden zone through a cave system. I got all excited about it, figuring we might get to be the first ones there. Somebody had seen it but had to log off before getting to explore it. That was just before the Lockdown, as people are calling it.

"We get to the cave, the three of us. Oh, we had a wizard with us. I got him excited about it, and he convinced Silleste.

"We get into the caves and right away start hitting stuff above our levels. But in small enough numbers we could handle it. You know, the usual kill something, back up a bit and rest up, then move forward again, slow and careful. We figured it was probably a zone tier higher than we were really ready for, but we were excited. And we kept running into stuff we could handle, if barely.

"Anyways, the other side is this like glade of trees surrounded by cliffs. At the center we find this big fountain that's like a huge boulder cut in half. Water comes out the top and spills down the rough sides but avoids the cut face, where a Rift is. We'd only seen a couple to Rift City, but we figured we'd found one nobody knew about. Eldemar, that wizard, said a secret like that was worth good money. He handed an illusion scroll to Silleste, talking about hiding the entrance.

"That's when trouble started." Altion rubbed at the links resting on his thigh, polishing one with his thumb, and looked away. I wasn't sure how long to wait for him to continue.

"The glade wasn't empty. Wasn't unprotected. There was a reason people hadn't heard about it. Probably nobody had gotten there far and lived. I don't know what they're called, but these ... things swarmed and attacked. They were smart, too. They kept between us and the way out so we couldn't escape. I don't know how many there were. Twenty, maybe?

"They looked a bit like dragons, but only about the size of German Shepherds. They weren't good at flying, like the way grasshoppers don't really fly, they just use their wings to jump farther, you know? But they attacked as a pack. Eldemar threw a lightning bolt off that hurt a couple of them pretty decent, but I couldn't keep them off all of us. Silleste and I had armor. Eldemar? Not so much. Before he went down he got off this fear thing that drove them away, but not long enough to matter.

"The Rift was the only way to escape. It came out in the mountains a ways north of here, but it was a one-way thing. We got though and there was no Rift. I didn't think they're supposed to work that way, but I guess they can. Or it closed behind us and we missed it.

"We found a trail, and it led us here. Once we got here we found a safe place. It was late and we were tired. So we logged and came back the next morning. Then the Lockdown happened. We did some local quests for a few days, and then we got attacked. So that's the story."

The timeline made sense. That last time she logged off she told someone she'd found a Rift and went through it, but left out the details or where she'd ended up. At least those pieces came together.

"So you got stranded here, got attacked by somebody Silleste thought was after her, and then I said hi. Yeah, I don't blame you for being suspicious of me at first. I'd have done the same. And then we get attacked. You said something about a pattern. Let's hope that's not what's going on."

And really hope, at that. All the more reason to find her quick. Tension gathered in my stomach, a nervous crowd gathered to watch trouble.

"Those guys were after something," I pointed out. "No way that was a random ganking. That woman wasn't somebody with hired backup for PVP raids. And they fired at you first." Hey, they weren't after me, nothing about it was my fault.

"Yeah, I was thinking about that." He still hadn't turned back towards me.

"Well," I said, straightening out. I didn't need to be facing him if he was just going to keep looking away. "If they are hunting her, then they don't have her. If that's the case, we need to find her first. Where do we go from here? You said she got on a ship?"

"Yeah. The Amethyst Rose. I caught the name as it left."

"So how do we track it?" Obviously not by footprints, but there had to be a way.

"I know a guy."

"You know a guy?" Hardly the most helpful answer.

"I've spent my time running quests and meeting people," he explained. "Networking. There's this bartender I know. Smugglers and freighter types talk to him. He'll know where the ship was going."

"Well, the last bar was fun. Let's go hit another one," I suggested.

"They're not all like that. I haven't seen much trouble here, all in all. Especially with so many Fed soldiers about. And man, they've been bringing a lot in. Seems like a quest event though. I'm guessing a planned storyline. Well," he said as he stood, "no time like now, right?"

We walked streets and alleys, crossing traffic carefully. We tried to be inconspicuous when we saw patrols, clanking squads of eight again, but a guy in chain mail can only be so inconspicuous. Sure, his cloak covered most of it, which helped, but only so much.

The bar itself was smaller. The single-story block building with rounded edges looked out of place shouldered between a pair of newer, shinier buildings. An actual wood door with an oversized handle led us inside. At least, it looked like wood. Might've just been a realistic synthetic.

Everything about the inside said dive bar in languages everyone should have understood. Glowing spheres floated just below the ceiling, getting light everywhere but never making any one space bright, or even fully lit. Booths lined the outside, with small tables for four sprinkled around the middle. A stage filled one corner, taking a decent amount of floor space for something not being used. Drones or little robots hovered around the bar, waving soft spotlights around at different drink bottles, and keeping the bar area the only adequately lit space.

"Get a booth," Altion recommended. "I'll go talk up the bartender."

A waitress in a short, slinky, sleeveless dress showed up almost right away. Spindly cyborg limbs on her left half contrasted with her curvy right side. What I really wanted was coffee, but I wasn't sure about risking Space coffee just then. I wanted regular coffee.

"What kinds of beer have you got?" I asked instead.

"We have every kind of beer available on Relkit III." As if that helped. I named one I'd tried at the Hunters' Hall, not feeling adventurous.

"You got it, sugar," she said as she turned and strutted off. Her metal leg ended in a heel she matched with a tall shoe on the other leg. Maybe some kind of inner gyro helped her balance. Her return with the beer was just as prompt as her arrival.

"Well, hello," a Fenurian purred as she slunk up close to my left and set a highlighter-green drink on the table next to my beer. "I'm Lunis. I'm pretty sure I haven't seen you here before." A loose-fitting tank top of super-thin silver material flowed from her shoulders to the booth seat. Extra short, red-dappled brown fur gave her an aerodynamic look.

"That'd be because I haven't been."

She leaned over my drink and sniffed, then turned her head up to frown at me. "And you're drinking that? There are so many better things you could be drinking." She sat back up and took a sip of her drink, picking it up in her left hand and drinking it like a human would, at least, and not just lapping it up. I wasn't sure I'd be able to take her seriously if she had.

She held the drink up to what light there was. "Mind you, around here you shouldn't trust a drink a stranger hands you. But you could share mine." She leaned over the table a little turning her body and pulling thin fabric across fur-covered breasts she pushed out a little. Subtle, huh? Where was her right hand? I grabbed it and held it with my steel grip, pulling it away from the box at my belt.

"Nuh-uh," I said, on to her game for sure now.

"Hey," she called out louder than necessary. "Let me go!" I was starting to hate bars here.

Three big thugs, one Mordian and two human, got up from two booths away without hesitation. One cue. A setup. Wonderful.

The Mordian's oversized hands crashed down onto the table. "What's going on?" he demanded.

"He started groping me and he won't stop."

"No," I protested. "I was not. She was trying to pickpocket me." I tried to keep my voice level. Extra Charisma or not, I didn't think it worked. This wasn't going to be something I could talk my way out of.

"You get your filthy hand off my girl," the closest human, a burly beast of a man in a vest checkered with pyramid studs, commanded. I had little doubt violence would erupt as soon as I did. So I didn't. Stall for time, I figured.

The Mordian grabbed the table and hurled it out of the way and across the room. It only didn't hit a man at a table alone because he ducked. It did smash into the cyborg waitress. While the table wasn't blocking me in anymore, that didn't make me less cornered.

"Hey . . . ," I tried, raising my right hand to wave him back, still keeping hold of the girl's arm in my left. "There's no need for this. Nobody's been hurt, it can stay that way."

The man who ducked the table rose to his feet sporting an enraged glare and smoothing out dark blue hair. Other bar patrons were turning to see what was going on.

"Um, no," the other human said, not looking less menacing for being shorter and slimmer than his buddy. "It can't."

Damn. Altion's back still faced me from the bar, where he continued to lean on one elbow all nonchalant. I was on my own here. "I'm not unarmed, how ugly do you want this to get? Why don't you just take her and leave?" If I could just de-escalate things a little, there could be a way out of this.

"Maybe you give us all your money and we're willing to forget this whole thing happened," the Mordian said. Their eyes all held the same thirst for violence, for inflicting harm. No, handing over money wasn't going to stop things.

I stood up—not too quickly—and shifted Lunis from my left hand to my right. She wasn't putting up much of a struggle, which wasn't sitting right. With my left hand free I snapped my claws out, hoping they weren't looking for a dangerous fight. I at least wouldn't be easy prey.

Their expressions hardened from tauntingly dangerous to determinedly deadly. The reason clicked hard and fast. I was holding sharp, serrated blades to the Fenurian one of them called "his girl." I had her hostage. She was just supposed to be bait, not in any real danger. Oops? So much for de-escalating.

Now knives came out—and a hatchet for the Mordian. Really? Who carries a hatchet into a bar?

"Look," I tried one last time, "I don't think any of us want this fight." The blue-haired man's eyes dropped to the knives and hatchet. He picked up a chair in one beefy hand.

"Let her go or you leave here in bags," Checkered Vest warned. So I shoved her towards the man as hard as a Strength 15 could. I really needed to keep putting points into that. She stumbled and Checkered Vest reached to grab her. His eyes widened as she slackened and slid to the floor. Blood coated and dribbled from the knife in his hand. He came at me screaming.

I had enough presence of mind to catch his knife slash with my Cyborg Arm Block, and I felt no pain as my silver Heath bar dropped a small amount. There was no question I was in it now.

I got one claw swipe on him before the others came at me, but a Melee Attack rating of 120/1000 and a whopping 16 points of Unarmed Combat skill means you can miss something right in front of you. I dodged a stab from the other human, also gaining +1 Dodge. The Mordian wound back with his hatchet until a chair collided with his head. You gotta be careful who you throw tables at.

The Mordian turned, leaving me two to deal with. From the small amount Checkered Vest's Health bar had dropped, he was at least my level, more likely a level or two above me. This was no newbie garden encounter.

I turned and dove over the booth seating, ending up under the next booth's table. A yelp of surprise from the booth's occupants suggested their displeasure at my intrusion. They had to have seen what had been going on, what right did they have to be surprised at this point?

The shorter human stepped up onto the seat I had started all this in, coming into view in time for me to draw my pistol and squeeze off a lucky shot that caught him in the face. He fell backwards, clutching at his face. Cursing myself for a fool, I crawled out from under the table. I really sucked at de-escalating. I put the pistol away, not wanting to draw more attention to myself as a threat.

The Mordian had already smashed the blue-haired guy's table with the blue-haired guy. Three other burly dudes were closing to get involved. The splintering sound of something breaking with jagged edges emphasized how out-of-hand things were getting.

Checkered Vest's berserker bellow announced his charge. I jumped up and over him only to smash my head on the ceiling. I came down hard on my knees. Someone else tripped backwards over me, smacking the floor hard with their head.

"Come on," Sir Altion said, dragging me to my feet. "Let's get out of here." He bashed away a swung chair with his shield like he was swatting at a fly. The chair-wielder went down from another chair hitting him square in the back. I bolted with Altion. The din behind us escalated to cascading roar as more and more figures joined the raging brawl. We ran like animals from a forest fire.

"You have a thing about bars?" I think he was teasing.

I clearly had more Stamina than Altion, but still we ran without stopping until we reached one of the landing pads. Fortunately, we never ran into any Federalist patrols.

The way the town sat on the outcropping, bigger ships docked along pads sticking out like broad leaves around the edge. Especially large ships squatted on pads far smaller than they were. The sheer amount of mass some of those ships should have had lent an extra flimsy look to the pads, which also served as a gentle reminder that game physics wasn't always real-world physics.

Altion lead me to a terminal building the size of a large warehouse. Reflective black glass rose easily a dozen meters tall along the entire front face. A foursome of Federalist troops, in blue uniforms rather than combat armor, stood sentry alongside oversized entry doors that slid apart for us. Model starships formed a convoy along the spacious atrium's vaulted glass ceiling.

A blue-skinned, lumpy critter sat behind a registration counter, blinking bulging eyes at us from a head that waved on a tentacle neck. Not one of the player races. A discordant hum undertoned a voice that couldn't quite handle hard consonants as it asked us our destinations. We didn't even have to wait in line. Better yet, no security screenings. Walking into an airport as armed as I was wouldn't ever happen outside the game!

Altion balked at the fare for two to Jentassa IV and asked how much I had with a sheepish frown. The big Knight having to ask the newbie for money. I warned myself not to tease him about it until the ship had lifted off. Admittedly, the amount was intimidating. He had about twenty times the cash I had. The plasma rifle was decent loot, and I preferred the better accuracy on my laser rifle. Plus there was the carbine. He took the looted weapons and ran off to sell them. Even after that, pitching in what I could left me with all of 4 silver. But we had enough together.

With no need to check baggage, an android directed us to a corridor for Landing Pad Eight. Another uniformed soldier stood at the corridor entrance, along with a civilian who checked our tickets before letting us through. I couldn't shake the feeling barred doors were about to close behind me. I had to remind myself I wasn't even in prison in real life. While I'd avoided thinking about it for a bit, I'd rather have avoided it longer.

I expected passenger starships to be graceful star liners, with sweeping wings and elegant lines. The corridor emptied onto the landing pad perch of something for which ungainly seemed understated. Four huge cylindrical engines hung from thick struts jutting out from a fuselage that could have been blocky parts of other ships smashed together into one oversized whole. An assembly of components that might as well have been ripped from other ships deemed too unsightly to keep.

A boarding ramp wide enough for a tank hung down like the lolled-out tongue of something that had vomited to death. Altion gave me the same querulous look I was sure I wore.

"Looks so inviting, doesn't it?" The knight asked. "Like walking into a dragon's mouth."

"Aren't you the cheerful one? Let's just get inside and hope they have chairs. And seatbelts."

Mordians in gray-and-white jumpsuits greeted us at the top of the ramp, checking our tickets yet again. No cheerful flight-attendant smiles on these women, no. Also, Mordian women were not my idea of attractive. I've seen prettier trolls.

The interior hardly inspired spacefaring excitement. Rather, words like "utilitarian" and "cheap" came to mind. No futuristic gleaming white bulkheads, but exposed beams and unfinished metal. Altion's boots clanged on the deck, although the crew wore softer shoes that padded heavily along. While my boots weren't actually silent, they certainly seemed that way in comparison.

A green-skinned Mordian steward with small, nub-like horns in a ridge over her forehead led us to a small cabin. "This will be your cabin for the trip. The flight will be about twenty standard hours. A deck plan next to your cabin door will lead you to the common spaces." She took the tickets and demonstrated the door would slide open with a wave of either of them before a sensor on the wall. The room was the kind of place you'd only call comfortable compared to a prison cell. Altion sighed in disappointment, or disapproval.

The wall across from the door would have been a good place for windows, but instead only offered buttress-like supports every half meter. Beds lined opposing walls, with a desk and chair next to each. A touch-screen display panel next to the door displayed the few "common" areas of the deck like the zone maps of early games. I tapped different areas to see what kinds of options there were. The dining hall and lounge were both listed as open "26/5."

"Well, at least we should be able to have a conversation here without being attacked, right?" I suggested.

"We'd better, or I'm gonna be ticked. Or I'd suggest one of us is cursed." Altion dropped onto a bed. I sat more lightly on the other.

"Hey, I think curses only happen where you come from." At least, I really didn't want to end up believing in space curses. "So, what do we know about this Jentassa, and any ideas why Silleste chose it?"

"I've only heard a little. Jungle planet, mostly. Humans and elves with some other aliens. It's a place she could blend in some among other elves, so maybe that's part of it. Or maybe she just took the first ship headed out." He shrugged and let himself fall back on the bed. "I guess we'll find out when we get there."

"Sometimes I miss being able to push a button and skip straight to the next zone," I grumbled, with little to do but wait. It wasn't like I expected the lounge to be filled with side quests I could do on the ship. "So, how'd you meet her, anyway?"

"Silleste?"

"No, the President." At least he had the decency to chuckle at my sarcasm. I thought it was kind of witty.

He laced his fingers beneath his head. I scooted back to lean against the bulkhead.

"Not that exciting, really. Fantasa'an has a few different starting cities. I started off in this castle on the edge of a rocky plateau overlooking this wide mix of prairie and forest. I'd gotten through the tutorial and some basic starter quests, got myself up to level four, and then had to decide where to go. I'd talked to some NPCs, and most of them suggested I head west, out along the plateau.

"But there was this one chick who talked about farm towns in the lowlands having all kinds of problems and needing help and complaining how their own prince never sent anybody. Their lands and the plateau lands are different kingdoms, and they don't get along. There was some lore about that in the castle, about how the castle had been built to fend off attacks.

"So I took this switch backed trail down and trekked through some woods. I think the forests right around there are more like level five to ten, 'cause I kept getting my butt kicked. That was back before the lockdown, obviously.

"She was also hunting some of those woods from a town further in. She . . . she showed up just in time, and suggested I follow her back to town. So we partnered up and worked on quests around there, met Eldemar, and eventually ended up in Space Opera Land. I hit level nine just before we met. Looking forward to seeing what I get at ten, which shouldn't be much longer at the rate trouble has been finding us."

"Yeah," I agreed. Level five didn't seem impressive, so I didn't say anything about it. Besides, he hadn't asked. If he wanted to know he'd ask. I'd figure out what to say then. I should have caught up some by then.

So, while there was no waiting for zones to load, there was also little to do but wait and rest for the trip. Unless we got attacked by pirates or something. As long as it wasn't some stupid space dragon or something. . . .

Chapter 13

"Wake up, sleepybutt. We're almost there." Altion loomed over my bunk, as if he wasn't big enough already. I stretched, again pleased to be waking up somewhere nicer than my cell. As if that narrowed much down though. Was that ever going to stop being the case each morning? Was it morning? Whatever. New system, new planet, new day. Plus, I'd gotten a sizable chunk of XP for "traveling to my first new star system," which pushed me over the edge to level 6.

Level 6 gained!
+23 Health
+19 Stamina
+8 Mana
+15 Focus
+5 Primary Characteristic Points
+10 Skill Points

Windows in the lounge faced to the ship's side, and the knight and I were far from the only ones gathered to gaze out as the ship passed a pair of planets orbiting each other close. A thin band of colorful rings surrounded the pair. Neat as it was, I wasn't sure if the physics would really work. Then again, science wasn't ever my specialty.

The ship fell into orbit around an orange and green ball. While we moved closer, I distributed points from leveling. I hadn't done anything to strength in a while, and after the recent brawl I wanted more. So, I dumped my five points of primary attributes there. Five skill points I put into Track and five into Pistol which had fallen behind Rifle.

"Attention all passengers. We have arrived in orbit around Jentassa IV. Off-boarding passengers proceed to the shuttle hangar for departure."

A short, slender Mordian came and led us to a line of shuttles, blocky affairs with stubby wings and beefy landing struts. Four other humans joined Altion and me on one shuttle. Four additional seats remained empty. The scrawny Mordian boarded with us as our pilot. At least the shuttle had seats and buckles.

A brawny man next to me buckled himself in and clung to the harness straps with a white-knuckled grip.

"You worried about the flight, or something or someone waiting for you?" I asked the guy.

"I heard shuttles get attacked by pirates sometimes," he explained.

Altion leaned forward as much as his harness allowed. "If you were a pirate, would you go after a Mordian ship? This shuttle is probably armed heavy enough to *be* a small pirate ship. Plus, do you see anything here that seems valuable?"

The man laughed a hollow, forced chuckle. "No, I guess not."

I patted the pistol on my thigh. "Tell ya what. If we *do* get attacked by pirates, Sir Altion and I here will cut you in on a share of whatever loot we get off them."

The man looked me up and down. I couldn't tell if he was reassured or not.

The view out a decent sized window distracted me as we came in over a broad orange desert. Once we crossed a tall, icy mountain range we dropped over an expanse of vivid green jungle canopy. Colorful creatures winged and soared above the treetops. Nothing I recognized from my Hunters' Hall reading. A broad river snaked its way from the mountains to some far-off, unseen destination.

We circled around a city before spiraling in to land. A sprawling city spread above the trees, as if built on mammoth, interconnected metal lily pads floating on a treetop ocean. The green carpet rippled across an expansive valley rimmed on three sides by low mountains. If there were any other settlements in the valley, they hid below the canopy.

The shuttle landed, and we disembarked down the scuffed ramp to a rooftop not far from a frosted-glass dome enclosure with two sets of doors. Few other buildings were as tall. I made out multiple lily pad clusters of buildings connected by bridges at multiple levels. We made for the dome and the shuttle left with a thrumming drone of overpowered thrusters.

The dome capped an empty shaft running down the core of the building. Open platforms all around the edge served as elevators. I stopped counting floors below at sixteen.

"So, you think we get attacked here?" I asked as we walked toward the nearest elevator platform. Just a flat square of dark metal, with no railings, seemed an appropriately inconvenient place for a gunfight. I needed to figure out how to upgrade my jump jets to full-on flight thrusters.

Altion grumbled. "I kinda hope not. That looks like a bitch of a fall, you know?"

"Yeah. I'm not sure I can jump all the way across." Not remotely. Fortunately, the platform lowered us to the ground without incident.

Outside, we explored a few streets while rounded hover vehicles zoomed alongside or above. Buttresses lining tall buildings provided ample spaces for hiding and cast a web of soft shadows in the bright, blue-tinted sunlight. A varied assortment of muted colors spread throughout the city. Bridges and streets and buttresses ranked with shadows as limited sources of gray.

Humans showed a distinct majority presence, followed by elves and a smattering of other races, including some I'd never seen before and weren't offered as player options. I enjoyed an extensive buffet of skin colors and hair colors and whether one had hair or scales or antennae or what have you. Fashions were even more varied, as were the color schemes. Not always colors that belonged together.

"I wonder what the local factions are like," Altion said, breaking the casual silence we had walked in since arriving. "It seems like there's at least two everywhere I've been."

"Yep. Easy way to include more local quests, right?" What would they be though? That was the real question. That and could I steer clear of them.

The knight nodded, and a grin spread across his face. Leveling up wasn't likely to hurt. But part of me felt like each quest was also a potential delay. Delays worried me. I realized my fingers were drumming on the handgrip of my pistol as I walked. I took the hand away and made it swing free.

"So, where do you think we go first, Space Ranger?"

"Hunter," I corrected. "A bar. We'll need to find out what's what and who's who around here. Bars tend to be the places for that, right?"

"Has been so far," he agreed. "And maybe this time—"

He stopped at my glare.

We had just gotten an idea of the general layout of our Zone—each lily pad part of the city was a numbered zone—when I noticed a figure following us. Altion gave no indication of having seen it, so I waited to confirm before I said anything. My first impression was right. Someone was following us. A human man in brown pants and a burnt orange sleeveless tunic, who paused behind things and then sped up enough to catch up a little.

Why should I have been surprised? Reflections and casual glances showed me more of the hairless man with an aggressive walk and an oversized, hulking pistol that could have been a sawed-off shotgun. It even looked like it offered two barrels. Upgrades to the tactical package were paying off.

"So . . . , don't look back," I warned, "but we're being followed. Human with a pistol that's had a steroid overdose. I'm thinking another player looking for someone to gank."

"By which you mean murder."

"Yeah. Not as much fun when people die from it." I was never going to see these games the same again. Mind you, I'd have to survive and get out of this one before any other would matter. "Let's look for an alley we can lure him into. I'd rather be the ambusher than the ambushee. Unless we see a place we can ditch him."

"Hells yeah," the knight agreed.

Dark alleys, on the other hand, were less plentiful here. What we did find was a large outdoor café plaza. Three streets and a wall of shops bordered a paved square raised a step from the streets. Round tables spread haphazardly, many topped with wide, disk sun shades that oriented themselves to follow the sun. People in various colors and configurations occupied perhaps a fifth of the seats, and a human waiter in a black space tuxedo strolled through with a tray of small drinks. A small orange lizard winged low across a mostly clear sky.

"Whatd'ya think, we stall here and see if we can wait him out?"

I wasn't itching for a fight. I'd figured out early on there wasn't a Consider system to tell me if a fight was winnable, and a few million players had been in the game longer than I had. Actually, I rather doubted anyone was newer than I was. That made me the official newbie.

But I didn't have a better plan for avoiding him, and ambushing him was getting trickier. I could get to a rooftop, but that wouldn't help the tank. We stood and faced each other, discussing the different merits of each table while also surreptitiously keeping an eye on our stalker.

He stopped under a doorway awning across the street, as if he were just another wandering shopper.

The street opposite the shops had a T intersection with a narrower street leading away. The street opposite the guy tailing us had heavier traffic.

"How long do you think he'll wait?" I asked, then noticed the man talking into a communicator. I swore softly and pointed it out.

We headed towards the more trafficked street. The back of my neck itched, exposed to a shot that could come at any time if the guy was willing to attack us in a crowd. Three lanes of traffic would at least give us cover if we got past it. I wasn't sure if I'd be strong enough to leap over it with a heavily armored passenger.

The close lane of traffic slowed, colorful rounded shapes a half meter above the ground. One, shaped like a minivan melted around the edges, stopped with a growing space before it and a line of traffic behind it. The rising-pitch whine of a horn blared.

Dread climbed onto my shoulders, weighing them down as men hopped out, two on the close side and two more from the far. Cops? I dared to hope, already chiding my foolish optimism. A variety of weapons came out from under long coats. Nope. Not cops.

We turned back in time to see four more hopping out of a similar hover minivan to join our original problem child. More long coats, more weapons, small and large. Not cops. I discarded a brief hope they were rival factions with us just caught in the crossfire.

Shots came from both sides at once, rapid-fire streams and bolts of reds and oranges. Screaming customers dove to the ground, their drinks and meals scattering. Somehow the initial barrage missed us both as we ducked down and flipped over tables for cover.

"If this is PVP, it's pretty damned well set up!" Altion complained.

Tables helped some, but some shots lanced right through. We returned fire, but much too quickly found ourselves taking damage faster than we could dish it out. I took one out, netting another 300 XP, but too many still gunned for us. Please, no grenades this time, I prayed.

They held their distance, spreading out along both flanks, pinning us in with an ever-improving kill zone. They also used tables for cover. One with a pistol grabbed a young girl for cover.

Metagaming is all about understanding the rules and code behind the game, figuring out what little flaws or foibles you can exploit. Shooting a kid would ding me with some serious faction hits, and would get me into a lot of trouble. But the guy was a good shot, and was taking me down too fast to leave alone. The key factor, however, was the kid. I've never played a game that started anyone as a kid, and the game hadn't given me any kind of age options. Everyone I'd seen that struck me as a player looked about the same age. The kid was an NPC. She had to be. I took the shot.

I also appreciate game mechanics that reward aim with increased chances of crits. The flashing "Critical Hit!" notification faded as he fell. I hadn't even hit the girl.

> **+300 XP (6600 total)**

Decent experience, suggesting these were my level or higher. Including that one, we'd taken down about half of them by the time Altion tossed me a healing potion. "I got one for each of us," he said as his health bar notched even closer to death, and his was doing better than mine. I drank it down while he pulled out his.

Healing potions are always good things. If someone offers you a healing potion, always take it. You can't have too many. This was better than just, poof, your health bar is better. It tasted like life itself, which I suppose it basically was. The rush that ran through me was more than exhilarating, and I felt pain vanish as it washed wounds away.

There were still aches, and there was still damage. Oh, was there still damage. Wounds disappeared, yes, but half my Health bar was a silver line still rather low. The potion didn't affect the artificial parts. Yeah.

Altion brought his potion up to drink it, and an orange line lanced through it. The potion shattered with sparkling red splatter as the orange beam of death continued into, and back out of, the knight's head.

"No!" I yelled ineffectively as his Health bar vanished, and he dropped to the too-regular sci-fi cobblestones. In the distraction of watching my first friend in the game die, knowing somewhere in the real world there was some guy dying with him, I got hit twice more, eating up a good quarter of what the potion had given back.

I ran. What else could I do?

I ducked and stayed low, weaving from table to table, knocking them over for cover. A little cross street led away. In the back of my head it had already been a Plan B, but that Plan B looked a lot differently then.

Shots missed me as I jumpboosted my way over the light traffic in the way. Another sign it was a game: people still drove by while a major gunfight went on right next to them. At least one shot hit a vehicle, which crashed into . . . something. No wasting time looking behind me.

I sprinted down the narrower street, just one lane each way with barely any traffic. I kept to the middle of the road, weaving to keep as many cars as possible between me and however many were pursuing. A horn blared at me. Dozens of shots missed me in the length of a block. One didn't. Slivers of red Health bar remained. Damage penalties reduced my speed, as if the pain wasn't enough punishment.

I took a diving leap, hoping to stay hidden by cars I dove between. I landed in a roll, gracefully rolling up to my feet and continued running.

Or, that's how it had played out in my head before I tried it.

Okay, fine. I faceplanted.

I scrambled to my feet and ran. At least my Stamina bar was dropping slowly, that was something.

"Don't let him get away!" someone yelled behind me.

I squeezed a few ineffective shots off before rounding another corner. They were keeping up, and I had thought my speed was pretty decent even cut down as it was.

I kept firing behind me as I ran, shoving my last power pack into the pistol on the fly. I rounded another corner, thankful for any moment out of their sight.

This alley was narrow, too narrow for a car. Yet no litter drifted about. No garbage cans sat around like lazy bums. So much for cover. It offered four doors. And a dead end.

I tried the first one, which buzzed and refused to open, as did the second. A sign hung over the third, "West End Salvage." Another sign declared it closed and the control panel next to the door didn't even beep or buzz. Nothing.

The final one swung open, and I lurched through to shove it shut behind me. I leaned back against it, finally allowing myself a moment to see just how bad my situation was as I heard them bang at one of the locked doors. Seventeen points of red Health left. I could almost do that in a single punch. The silver bar offered a whopping 4 cyborg HP.

The door locked with a beep and a sturdy clunk.

Darkness surrounded me, lit only by a green indicator glowing and fading on a forklift robot against the far wall. Nightvision let me see most of the space although far too many deep shadows lingered. Stacks of containers and large boxes in arbitrary piles spread around me. Drums on pallets sat in short rows. Even in space I can recognize a shipping/receiving area. A window suggested office next to the industrial robot.

Pounding on the door at my back echoed in the tall space. Angry voices grumbled then receded. I was safe. I guess they couldn't pick electronic locks.

"So, this is where we have a conversation about who you are," a menacing voice explained, "and who sent you." Figures stepped out of the omnipresent shadows.

I didn't have the time to count them, but at least ten moved into covered positions as overhead lights clacked on. Glare protection was a nice upgrade benefit. If they counted on me being at all blinded by the light, they'd get no benefit from that. On the other hand, I saw a lot of rifles pointed my way. One heavy one perched on a tripod. Light gleamed off metal parts on all of them. Biohazard symbols became visible on dusty drums around me.

"What?" I know, I'm cool, huh? At least I wasn't out of breath. That would have looked even worse.

A big guy stepped forward, the pistol in his hand dwarfing the one I realized I was still holding. I let it drop and raised my hands.

"What do you think you're doing here?" He stood at least a head taller than me and was either an android or a cyborg bent on replacing as much humanity as possible. "You've either stumbled somewhere you really don't belong or you're in for a supernova of trouble." Chunky metal fingers clenched into a fist. Was that bulky gray armor worn or built in?

"Hang on, Jorraq. He's one of us." One of us. I wiggled alloy fingers in as much of a wave as I dared. One hit point per second of natural healing meant a labored creep on the red Health line. The silver one didn't change at all of course.

"My name's Max. nobody sent me. I'm not working for anyone. I was jumped by a gang and this was the first place I could find to maybe hide from them."

"Do you buy that?" the woman behind the tripod-mount asked. I recognized the implant over her eye and temple. Hers was still the level one version.

"Maybe," another said.

"He does look pretty beat up," the one who'd recognized my cyborgness added. The right half of his head gleamed gold. Dark hair spilled down the left side.

"So . . . ," Jorraq, the leader, stared. "Max. Gang, huh?" Given my track record so far of de-escalating situations I wasn't exactly feeling comfortable.

"Or something," I confessed. "Actually seemed more like hired thugs. A couple cars of them."

"So not Federalists? Not troops?" Ms. Tripod Mount's voice shook.

"No. No uniforms, but they were disciplined and knew what they were doing. It was a coordinated ambush. I don't know why. They killed a friend of mine." My only friend. The orange beam vaporized healing potion and brains again in a flash.

"Where are you from, Max?" Jorraq crossed his arms with a whir of heavy servos.

"Relkit III. I've only just got here. I came on a passenger liner. Gotta say, so far not impressed with this planet." Honesty. It works sometimes.

I'd tried a similar line my first morning at FCI Otisville. The reply then had been, "You aren't supposed to like it here." Seeing as how this wasn't a prison planet, it had to get a better response here, right?

"And you have no idea who you've crossed?"

"I just got here. Really. We got off the ship and were looking for a bar. We were being followed before we found one. At first I thought maybe it was a . . . mugger." Keep things simple.

"And why should we trust you?" I hate questions like that.

"There's a way to find out," one of them suggested. That didn't make me feel any better.

Chapter 14

They led me at gunpoint past the forklift robot through the office door. A computer terminal sat neglected on the one desk while a stack of dusty boxes sat on the chair in the corner. Through there, in another warehouse space, a wide cargo elevator carried us down. As big as it was, the dozen or so of us were a snug fit. Someone stripped me of my rifle.

When the elevator stopped, someone shoved me ahead into an arena with a sloped floor. I slid down to the dirt floor; the others moved to take positions around the outer edge behind a battered railing.

Five silver hit points now. So, there was natural healing for it, but about a point per minute. I'd never spared the time to notice before. The red bar was longer but still only one third full. At least normal healing added up. That narrow silver bit worried me.

"An arena?" I complained, taking in my surroundings. At least they didn't line the thing with Medieval weapons. "I was just nearly murdered in the streets. Half of me barely works." How was that at all fair?

"He's right," the man with the golden head said. He picked up a white case with a red cross on it and hopped over the railing.

"You really are a mess," he added, extending a gold hand for me to shake. "I'm Grovan. Let's get you a little patched up, eh?" Like I was going to complain, even if just a temporary fix.

The first aid kit offered an array of hardware and tools, none of which looked like anything a surgeon would use. Some dripped oil or grease. Light from banks of overhead lights suspended or hovering high above us glimmered in slick grime.

"So, what, you patch me up and then I fight something?"

"You're a bright one, aren't you?" He set to work on my arm first before I saw more of me wasn't flesh than I'd realized. My armor vest showed wear reflected in the 12 of 50 durability remaining.

"And this proves you can trust me . . . how?" The more games progress there still only seems to be two kinds of quest. You either fight something or you run errands. Games had evolved from following a storyline by going from waypoint to waypoint clicking to "interact" with objects, to VR goggles which really just stepped it up from clicking a button or lever to poking at it. Conversations had come a long way from selecting dialog from a menu, but just then I'd have preferred some kind of puzzle to another combat.

"Well, if you die we don't have to worry about it. If you win then at least you're tough enough to warrant some respect."

"Oh. What am I up against?"

Rather than answer, he finished his work, leaving my silver health bar at 50%: 48. I'd healed up more bio-health along the way, so the two bars were almost equal. He hovered his way back up to his spot.

Metal fists came down on the railing all around me, banging out an ominous, slow, dirge rhythm. Just the cadence for chanting to although not a word was spoken. A door, opposite where I'd come in, ground and scraped its way open.

The banging stopped. The trial was about to begin.

Quest: Earn the CyberRogues' Respect

The CyberRogues don't trust you yet. Win a trial by combat to earn their grudging respect.

Grudging respect, that was reassuring. Nobody had said anything about rules, but to-the-death seemed all too implied.

What crawled out didn't need a door that big. Skittering down the opposite slope on ten metal legs and brandishing over-sized lobster claws and a scorpion tail it was equal parts insect, robot, and nightmare. The long tail swayed over its back like a cobra.

If ever there was a time for that gelcaster under the rifle I'd sold for space fare, this was it. As it was, Jorraq held my rifle in one metal fist with a smug grin. Jerk. I didn't see who had my pistol.

The thing zig-zagged as it undulated closer, body leaning one way and tail covering the other back and forth. I needed some kind of edge.

I crouched down with a plan and waited until it charged forward. The cyber nightmare decipede rushed at me faster than I expected, but I still got my move off. My claws snicked out behind me as I leapt with full boost. I put all that inertia into a power attack.

> **Race Ability Unlocked: Cyborg Leap Attack**
> Leap attacks add Strength to base melee damage and add your Jump Distance to Crit Chance and Crit Power.
> Cooldown 60 seconds

> **Leap Power Attack Critical Hit! 268 Damage!**

My claws slashed right through the thing's tail, severing it near the halfway point. Based on the sounds from my audience, I'd impressed at least some of them. Hey, I was impressed, too

I turned when I came down and it had already turned, too. That much damage should have come with a stun effect since it would have flat out killed me. No. The damned beast was down a fifth, at best. How tough was this thing?

It charged again, not any slower than before and before my jump cooldown was over, let alone the much longer cooldown on Leap Attack. I dove to the side to swipe at it while dodging. It almost worked.

For something waist height, it had long reach and over-sized pincer things big enough to grab my arm. The next thing I knew I was on my back in the dirt while curved loppers tried to take off my left arm. Blood spilled out around the pincer's edges as 46 Health vanished all at once. The 6 Toughness from my jacket only did so much.

Power Attack was available again, and I took advantage of that, bashing its elbow as hard as I can. Thanks to the strength I'd added that meant 60 damage in one punch, minus whatever its Toughness did to reduce that. It dropped me, and I flopped to the floor.

Its follow up attack missed me, fortunately, which gave me enough time to stagger to my feet feeling short on options. It skittered back, snapping pincers at me. I braced myself for the inevitable charge, setting myself up for one desperate play.

Ten legs meant it skipped from standstill to full-on sprint without bothering to accelerate. I'd wanted more time. Or a pike. I jumped over pincers swinging in from both sides and landed on the thing's back. Without its tail to cover it, I was hoping its pincers couldn't reach up here. I went primal on the damned thing, stabbing and stabbing with my claws until robot legs gave out from under it.

+500 XP (7100 total)

Quest completed: Earn the CyberRogues' Respect
Quest Rewards: Reputation increase with Jentassa IV CyberRogues +250XP (Total 7350)

"Not bad . . . not bad," Grovan said once he'd slid down to me. The crowd relaxed, and a murmur of conversation spread around them. I couldn't hear it well enough to gauge any kind of verdict. If I came across a hearing upgrade. . . .

He waited, arms crossed, while I crawled down. Overhead lighting dimmed once was nothing interesting to watch.

"So, now what?"

"Now we're going fix you up, and then we're going to celebrate."

Fixing me up sounded good. Celebrating? I haven't partied since my arrest. A little downtime didn't sound like a bad idea. Especially if I could win these people over enough to get help from them. As long as it didn't mean some tedious side quest.

Grovan started repairs with his first aid kit. The rest wandered off through different doorways. He worked quickly and efficiently, and I waited quietly while he brought the silver part of my Health back to full.

"I think I need to learn to do that," I admitted once he'd finished.

He scoffed. "Yeah, you probably should, if you're going to keep getting beat up like that. Invest in some armoring, too."

Invest. Like that was going to happen with the meager resources I had left. But I nodded at his advice and followed him up when he climbed out of the arena pit. Time to find out what kind of party these people threw.

We passed through corridors with shadowy overhead pipes to another elevator down.

"How big a place do you have down here?" While the automap function gave me an overhead view, it lacked scale.

He chuckled. "I don't know, actually. We keep expanding. I've lost track. But we've got tunnels connecting different parts of the city. Sometimes above ground travel . . . just isn't safe."

I couldn't argue that.

"So what's going on around here, anyway?" Factions, right? Was this a resistance-versus-soldiers kind of place, too? Or was there something I should be more concerned with?

"Time for that later." He pressed his hand to a touchpad and a gray door slid open with a full-on starship swish.

How to describe the room he led me into . . . about forty people sitting at long table, drinking, laughing, sharing stories. Yells and cheers rose up around a gambling table in one corner. A woman danced on a stage, half her body reflecting and refracting light like crystal. Lights hovered over the tables and robots zipped about with food and drinks. A pair of androids battered each other in a corner boxing ring.

Picture a Viking longhouse full of Norse warriors chugging mead, but put it in space and make them CyberVikings. Yeah, it was like that.

Grovan led me to a table and ushered me to an open spot . . . right across from Jorraq. Between Ms. Tripod Mount and a guy burlier than Jorraq who might've been assembled out of industrial robot spare parts.

"Welcome, Max." Jorraq's words were cordial enough, but flat and emotionless. "I don't want you thinking you're one of us—far from it. But you can stay for now. We'll figure the rest out tomorrow. Tonight, relax. That was a decent show earlier."

"Thanks. Are you the one in charge here?"

"Yes. And no. Technically I'm third in command."

"But right now, what he says goes," Ms. Tripod Mount added. A robot gave me a plated slab of meat and a mug of something foamy. Utensils rose out of a dispenser in the table.

"One thing we should warn you about, Max," Jorraq said before stuffing his mouth. I waited while he chewed. He was a patient eater who chewed thoroughly.

"Inquisitors," he continued after drinking from a mug like mine. I took the chance to try it. It wasn't mead, but a golden, bitter beer. Harsh stuff. It fit the setting.

"Usually we'd see one or two a year. They'd show up and grab some people up for whatever sin they cared about that year, spout out threats, and then leave. Then a whole squad of them showed up a few months ago. Still here. They don't say much, they don't preach anything. They're just rounding up cyborgs. Don't seem to care much about anything else though. Marshall Stants' thug army deals with everything else."

Ms. Tripod Mount shifted on the bench next to me and her jaw clenched in anger.

"Stants?"

"You really aren't from here," she said next to me.

"I said that."

"He's the governor," the industrial heavy on my left said.

"The people that attacked me, you think that was Inquisitor related?" I hoped that was it, or else there would be yet something else to watch out for.

"Nah," Jorraq said. I tried the . . . steak. It wasn't beef, and it didn't just melt in my mouth, but I was hungry and I enjoyed it. "If it was Inquisitors, you'd know. Flashy red powered armor, nothing subtle about them at all. Plus, you wouldn't be here."

"And that's why all the tunnels?"

"Yep," Ms. Tripod Mount said.

"So, I've got names for a couple of you, but you are . . . ?" I asked her.

"Anassa." Not really a talker, that one.

"I'm Kirk," the guy on my left added with a jovial smile

Other than Jorraq, others nearby didn't talk much, to me anyway. Conversations waged down the table in both directions. But Jorraq showed an interest in me. I got a basic city layout from him, and he suggested I could buy better gear than I had from one of his guys. "Oh," was all he had to say when I explained how broke I was.

They offered me drugs in chip form I didn't have a port for and would've declined anyway. I had more of the beer, but stayed sober. Several around me threw sobriety to the wind. Anassa excused herself earlier than most. Kirk led me to a storage room with a cot in it.

"Someone'll come get you for breakfast," he said before the door closed behind him. An indicator over the door control switched from a soft green glow to "LOCKED." I'd only earned so much trust.

The door beeped when it opened hours later. A night of rest had healed me up, and I felt ready for whatever the day had to offer. A string of quests to grind through seemed likely enough. In a game where life wasn't on the line I'd be more intrigued.

"Breakfast," Anassa stated before striding off. I hustled after her. She led me down more corridors, still topped with overhead pipes, into a barracks chow hall. This looked more like the chow hall at Otisville. Spartan, utilitarian tables and benches in a room where no expense had been spent in decoration.

She led me to a serving line where I picked up blue sausages, something that tried to be cornbread, and something that probably wasn't scrambled eggs. "Jorraq's over there," she pointed out once I had my food. Then she left. So, I strode over and sat across from Jorraq, the only one sitting alone.

"So what's up with her?" I tried.

"She had a brother."

"Ah." Had a brother. Now has a problem with Inquisitors that are hunting cyborgs. I didn't need to press for the rest.

"So." Time for a different topic. "I'm hoping you can help me. I'm looking for a friend of mine. An elven woman who came here...probably about five days ago."

"Not too many elfs come here," he pointed out before popping a chunk of cornbread in his mouth.

"She thought someone was chasing her, so she might be trying to lay low. I'm getting the impression you guys know the best places to do that, so maybe you know somebody who's seen her?"

"What's she look like?"

That was a good question, wasn't it? God, why hadn't I asked Altion that before....

"Friend of yours, huh?" He noticed my hesitation.

"Okay. I'm a friend of her parents." Who should've given me a description... this was going to get bad. "They think she's changed her appearance." There, I hoped that'd tide him over.

"Well, if she's on the run that's a good start. But still an elf?"

"She won't have gone so far as surgical changes. Her name is Silleste, that should narrow it down, right?"

"That'll help, sure. It's not something I can help you with directly, but I know someone who probably can." His expression blanked and I figured he was using an implanted radio. It continued for a while. I tried not to fidget, and focused on finishing breakfast.

"Okay," he said after I'd finished, "Anassa is going to take you to our Commander. I've let her know you're coming and a little about your... situation. Anassa will be here shortly. I've got work to do." He stood and left, leaving his finished tray. I'd noticed where the others were stacked, so I brought his and mine and added them.

Anassa came a few minutes later. A stubby carbine sat slung over her shoulder, and she held my pistol in one hand and my rifle in the other. Both hands were a smooth, matte gray. Her dark flak jacket was open, just a black bikini top underneath. An NPC designed by a man, I'm guessing.

"Follow me."

More hallways and tunnels and then we came to a long, narrow one. This one had thick pipes along the side and just metal framing overhead. Small lights at intervals along the walls at the floor gave just enough light to navigate by, which for me meant plenty. Enhanced vision was likely the rule rather than the exception here. Light to navigate a straight, longish tunnel? Must have been built by or for people with normal eyesight.

The corridor ended at another more like before, and this led to an elevator up. Two more corridors later she stopped at a door, opened it, and ushered me inside.

Chapter 15

Three computer screens took up most of the desk in the center of the office. The woman behind them folded them down one by one and gestured to a chair. I sat.

At first glance, she seemed out of place. She appeared human, except for her solid chrome eyeballs with no pupils or irises. A little disconcerting. A military officer jacket, complete with ribbons and medals, hung open over a basic black shirt. Straight black hair hung to her shoulders.

"So you're Max."

"Yes I am." Off to a good start, huh? I could have sworn I was more charming than that. Was the game actively stifling me until I dumped enough points into Charisma? How's that for a creepy thought?

"I'm Commander Trell. Jorraq told me about the woman you're looking for. One question I've asked myself while you walked over: if she's being hunted, how do I know you're not the one hunting her?" To be fair, she wasn't the first to ask that, was she?

"Well, on one hand, maybe it doesn't matter," I suggested. "Then again, I don't think I can prove I'm not, so it's just my word that I'm not. But if I was a hired bounty hunter, I'm pretty sure I'd be better equipped." I waggled a chrome finger through a ragged hole in my jacket for emphasis.

"I'd hope so."

"So, what now?" I sighed, I knew what was coming.

"Now I offer you a deal. I've got a network of spies and informants throughout this city. I'm pretty sure I can find her for you. But first you're going to do something for me."

"And what's that?"

"Marshall Stants has a long-range sensor array on a rooftop. I have a ship waiting to deliver some cargo. But the array is specially calibrated to detect stealth ships. The kind my smugglers prefer. Where the array is situated, we can't just shoot it, and taking it out from a ship poses other problems. So I need someone to get on that rooftop and take it out for me. It'll take some time for them to replace it, and in that time I'll get my shipments through."

"Okay." Should I have taken a quest like that without knowing more about it? Probably not. I'm not sure how much choice I had.

Quest: Destroy the Sensor Array
The CyberRogues need a rooftop sensor array destroyed to allow their smugglers through.

The door opened and a scrawny woman with a chrome skeleton of a left hand walked in. Chrome plates suggested implants where her ears should have been.

"This is Sira. She'll teach you what you need to know."

I followed Sira to a small warehouse space littered with crates and drums, some stacked on pallets and some individually.

"Do you have any experience with explosives?"

"Explosives? No."

"Great. You're going to learn, then."

One of the greatest mercies is this game lets you learn skills far faster than in real life. We worked through dinner and well into the night, but by the time we finished I'd gained Engineering and Demolitions skill at 10 each, and gained a new class. Just like that. It left me wondering how many I could have? Was there a limit, or some increasing cost I wasn't aware of?

Class gained: Rogue
+5 Agility, +2 Charisma
+50 Focus
+10 Evasion, +10 Crit Chance, +10 Crit Power,
+5 Melee Attack, +5 Ranged Attack, +10 Speed
+10 Sneak, +10 Dodge, +10 Pickpocket, +10 Pick Locks

Regardless, the added class came with incremental bonuses. She'd also given me a lock picking kit, good for mechanical and electrical locks.

After all that she showed me to an empty bunk in a barracks full of people already asleep. None of them snored, and sleep came fast, a Hunter ambushing prey. In the morning she came and got me for breakfast. I hopped out of bed all rested and ready to go. Eager to go, to be honest. The sooner I got this done the sooner I'd be able to get back on Silleste's trail. The longer delays got, the further behind I'd fall.

We took more tunnels and up another elevator. One final hallway took us to a storage room full of barrels and kegs. I followed her through the bar it connected to. Nobody was there this time of morning, so we proceeded to the street.

"This is where you'll come back. when you're done. I'll make sure the bartenders know to keep an eye open for you. We're better off sticking to side streets. Avoid high-traffic areas, that's where you'll be more likely to stumble into Inquisitors." And who knows who else.

We did have to cross one larger intersection, but we melded into thick pedestrian traffic. Rush hour happens in space, too.

More crossings waited ahead, with towering skyscrapers rising to either side of a broad thoroughfare. Something caught my eye a few floors up a rounded tower across the intersection.

A body. Fastened to the wall. Strung up, in fact. Bent and twisted metal limbs splayed from a torso largely flayed of flesh. The face stripped to a white skull. I shuddered.

"Please tell me that's not Anassa's brother."

"It's not. I don't know who it was. Somebody gets strung up like that at least once a week. There are other spots. Examples."

". . . of what?" We finished crossing the intersection and followed a line of people towards the next side street. Two elves in environment suits, sans helmets, complained to each other about the traffic.

"The sin of cybernetics." We rounded the corner, and she didn't offer more. I didn't press.

Six blocks later she stopped us short.

I didn't need her identify the figures walking the next street. The four soldiers flanking them weren't that unusual. Typical light armor with respectable looking rifles. No, they weren't the attention getting ones.

No, the other three were the ones that held my gaze. Mine and the pedestrians who hurried out of their way. Big, bulky powered armor suits a thick-helmeted head taller than everyone around, vivid crimson. Heavy boots tromped the street as they marched. Two of them held rifles too big and cumbersome to look practical, but these space marine types toted them as if they were plastic props.

Swords hung at their hips. The middle one carried a banner. Space Paladins. Had to be. The Imperialist stormtroopers I'd seen on Relkit III had nothing on these guys.

"We can't fight them. Not three with support."

"If it was just one?" Hey, I wasn't suggesting trying to split them, but I wanted to know more.

"Maybe. If we had a perfect ambush and we could lure one close enough to the bomb in here," she thumbed at the pack on her back. "I don't think your rifle would scratch the paint. But the armor and weaponry are only half the problem. They have mystical powers. They'll paralyze you and command you to your knees. And you'll be on your knees."

She pulled me further back. Space Paladins, all right. That'd be a prestige class for sure, if it was even available to players.

We waited a nice long time before venturing forward again.

"We have to be careful from here on out. This is a more patrolled area." Of course it was. The quest couldn't be easy.

She wasn't kidding, either. We had to duck aside for a hover APC that passed about three meters above us. A double-barreled belly turret looked like it'd one-shot me for sure. Damn, I needed better armor!

We veered into a small park with fountains and blatantly holographic flowers. She led me to a bench and had me sit next to her.

"There's your target," she said, pointing it out with a nod.

The building sat across the park, a squat tower twelve stories tall, at least two floors taller than the buildings for blocks around. White buttresses divided columns of black windows. Four soldiers stood guard at the ground-floor pedestrian entrance. It didn't scream out fortress or even military installation.

"The array's at the top. Get up there, place the bomb, and get down before the timer. The timer's max setting is fifteen minutes."

I already knew it wouldn't be that easy.

She passed me the wrapped bundle I put into my pack, and she left. Not even a "good luck."

All I needed now was a plan.

The buttresses tapered into the building about halfway up and didn't look climbable. I started by making a circle of the building. A rear loading dock had two small gun turrets where I expected cameras to be. So not that way.

I found a cafe off one side of the park I could sit and observe the front entrance for a while.

I considered the skills they'd given me: Demolitions, Engineering, Pick Locks, and Pick Pockets. The first one for the bomb, obviously. Engineering included where to place bombs, but also how to interpret building plans and layouts and mechanical systems.

If I could get inside, the ventilation system might get me get to the roof. Pick Pockets suggested swiping something. Like an access card. What, just walk in? With no disguise skill, wasn't the whole cyborg thing going to be an issue? Then again, this quest seemed designed for cyborg rogues, so there had to be a way.

I watched the people going in and out throughout the day. The android cafe waitress didn't mind me being there as long as I ordered something. The cheapest hot drink took the last of my funds. I already knew I wasn't going to be buying my way up there.

While there weren't many, the occasional cyborg did come and go. I took a walk to pass the entrance, confirming a security card opened the door. The soldiers weren't stopping or questioning anyone. The beginnings of a plan assembled.

First, I spent the afternoon pick-pocketing. Grind the new skill up, just like in pretty much every other game. Out of ten tries, three came up with nothing, two failed in ways that got their attention. In one case I knocked the man out. In the other, I ran. Having a decent speed is a good thing. I also netted a personal communicator and 63 silver chips. More importantly, I raised the skill from 10 to 15.

By afternoon's end more people were leaving, although some still entered. I picked a target, a human guy in blue pants and gray tunic, and followed him. I even gained another point in Tracking. The game knew what I was up to. Three blocks to a bus stop. A few people waited at a bench no one sat on. I moved in next to my mark while two other people joined the line.

The bus hovered through an intersection a block away. It was time. I bumped into my target and got the card. "Hey, watch it," I said over my shoulder as if someone had pushed me. The guy bought it while the chubby bald man behind me offered a confused shrug. I pocketed the card, pulling out the communicator as if that's what I'd reached into my pocket for. I flipped through the menu on its screen, a perfectly ordinary thing to do.

The bus came, and my mark boarded with those before him. "Nah, go ahead, I have to get this," I explained to the bald man behind me. Another shrug and he boarded. I walked off.

Phase one complete.

The evening rush hour was winding down by the time I made it back to the tower, yet people still entered. The guards still ignored them, no doubt waiting for the buzz of someone's access card denied. I swallowed and stepped forward to take my turn.

The guards shifted on their feet, but didn't turn as I passed between them to the door. I waved the card before the scanner and an indicator above it blinked green. The door slid open.

The lobby inside seemed simple enough. Information kiosk to one side. A single, bored-looking guard shifted his weight side to side. Computer terminal kiosks in paired rows formed an aisle to a bank of elevators. Tempted as I was to see what information the terminals offered, acting like I knew where I was going felt safer. I strode forward to the elevators and tapped a button to call one. Just like I would anywhere else.

Footsteps clacked on the hard floor as a door slid open. I stepped inside and let it close behind me. I wasn't interested in sharing an elevator with someone who might ask questions.

The elevator beeped at me. "Level?" a feminine, computerized voice asked.

"Twenty." Would it let me go straight to the top?

"Scan access card."

The sensor was obvious, so I waved the card like I had at the door.

"Access denied. Level?"

"Roof?" It had to be worth a try, right?

"Scan access card." The result wasn't surprising.

"Access denied. Level?"

I looked up, wondering how far my stolen card would get me, when I spotted an access panel in the ceiling. A button next to it looked like a control for it. It was about a half meter out of my reach, so I poked it with my rifle. I guess the designers assumed reach would be a sufficient deterrent. There wasn't a card scanner next to it.

A click and the hatch released, popping up an inch but not opening all the way. So, I jumped for it, pushing it out my way. It smacked open louder than I would've preferred. I lowered it closed and pushed until it clicked back into place.

Recessed hand and foot holds provided a ladder in the wall. A long climb up, but better than trying to climb a cable. Especially since there wasn't a cable to climb. The car's roof was barren except for the hatch, some motors, and emergency brake mechanisms.

A familiar beep sounded below. "Level?"

"Fourteen," a woman said, and the car started up smoothly, no jerkiness here. It accelerated swiftly. Good thing I wasn't already climbing.

The car stopped, and I moved to the ladder before it whooshed back down to the lobby. I'd made three floors when it rushed towards me again. was it coming faster than before? I hurried. Could I outrun it?

It stopped on 18, not far below me at that point. I didn't stop or slow down until a stenciled sign identified the final door. "ROOF."

What the door didn't have was any kind of control panel. But I found the actuators that controlled it. With some engineering tools courtesy of Sira I tried to activate them. Several sparking failures netted me a +1 in Engineering before the door slid open.

The rooftop spread out around me, a prairie of slender antennae spattered with HVAC blocks. Towering over that, the one tree in the prairie: a large satellite dish bristling with other sensors. My target.

I rounded an HVAC unit the size of the elevator housing I'd stepped out of, to come face to . . . it didn't have a face. An iridescent black blocky thing on six chrome legs skittered away about five feet back while a stub-nosed turret towards the front swiveled towards me.

Of course the thing wouldn't be unguarded.

I leapt up and back as it spat red bolts at me. I came down on top of the thrumming air conditioner and readied my rifle. I was all set to jump over the thing, raining lasers on it from above, when the damned thing climbed over the edge to face me. I still jumped, but backwards. Three shots were all I could get off before coming down behind more cover. Not a single shot hit.

I had seen, however, the rooftop equipment wasn't spread evenly. Empty, open killing grounds lay between clusters.

A peek around the corner revealed the security drone climbing down and heading my way. It couldn't jump, and I was faster than it was. Hit-and-run it was. I missed it again, but it didn't, hitting me for 32. At least my rifle hit a little harder. I ducked back and back tracked one corner. I aimed, ready for it.

This time I hit the thing solid. Forty points of rifle damage inflicted a disappointing change to its health bar. Back around the corner and I jumped on top of my cover to hop down the far side. Rogues attack from surprise, Sira had pointed out. I hoped it wouldn't see this coming.

Sure enough, I rounded a corner behind it. With any luck, its rear armor would be lighter. Quick aim before it reached the corner and. . . .

Ability unlocked: Rookie's Sneak Attack
When you attack from a concealed position or from surprise, you have increased chances to hit and deal additional damage. Your attack rating, Crit Chance and Crit Power are doubled for these attacks.

Sneak Attack Critical hit! 94 damage!

Well, that was better than 40. Now it was down about a third, but it's turret swiveled. I got off another shot as I ducked behind cover, but missed.

Rifle Skill +1 (18)

I fell back to another corner but didn't have enough time to aim before having to fire and duck again. But I had a new strategy now, so once around the corner I jumped up so I could cross back behind it again.

Another sneak attack shot, and it was down past half. This could work.

I fell back again until the leap cooldown refreshed, and I kept going with my pattern. It didn't seem to learn. I gained another point of Rifle before it died.

+250 XP (7600 total)

Level 7 gained!
+23 Health
+22 Stamina
+8 Mana
+15 Focus
+5 Primary Characteristic Points
+10 Skill Points

Another level, good. And healing came with it, so back to full all around. Nothing on my character sheet suggested classes gaining levels independently.

So having more than one class just meant extra capabilities. You'd think the tutorial would have said something about that.

On a hunch, I checked out the remains of the drone. Inside I saw parts that looked familiar from watching the repair work Grovan had done. A couple of minutes and I had several useful looking bits and pieces in my pack, along with a point in Scavenge. That was bound to come in handy.

I didn't know how much time I'd still have up here, so mission next, skill points later. I jogged to the sensor array.

The main dish dominated it but wasn't the only major component. Seven smaller dishes I hadn't noticed before contributed. Four metal framework legs supported the whole assembly, which was gimbaled so it could be aimed. Figuring out the best place to put the bomb didn't take too much inspection. Still, no flashing icons marked the spot, so I made sure to check the thing out from different angles before climbing a maintenance ladder.

The bomb in my pack came with straps and a magnetic mounting plate. Affixing it took seconds. The timer, that warranted some thinking about. I had a remote detonator as well, but Sira had warned me it could be jammed if the bomb was detected. Hop down, jog back to the elevator, ladder my way down. . . . Fifteen minutes to be safe sounded good.

My math hadn't counted on guards waiting at the elevator door.

Chapter 16

Four of them. I so had to get grenades. Even the gelcaster might have given me an edge if we hadn't hocked it for passage here. I ran back for cover as they fired red beam laser pistols. Not too unlike my own.

Finding places for cover wasn't too hard, but avoiding four of them fanning out didn't seem likely. I ran to get some distance before remembering something. I boosted myself up on top of another humming equipment box. Just because the robot could climb didn't mean they could. If they'd even think of it. I flatted myself out

With a good view of the sensor array.

"Whatever you do," Sari'd warned, "don't be on that rooftop when the bomb goes."

I waited for ten long breaths, which seemed an eternity. I lowered myself down and crept back to the elevator. If they kept spreading away, I'd be behind them now. I was right.

I got to the elevator in time for it to open and disgorge three more black security drones.

This was not a quest for newbie rogues!

I spun and ran for a different cluster of covering equipment, desperately needing a plan B. Time was leaking away fast.

A peek back showed two of the drones had followed me. I circled around and saw them split up. Well, I'd handled one before. Could I finish it off before its partner joined in?

This time I tried a different ambush. I needed to do damage faster. I peeked again to confirm where my target was, and I leapt. Time to put all the modifiers I could think of into play.

Sneak Leap Power Attack Critical Hit! 308 Damage!

My claw ripped open the little turret on top. From my new position standing on the thing's back it only took two more rifle shots to finish it.

+250 XP (7850 total)

One down . . . five to go? Plus the four guards? Not at this rate. I made another try for circling back to the elevator, but a pair of guards spotted me and pinned me down. I traded fire with one, not scoring a hit but taking one while gaining another point of Rifle. Another pair showed up from the side, boxing me in.

I still had one way I could go, so I fell back to the array. I made it a fighting retreat and did more damage than I took. One dropped, for another 200XP, but robbed me of about 20% of my Health in the trade.

What were my options? They ranged in an arc between me and the elevator. The closest building edge was behind me, but I had nothing to climb with. Nothing resembling a fire hose, and no good sources of long enough cable I could rip out.

What was I going to do, jump across to another building?

I considered that while swapping for my last rifle power pack. Fighting my way out of this wasn't going to work. I thought back to my recon of the building and its surroundings. It'd mean four lanes of traffic to a building four or five stories shorter. Twelve to fifteen meters across and about that much down. Jumping distance was based on speed, in turn determined from Agility, with a times four multiplier from my boosters.

Insane as it was, I couldn't come up with a better option.

The detonator clipped to my belt beeped. Thirty seconds. Crap! How had that much time passed? Not fair!

And that settled it. A couple more shots for cover and I sprinted like, well, like my life depended on it. At the edge I launched into my booster-assisted jump.

The explosion was deafening, and I felt the blast hurl me forward while it kicked my health bars to frighteningly close to nothing. Experience notifications, and my life, flashed before my eyes as I slammed into the rooftop.

Level 8 gained!
+23 Health
+22 Stamina
+8 Mana
+15 Focus
+5 Primary Characteristic Points
+10 Skill Points

Since my bomb had killed the guards and drones, the game gave me XP for them. No complaints about that! And Healing to boot, thanks to leveling.

I spotted this building's elevator access door and hurried over to it. It took a few tries to open it, but I gained another point of Pick Locks. The door opened to the waiting elevator I'd called in the process.

Once inside, I spared a moment for reviewing my character sheet.

Name: Max McAlloy		Level: 8		XP: 9350			
Primary Attributes		**Secondary Attributes**		**Tertiary Attributes**		**Skills**	
Strength	20	Health (CON)	236	Ranged Attack	133	Unarmed Combat 16	
Agility	28	Stamina (CON/STR)	364	Melee Attack	128	Dodge 25	
Constitution	23	Mana (WIL/Mag)	70	Evasion	143	Pick Locks 11	
Appearance	10	Focus (Will)	174	Toughness	0 (52)	Pick Pockets 15	
Intellect	17			Resistance	0 (72)	Pistol 15	
Magic	0			Melee Damage (STR)	20	Rifle 20	
Willpower	15			Magic Damage (MAG)	0	Sneak 34	
Charisma	17			Crit Chance	34	Demolitions 10	
				Crit Power	29	Engineering 12	
Boosted Jump	x4			Mitigation	0	Scavenge 1	
Claws: +50% Melee Damage				Speed	48	Track 36	
Nightvision	60					Bribery 5	
						Haggle 2	

Two levels to allocate. Wow. I had ten points of Primary Characteristics and twenty skill points to spend. First, I bumped up Strength and Agility. I kept needing more Strength, and Agility fed into so many combat numbers. Skill points were tougher. I decided on Dodge, Pick Locks, and Pick Pockets: ten, five, and five. The Stamina number made sense and explained why I never seemed to run out. I wasn't sure what its recovery rate was, but I had enough to last through some fair exertion.

The elevator asked what level I wanted, and I asked for the lobby. A registration kiosk sat unattended. I strode through the empty lobby and out to the street. Getting back to the bar to meet back up with Sira took a while. I avoided patrols of soldiers and one pair of Inquisitors. But I gained more Sneak along the way.

The bartender recognized me and offered me a free drink while I waited for Sira. About half the seats were taken, and I sat at the bar in the middle of the biggest open space I saw. The patrons looked like they were trying not to see me.

Sira showed up about an hour later and aside from a short, "Congratulations," didn't speak as she led me back to Commander Trell.

Quest completed: Destroy the Sensor Array
Quest Rewards: Reputation increase with Jentassa IV CyberRogues +500XP (Total 9850)

At least I was making progress at leveling. That might make the delay on my real quest worthwhile.

Sira closed the door, leaving me alone with the Commander.

"Sit." Two empty chairs faced her. I plunked myself in the lower one.

"You did well. I'm pleased. You might have a future with us." She fidgeted with a data chip.

"Thank you. I appreciate that. And under other circumstances, I think I'd jump at that. But I'm not really here under normal circumstances. I have a mission, and I have to put that mission first."

"The elf girl, yes."

"Were you able to find her?" Or would I have to do another side quest to find out?

"Yes and no," she replied, sliding a datapad across her desk. The screen showed a hard-looking man with a black crew cut, Marine style, high-and-tight.

"This is Gelrick. He's a local bounty hunter. He's got her, although I don't know where. He's a dangerous man who gets hired by dangerous people."

"But you know where to find him?" Fantastic. I wasn't the only one looking for her. Why would a bounty hunter take her, unless he knew who she was? I refused to believe this was all about covering up the Rift she and Altion and their wizard friend had stumbled across, which seemed the only other option.

"Yes and no, again." She took the datapad back and switched it to a map of the city. "There's more. It sounds like he hired the men who attacked you and your friend."

That couldn't be good.

"As for where to find him? He has a ship he keeps at a private docking port. He's also a regular at a casino called the Lucky Star. Not a nice or gentle place. I've marked both locations on the map for you."

"Gelrick fights hard and dirty. If he gets the drop on you... don't let him do that. You'd never be seen again. He wears distinctive red boots and goggles on his hat. Watch that casino and finding him probably won't be hard."

"Dealing with him once you do... that might be. But that's up to you." She slid the datapad, along with a 500-silver piece chip, across. "For your help. I appreciate it. If you find yourself looking for work, you can come back to us."

At least I had a lead, the best lead yet. Not just the planet, but I was in the same city she'd come to. This Gelrick had grabbed her within the last week or so. He either still had her, or he knew who did.

And bounty hunter was better than assassin. Somebody wanted her alive. Other than me.

"Thanks." I stood and took the pad and chip. Both fit in the belt box, although the datapad shouldn't have. Once again, no reason to complain. Take what benefits I can get, right?

She pushed a button on her desk and Grovan came in for me. "Come on," he said as he strode away.

Grovan led me to a workshop where people with assorted percentages of humanity worked at benches with tools that whirred and sparked.

"Give me that jacket and vest. Those needs help, to start with." I handed them over and he passed then along to a heavyset woman with lenses and sensors all over her head.

"So, you've got some money, and we're supposed to get you some upgrades before you go getting yourself killed."

"Thanks for the vote of confidence."

The woman scoffed as she got to work on my jacket.

"First, some repair tools. I'm not going to follow you around and put you back together.' He handed me two tool kits, a small first aid one that finished off the space in my belt box, and a larger kit I put in my pack.

"Those, with the Engineering you picked up, will let you fix yourself up, along with small repairs on ships. Now, sit." He patted a stool next to an unclaimed workbench. I did as he asked, and he got to work.

After fifteen minutes, I approved of both upgrades:

Tactical Package III

+6 Intellect, +6 Willpower, +15 Crit Chance

+15 Evasion, +15 Ranged Attacks

Quadruple nightvision range (80m)

X20 vision magnification

Toughness Package I

+10 Toughness, +10 Resistance

+100 Health

"Nice. Thanks."

"You're welcome."

I got my jacket and vest back. The jacket was now a mix of dark gray and green, and felt lighter weight, although the stats didn't change. Both all repaired. Both had needed it. No bill for any of it. "Keep it," Grovan had said when I'd asked him how much.

After that Grovan led me a to a room, a room of my own this time. It wasn't much, just a cot and a desk, but it was nicer than just being tucked into a storeroom. They didn't even lock the door. I was tired, and sleep came easy.

Chapter 17

Sira led me to the surface, through the ever-present tunnels and elevators. Which parts of the lily pad city we passed through I couldn't say. I'm not sure the underground geography corresponded to the surface. Who knew? I didn't ask. This time we exited into an alley. Not the one I'd came in from. She shook my hand with a fleshy one. Only her left was alloy.

"Good luck. I hope I see you again."

In another life I might have asked her out.

"I'd like that. It'll depend on how things go." This wasn't that life. But who knew, maybe once I had Silleste I'd bring her back here for quests. If nothing else, having a place to lay low would be good, and these people seemed to have invested in "lay low." Plus, it didn't have the evacuation feel of Outcrop. The factions here might offer more variety than Rebels vs Federalists.

The increase of troops so clear to see in Outcrop wasn't happening here. Or had it just not happened here yet? If it was a planned event, it might have been tied to quests there, and something avoidable here. Yeah, bringing her here was an option.

I slid out my new datatab and pulled up the map with its two marked locations. A blinking red dot showed where I was, so navigating wouldn't be hard. I'd had a better GPS app in reality, but this wasn't bad for a game interface.

I swung by the hangar the ship was at first. It was locked up tight, and the main entrance was too out in the open to try picking it. At least I didn't see guards patrolling or blatant security cameras. Still, better off not getting too close yet.

The hangar sat in the outskirts of the city, a slummy area with aging buildings, pitted and worn. Safe enough seeming by day, probably not so much by night. An apt place for a bounty hunter to stash his ship.

The city spread out more than I'd realized, and the casino wasn't nearby. Between the time it took to get to the hangar, then crossing half the city again, it was late afternoon by the time I got to the casino.

Hover taxis were an option; I'd seen a few, and I had money to work with now. But could I trust the drivers? I still didn't know what rival factions this city had, other than cyborgs and Inquisitors. The monorails and hover busses felt too public for a cyborg. Besides, I covered ground well without getting tired. High Stamina was a good thing, and I had plenty.

The Lucky Star sat surrounded by a parking lot arrayed with hovering and wheeled bikes more than cars. At this point, about a third of the spaces were claimed. The building itself was a decent height, but with no windows I couldn't tell if it was one very tall floor or two normal ones. I circled around, curious about the acutely pointed corners. If I had the image right in my mind, the overhead view would be a six-pointed star.

Yeah, lots of originality going on there, huh?

The entrance was obvious and appeared unguarded. I took position at a bus stop with a clear view. For all I knew he was already inside. If I didn't see him after an hour I'd go inside and wait there. For the moment, out here was safer. I had a clean line of sight, something I might not have inside.

And then I saw the guy. Commander Trell wasn't kidding about him being easy enough to recognize. The boots alone would have done it. Blood red clear up to his knees, swinging one in front of the other with confident swagger. At the same time, he walked like a woman in tall heels. A dark purple armor vest over a black t-shirt and gray cargo pants seemed identifiable yet nondescript at the same time.

The cap was straight up biker leather, dark blue with a short black brim. The goggles resting above the brim lent a steampunk flair to it. What if this was another player and not an NPC? That gave me pause while he walked in.

A large pistol sat on his right hip, while a smaller, sleek one lurked under his left arm. At least that suggested no weapon scanners going in. And two kinds of pistols, not paired one on each hip. Armor, but nothing heavier than mine. Admittedly, mine was probably more entry-level than his.

He was human, so I had advantages with built-in toughness, the tactical package, the claws.... But what level was he? Higher than me, no doubt there. So in a fight I'd better have a way to get the drop on him. Defending myself against a PVP ganker was one thing. Flat out murder? Crap. What options were there for taking him alive? If he was an NPC he might surrender. Would a player? Would I?

What was I getting myself into? I'd seen a lot of danger in this game already. If game was even the right word. The stakes were on the high side for a game. Prison might not have been fun or entertaining, or have anywhere near as much to see. Not that prison is all that safe, either. But I hadn't made enemies there. I didn't have friends, but I didn't spend as much time looking over my shoulder as I had here.

And there was Agent Wald, who didn't say much. Plus the other agents when they'd strapped me into the chair my meat body sat in. Would they have let me say no? Would they have let me go back to prison knowing what they'd told me? Or would they have called that a national security risk? I'd believe Wald disappearing me without fretting over it. She didn't strike me as a woman driven by her conscience.

She reminded me of one of the cops that arrested me. They'd bashed in my dorm room in Earhart Hall with a battering ram. Can you believe that? SWAT officers and this short policewoman with curly red hair.

For a hacker in his dorm room. I'd only been out of bed for a matter of minutes. The dorm cafeteria was still serving breakfast, and I was debating which pair of jeans to put on when the door banged open. One minute I'm standing there in my boxers, the next minute the redhead has her knee in my back while she's cuffing me.

None of that mattered anymore. Now I had to find the president's daughter, who that guy in the casino had snatched off the streets. He was my only lead on finding her, and I was stalling outside. It was time to go inside.

Sounds hit me first. Slow bass beats behind a quick rhythm in music loud enough to provide privacy but soft enough to allow conversations. A Mordian bouncer grunted at me as I walked past into a cavern where bright lights danced among shadows.

Three stairs led into the recessed center space dominated by a round stage. Gambling spaces filled the wings radiating out. Six dancers, one facing each triangular wing, worked around poles. Two were men, one in a soldier's uniform. A topless Elf woman with a river of green hair and alabaster skin, halfway into a striptease, put her foot over her head against the pole. Her skirt, two narrow panels front and back, just barely covered a wide-split crotch while she undid the back of boots most of the way up her thigh.

Each dancer had their own spotlight. Otherwise shadows lurked in the center. Not deep shadows, but enough to suggest discretion. To my nightvision, faces came clear as if full daylight.

Except for the entrance behind me, the inner corners where the wings merged sported peninsula bars where more seats sat empty than full. A good place to sit and observe without drawing notice. I picked one with a view of the door. The last thing I needed was my prey slipping out unnoticed. A white-furred Fenurian bartender didn't blink an eye as she made change from my 500-silver chip after I ordered cold beer, "something sweet." Humans waited behind the other bars.

A fair amount of space separated the different gaming areas. Each wing offered a different game, each run by one or more chrome androids in spiffy black jackets. Magnification bridged the distance, and it didn't take long to find my prey with his distinctive cap sitting two wings to the left leaning over a roulette variant.

The beer would have impressed me if it hadn't been as sweet. I should've left that part out, but I didn't want the cat-man asking me what kind of beer. I never thought I'd so miss old-fashioned drop-down menus. Blue smoke wafted from a shared hookah on the far side to cloud the ceiling, and hover drones providing most of the light. I didn't see the surveillance cameras to catch cheaters—but they'd be there. I wasn't here to ply my new rogue skills that way, so not my concern.

A tall figure in a hooded cloak sidled up next to me and sat on the stool to my right. Slender hands dropped the hood to reveal a man's face full of angles and sharp lines. Elven ears poked out of black hair and a curving, black sigil tattoo claimed most of his right temple.

"I'm Gerendish," he offered with a deeper, richer voice than I expected. "I'm a technomage. You new here?" He ordered Allurian Ice Wine, which came served with dry ice. Nice touch.

"More or less. I'm from Relkit III."

"Is this game amazing, or what?"

"It's something, all right." I took another drink of my beer. I wasn't in the mood to be social, but I also didn't want to be rude. Technomage sounded like a useful ally.

"To think I was a fat accountant before this."

"College student. Kinda alarmed at not being able to log off though."

"No loss for me. Here I've got power I'd never have out there."

"You aren't worried about what happens to your body out there?"

"I've been in more than six weeks now. If something out there mattered it would have happened by now. Either my body's on life support or I don't need it anymore. I could spend the rest of my life in here."

Six weeks? The game hadn't been out near that long. Time was passing faster in game than out, no surprise there. That's a standard enough game trope. But how much?

His fingers drew glowing symbols in the air in front of me.

Technomage Protective Aura

An invisible energy field surrounds you, protecting you from harm. Is it a magical spell? A force field? Who's to say. . . .

+100 Toughness, +100 Resistance

Duration 1 hour

"There, have a defense buff. If you're going to be in this part of town, you're bound to need it sooner or later."

Who was I to turn down a free buff? And a decent one, at that.

My prey left the roulette area. I had to turn to keep an eye on him, while trying not to seem like I was ignoring my new friend.

"So, you got a name?" He offered a delicate hand. The black armor on his sleeve wasn't fantasy chain mail. His grip was firm, but strength was not his strong point.

"Max. Max McAlloy. Technomage, huh?"

"Yeah. It's a prestige class you can only get in this World. Every World has them, and they're all different. They come in tiers. The first tier unlocks when you hit level 10. You haven't hit that yet, have you?"

"I'm pretty close." Lying probably wasn't going to get me anywhere, and if he were going to attack me he wouldn't have buffed me first. Unless he planned to spend an hour befriending me into complacency and figure out what I could do while he was at it.

This game was getting to me.

My prey still sat playing cards with three women. With the magnification the tactical package offered I saw them at least as close as he did. Their laughter wasn't genuine.

"Well, I've got some quests I need to wrap up. You could come with, get some power-leveling in. . . ."

"That'd be cool. I'm actually in the middle of one myself. I'm waiting for someone. But I'd be happy to do some teaming up later, maybe. Are you going to be here again?" Could I recruit him to help? Could I trust him? It wasn't like I had much to offer him.

"I'm in here most nights lately. I can make some good money in here. Swing by tomorrow night and we'll see what we can set up. Take care, Max McAlloy." He finished his drink and set the frosted-glass cup on the bar. His cloak billowed behind him as he walked away. Help would have been nice, but there wasn't time to figure out if I could trust him.

The three women collected up chips and straightened outfits as they rose from the table.

Where was Gelrick?

I slid off my bar stool. I still had a clear view of the exit and had been looking that direction after Gerendish. So, I shifted the other direction, scanning crowds for his face or his hat. A gun barrel pressed into my side before I'd scanned half way.

"Don't make any sudden moves," he warned. So much for not letting him get the drop on me. What special moves did this guy have? Would my Evasion score even matter for this?

"Yeah, I hear you." If only this once de-escalating something worked.

"We're going to go outside, you and me, and we're going to talk about who sent you."

"I don't know what you're talking about. Sent me?" Did he mean in game or out?

"Don't mess with me." The gun pressed harder. "Now move."

He walked behind me, keeping close. If the bouncer at the door realized what was going on, he didn't show it. I didn't want the Mordian involved, either. Gelrick guided me around between two star arms and turned me around.

The pistol under his arm was still there. His gloved fist clenched the bigger, meaner one.

"Now, who sent you, and why?"

"To the casino? I saw it on the map." Not a lie.

"You're looking for the girl, are you?"

"Do you know where she is?" Time to try a different tack.

He stepped back, and his expression changed from stern to . . . uncertain?

Another step back and the gun looked a lot bigger inches from my face. "You can tell me who sent you after her, or I can vaporize your head."

"Is she alive?"

The barrel pressed against my forehead.

"She's alive, but she's not on Jentassa. You aren't going to find her." I had to step back against the pressure on my forehead.

There was no talking my way out of this. He wasn't going to tell me where she was. But if she was off-world, he either took her on his ship or I was back to square one. Unless I died.

"Look," I raised my right hand good and slow and waited for his eyes to follow it with a lean of his head. Pick Pockets is as much about distraction and misdirection as it is about deft fingers. His pockets weren't the goal though.

I stepped aside hard to the right. In the same motion I slashed at his hand with claws that slid out on the way.

Class Ability Unlocked: Rookie's Feint
Tricking your opponent is a classic Rogue move. Adds your Agility and Intellect to your next attack check.
Cooldown 10 seconds.

Sneak Attack Critical hit! 96 damage!

He wasn't expecting that! After whatever Toughness he had reducing it, he took a decent chunk of Health, but not quite 20%. His blaster shot hit but the defense buff dissipated most of it. I'm sure it would have done a lot more than 21 damage otherwise.

He also wasn't expecting that. He caught me with a surprise kick that knocked me down before he ran off.

I hurried to my feet and sprinted after him. He was fast, but I was faster. I tried a pistol shot on the run and wasn't surprised it missed.

He jumped on a bike which rocketed up into the air.

Crap!

Other, similar bikes sat all around. It took an agonizing amount of time to hot wire one before it started and I took off after him.

He flew up for straight-line speed, which made him easier to find. All that magnification helped.

Pilot Skill +1 (1)

I drew my pistol. If I stopped him now, before he reached the main core of taller buildings downtown, I'd have a better chance. My tactical implant tracked headings and speeds and helped aim, but racing along on a flying bike I was controlling with one hand wasn't a good combination. My shot missed and just confirmed for him I was coming after him.

I tried a couple more shots, but he swerved more. That wasn't going to work, not at this distance and speed. I put the gun away to focus on speed, but that let him do the same. I heard somebody say once when everything else was equal, a race came down to who was the better driver. In this case, pilot. Almost by default that had to be him.

He reached taller towers and swerved around one. I raced to catch up and hadn't lost him yet. Corners came hard and fast now. I clipped the edge of a building taking a turn too fast, too wide. Yes, he was the better pilot. I know, you're shocked.

Traffic wasn't heavy, but came at different levels here. Ground traffic streamed below us. But he dove between horizontal layers of traffic crisscrossing at different elevations.

Up and over, hard left.

Diving down through cross traffic, I had to go wider to veer around. The guy was a maniac. Or just fearless.

Skill gains came, piling up on each other as I just avoided being pancaked by a hover truck. People on a balcony dove for cover.

He dodged up through another intersection, too many moving vehicles for my implant to give me a safe path through. That left me no choice but pass under it and correct a block later. Suicide wouldn't help, but if he got away would I ever get another chance?

I grazed another wall rounding a corner into oncoming traffic. Hover cars and bikes dodged up and down away from us. One crashed into ground traffic below, but I wasn't about to look behind me to see how bad.

I followed him up and around a dark green tower into a long straightaway. He pushed for speed but I drew my gun, feeling it come alive through the weapon link. Targeting displays lined up and I grazed his bike. That distracted him, and he juked and danced. Neon signs streaked past on both sides, which gave me an idea.

I fired to his right, just trying for close. If I happened to hit him, that'd work too. As expected, he dodged left, clipping a sign that exploded in a shower of sparks.

His bike shuddered, damaged, and he reached the end of the long buildings and turned again. I made the turn following him, but not by much. Now black smoke leaked from his bike.

He dove through yet another layer of cross traffic, which closed up and blocked me. By the time I slipped around I didn't see him anymore. I'd lost him! Yes, I swore.

I had to think! And then I had it. I knew where he'd head for as soon as he thought he was safe. I zoomed up for altitude and a clearer view. The city spread under me and I got my bearings.

Scanning the line between where I was and his ship was . . . there. I had him.

He was out of rifle range, so I only saw one other plan. I accelerated as I angled down at him, maximizing for speed. Faster and faster until just holding onto the bike was a challenge.

He leaned low over his bike, trying to eke all the speed he could out of it as it smoked more. He didn't look back, and he didn't look up. Nobody looks up.

I rammed him from above, knocking him off his bike and sending them both into the ground. His bike exploded on impact. I leaped up and back, hoping my boost would counter enough momentum for me to survive

Chapter 18

I woke to a reassuring XP notification. I hadn't died, he had.

+500 XP (10350 total)

I had all of 9 silver cybernetic Health points and 16 red ones. Ouch didn't begin to cover it. I'd never felt so much pain.

"Are you okay?"

A horn brought my attention to the here and now. Traffic had stopped around us. A woman stood next to her car, communicator in hand.

"Yeah, I'm fine," I lied as I got to my feet. Any crash you can walk away from, right?

Authorities would be here any minute, so I couldn't spare attention for the woman. I limped over to the bounty hunter's corpse. His condition was obvious. My armor was battered, his was flat-out destroyed. As was his head. Unbroken bones you could probably count on one hand. Heck, you'd probably hold them all in one hand. He hadn't literally splattered, at least. Still, I shuddered. Thank you, Technomage Protective Aura.

I grabbed the two pistols first before finding money and a pair of data chips along with a hand computer on the brink of destroyed.

Item acquired: WarTech B-220 Blaster Pistol	
A heavy but well-balanced pistol, tough and reliable. Weapon Link compatible.	
Range	60m
Accuracy	+10
Damage	55
Shots	20
Durability	31/65

Item acquired: LasTech S-90 Stun Pistol	
This sleek and compact pistol is legal on some worlds which ban more lethal weapons. It inflicts stun damage that can incapacitate but not kill.	
Range	40m
Accuracy	+10
Damage	65*
Shots	20
Durability	6/40

I hobbled away to avoid questions. Or space cops. Or pretty much any other attention. A looted silver chip bought bus fare. I only drew a few stares on the bus. I rode it to the outskirts enough to find dark corners to prowl. Past Gelrick's parked ship. I wasn't ready to linger too close to it yet.

I healed up resting on the bus, but that pesky silver bar didn't heal much on its own. I gained three more points of Engineering in the hour it took to fix myself up.

Next I tried my hand with the little hand computer. No dice. I wasn't going to get it working without replacement parts. Which I didn't have. The bits scavenged from rooftop drones helped with my self repairs, but weren't computer components. So, I turned to the two data chips, plugging them into my data pad in turn. It wasn't a full-blown computer, but as a data reader it opened both chips.

The first chip offered recent star charts and navigational data. I only looked at that long enough to identify it. A second directory listed profiles for several mercenary groups on different systems. One group it listed as operating out of the Jentassa system. Sure enough, it included a picture of the man who had followed Altion and I, herding us into the trap that killed my friend.

That answered that question. Yes, they were connected.

The second chip answered how they were connected. I skimmed through log files relating to past jobs, people I'd never seen or heard of, before finding two video logs.

The first opened with a picture labeled as Silleste. It showed an elven woman's heart-shaped face with soft features, rounded angles and soft lines. Vivid green eyes looked out under brown hair with gold highlights in a cute pixie cut. Pointed ears rose several centimeters taller than human ears.

"This is your target," a man's emotionless, deep voice said. "Her name is Silleste. She is an Elven mystic. It is imperative she is captured alive and as unharmed as possible. But she is dangerous. Once captured, she must be kept sedated. She is to be considered armed and dangerous even when restrained.

"I have transferred ten thousand to your account. The remaining forty will be paid on delivery. If she dies, your life is forfeit. Exercise caution."

As if that final sentence would be necessary. I wouldn't have needed to hear it.

So that confirmed he'd been hired to kidnap her. No mentioned of Altion though. One thing it did not confirm was when and where he found her. Had it been here after she'd fled here, or had he been behind the attack on Relkit III? If so, he must have followed her. She hadn't been here long, so I suspected he first tried for her there and chased her here.

I tapped on the second file.

"I've got her." Gelrick's voice.

The face at the other end belonged to an android without question. The head looked carved, a skull shape of gunmetal gray. Metal eyes glowed red in the centers. No mouth parts moved when he spoke, but the voice was easy to recognize from the first video log.

"Were there any issues with the capture?" No emotion showed on the face, either.

Gelrick hesitated before answering. "She shrugged off stun weapons. She fell to gas, however. I see now why you suggested keeping her sedated. Which I am."

"Good. Has she been harmed?"

"Nothing more than bruises."

"Excellent. Bring her to Hor'chan. I will have someone meet you at the starport with payment." Finally, a location.

"Very well. I will see you in . . . two days."

She'd been there a few days already at least then. The android stressed her condition enough I figured she was safe and alive. As long as she hadn't ended up in a slave auction or something.

"Good." The transmission ended.

Now I knew where to go. And I had updated navigational data to get there. I just needed a ship. And I knew just where to find one.

I made my way back to the hangar where Gelrick's ship waited, all alone and ownerless.

Still no sign of guards patrolling. It might have been a common rental storage place. I supposed it was. No just walking up with a stolen access card and waltzing in. I hadn't found one on him. A keypad controlled the door. The data chips hadn't included an access code. He'd either memorized it or saved it in his little computer, inaccessible either way.

Good thing I'd switched from Hunter to Rogue, or at least added Rogue. Time to put those skills to use. Grand Theft Spaceship time. . . .

Overhead light made sure the door wasn't a place to hide while I worked, so standing there fiddling with the keypad would be a sure-fire way to get in trouble. That meant a distraction. Redirect attention. Something just around the corner, something for people to watch.

But what did I have? A car wreck would do, but short of shooting a car I wasn't sure how to cause one that wouldn't kill someone. Plus, shooting a car would make me the center of attention. Not what I wanted.

Pieces clicked into place until they formed a plan. I strode off to find the right ingredients.

First, I needed a car. Hover vehicles were more common. Most rooftops seemed to include landing platforms. But ground vehicles were still common enough. Many of what I'd seen had been more about cargo and public transportation. Trucks, busses, taxis. But regular cars still plied roads. Not parked as ubiquitously as in the outside world, but still common enough.

It took several blocks to find the right one. Parked along with others. Not too well lit. Common looking. But I found it. It took several tries, gaining a point of Pick Locks, before the door clicked and whooshed up and open. I slid in and pulled the door closed.

Getting it started took more trial and error, and I gained more Engineering before the car buzzed to life. I drove it away to a different quiet spot. Next came what turned out to be the harder part. I had to override navigation controls. I didn't have the computer skills to do it, so it would have to be another application for Engineering. I was getting a lot of use out of that one. I set to work, hoping I'd be able to pull it off.

Ten minutes later I drove off once again, now heading back towards Gelrick's ship.

I stopped a block away, lined everything up and waited for the right opportunity. Timing would matter. Get that wrong and I might end up killing someone. I opened the door and counted down. I tapped the button and slapped the door control as I rolled out of the car. It accelerated away with an electric whine.

I didn't stick around to see if it worked or not. I couldn't afford the time. Either it would, or it wouldn't. I couldn't do anything about it now. I sprinted off, circling the hangar building the other direction. The car would either cross the intersection and crash into a building, or it wouldn't make it across. Whichever happened would give passersby something to pay attention to other than me kneeling in front of a door fiddling with its controls.

I rounded the corner to the entry door. Yelling and confusion a half-block away meant my diversion was having some effect. Would it be enough?

I pulled out tools and started on the keypad. No immediate signs of anti-tampering alarms, but at my skill level I wasn't about to take that on faith. Better off assuming time was a factor not on my side.

The door slid open, and I hurried inside.

Lights hummed to life, illuminating my prize, finally a space ship that looked like one. Blue and gray with red trim it sat, a wedge shape on three landing struts. Angled sides came together with small turrets. White lights lining the edges of a boarding ramp were a welcome sight. The door at the ramp's top opened at my approach. I'd expected to have to Engineer my way in, but I wasn't about to complain.

Exploring the ship would have to come later. A central lounge space connected to a small cockpit with seating for two. Pilot's controls marked one spot while the other featured an array of display screens. I spotted a chip slot and labeled that one the navigation chair.

I slid into the pilot's chair and control surfaces glowed to life. After a quick survey of the controls, I identified basic flight controls and power systems, defense shield controls, the navigation and sensor displays, and targeting systems for the two turrets.

What I didn't see was anything about how to open the wide hangar door. I could see the door through cockpit windows, looking down the ship's nose, but no sign of door controls there, either. Leaving the ship to open them wasn't very appealing, anyway.

Some quick taps on controls and I found the targeting interface. A quick drag of the finger and a tap to select the door as a target was easy. One press on a FIRE indicator and both turrets spat red laser beams that burned gashes into the door. The door disappearing in a small explosion would've been nicer.

Well, there's always the brute force approach, right?

First a little upwards thrust, enough to hold the ship off the floor and retract the landing gear. Add forward thrust... and bump into the door ineffectually. If I threw full thrust forward, would I be able to pull up in time to not crash into the building across the street?

I leaned forward and craned my neck to peer upwards. A scaffold of joists and beams held up the roof. I gauged it as less solid than the door, something I don't think I'd have been able to do without points in Engineering. So my brain was capable of things it wasn't before far too little real training. Tell me that's not disturbing. So, fine. I scored it back and forth with laser beams that vaporized roofing in narrow slits. Then I threw full power into upwards thrust and smashed through the roof.

It took about a minute to reach orbit. Acceleration pushed me back into my chair enough to notice, but not enough to bother me. The ship was more complicated to fly than a hover bike, but I gained two more points of Pilot while ascending.

Orbit happened more or less automatically, which was fine by me. Space flight was one area I didn't mind having the details simplified for. I'd played other games more dedicated to space fighter combat, where the physics were all too realistic. I'd never gotten the hang for managing thrust to get the right directions. This ship flew more like a simulated plane than a spacecraft. Fine by me!

With the expansive star field above me, and the sphere of Jentassa IV spreading out under the ship's pointed nose, I slid over to the navigation chair. At least once I had Silleste we could be pilot and copilot.

I thumbed the data chip into its slot and the screen prompted me to update existing navigation data. I tapped to confirm and waited while it loaded. That also took about a minute. After that, the interface was easy to work. I found the screens to query the database for the planet I wanted.

One display updated to show a star map, with indicators for current and destination locations. A dotted line connected the two. A dozen or more systems lay closer than Hor'chan. Fuel status showed 90% and fuel required for jump listed as 60%.

The database offered an entry on Hor'chan, which was nice.

Hor'chan	
Position	4 of 7
Size	13,875 km
Gravity	Standard
Atmosphere	Standard
Land Percentage	18%
Land Surface Area (square km)	108,900,000
Geograph summary: Hor'chan is an ocean planet with no true continents. Twenty-seven major islands and six major island chains account for 90% of planetary land area.	
Geopolitical summary: Each island state has its own government, each reporting to a Central Council. Each sovereign island sends one Councilor to the Central Council which meets monthly for two-week sessions. The Central Council does not have authority to create or impose laws affecting only one sovereign island. TRAVEL NOTE: visitors to Hor'chan should be certain to check local regulations upon arrival, as they may vary from island to island.	

How's that for an ideal place for criminal hangouts?

I set the system to plot the jump. Surprise, surprise . . . it took one minute. I sensed a pattern here.

Once it plotted the course, the main nav screen switched to a local system view. A dotted line marked the course from current position, past two gas giants, to a dashed ring around the system labeled, "Minimum FTL distance." I set to follow the suggested course and engaged the autopilot. An estimated duration countdown began at just over one hour, ending the one-minute trend.

With some time on my hands, it seemed a good chance to explore my new ship. The lounge served as the central point of the ship. An oval table claimed the center of the lounge, with four comfortable-looking padded chairs surrounding it. A galley-style kitchen space sat opposite the entry ramp airlock towards the back.

Two doors on either side ahead of the kitchen and airlock led to staterooms. The forward most two, where the ship was narrower, sat closer to square except for angled outer walls. The other two, middle more, were more rectangular, narrower and deeper. And smaller.

I was about to investigate a passageway leading aft when insistent beeping from the cockpit stole my attention.

"This is Jentassa Defense Force Squadron Fifteen hailing Gelrick of the Dark Raptor."

Dark Raptor. So that was the ship's name. I hurried into the pilot's chair. The local navigation display showed a diamond formation of four dots departing the planet behind me. Only one other ship registered on the display. But they were talking to me.

I thumbed the comm system. "I'm sorry, who?" Could I increase speed in a subtle enough way they wouldn't notice? No, probably not.

"I repeat, this is Jentassa Defense Force Squadron Fifteen. Gelrick, you are ordered to stand to, set station keeping, and prepare to be boarded."

"I'm sorry, Gelrick who? There's nobody here by that name." I said the last part convincingly. It was true after all. Sliders shifted power between engines and shields and weapons. Power output displayed 50%.

The diamond constellation increased speed, making my decision for me. I dialed power output to full and slid most of it to thrusters, directing some to shields. Sliders for front, aft, and both sides adjusted power allocation. Each slider defaulted to a center position, even distribution. I shifted everything to aft.

Secondary navigation and sensor displays also toggled to weapons controls. Primary weapon control sat with the navigator, but on my side and close enough I could reach. A red circle around the ship suggested firing range. My pursuers would still need to get a lot closer before crossing that circle. I prayed their range wasn't longer than mine.

"Computer," I tried, "how long until they're in attack range?"

No response came. Figuring out how to calculate that wasn't the best use of my time just then. If I boosted engine power more, I'd either get away or give myself more time. Thrusters at 100% used about 80% of the total power available, but I didn't see a way to push more than that. Not from here at least, and now wasn't the time to run back to find the engineering compartment.

One gas giant hung about fifteen degrees off course. Could I do some fancy maneuver there? With a Pilot skill of 7? Not likely.

I trained the sensor display on my pursuers, which gave me a visual. At maximum magnification they looked like stub-winged fighters. A colored bar chart next to each one suggested power output in red, shield output in blue, and I guessed the third yellow one was weapons power. Labels explained power and shields, but the yellow column lacked a label. Overall power level dwarfed the other two, suggesting most of it going to speed, like me.

A 100,000 km label appeared next to the weapon range circle. The ships chasing me passed the 200,000 mark and were closing. The FTL zone line still lay a long distance ahead.

What other resources did I have? I checked the computer interfaces in reach and found a ship recognition system. I dragged one of the ship images onto that icon and up popped an entry.

> **Corval Class Light Interceptor**
>
> Light interceptors are best suited to combat against small, fast moving targets like other fighters. Often used for defense screening and for intercepting incoming attack fighters they are fast and nimble.
>
> The Corval class is a common human design. They carry light shields and minimal armor, but are difficult to hit and may carry sophisticated jamming equipment to prevent targeting systems locking on. Partial wings allow for limited atmospheric capabilities, along with providing optional hardpoints for heavier strike missiles.

Wonderful. Fighters gaining on me. Four of them.
180,000 km.

I considered the gas giant again. But what options did it give me? How did "limited atmospheric capabilities" compare to whatever my ship could handle? Streamlined as it was, they wouldn't have to follow me in. They could wait me out in orbit. No help there.

160,000 km.

They were going to catch up before the zone line. When they did, they'd shift power to weapons. Would that reduce their speed at all? I had power left after full thrust, so it seemed safe to assume they did, too. Would it enough against my shields? I had no way to gauge shield strength.

"Light shields and minimal armor." If I fired at them would they increase power to their shields? Would they take that from speed or from weapons? Either one would help. But where would I take power from? Certainly not speed. I needed every bit of that I could get. Without knowing how good my shields were, how was I supposed to know how much power I could shift from them?

140,000 km.

I bled power from shields into weapons. After some juggling, I had the starboard turret at full power and all the shield power to aft shields. One engine hit would screw me. At least I had time to figure out the targeting system more than just selecting a door right in front of me at point blank range.

"Target acquired. Target out of range," the system warned me in flashing red text.

120,000 km.

They weren't dodging or evading. They knew they weren't in range yet. What else did they know? Just as important, what didn't I know?

"Target locked." They hit the red line, which flashed three times and turned green. I fired.

And missed.

I fired three more times before my target started actively evading even though none of the shots came too close.

Gunnery Skill +1 (1)

My target fighter fell behind the rest as its evasive maneuvers took away from straight-line speed. I switched targets, going after each one and then jumping from target to target. I had to keep them busy. Every little bit helped.

90,000 km.

They weren't firing yet. Did I have a range advantage? Or range affected accuracy, and they were waiting for some optimal range. It didn't matter which. The longer before they fired the better. I kept firing, scoring more Gunnery but not scoring any hits.

80,000 km.

Now they fired, all in unison. Only one hit, and the shield strength indicator shortened while the red line traced across my shields. It crept back up when the hit stopped, but nowhere as fast as it had gone down.

Dodge or fire? I couldn't do both and expect much. Not with such beginner-level skills. Oh, for evasion macros. . . . I fired more. They dodged in every direction, avoiding my shots but sacrificing speed. They still closed, just not as fast. Whichever one I fired at dodged more while the rest fired.

More hits dragged down my shield strength. The shield indicator was down half, and blinking, by the time I hit a fighter. It spun and exploded and disappeared from my display.

+250 XP (10,600 total)

The three remaining fighters backed off to 75,000 km. They didn't stop firing, and a shot got through shields. The shields hadn't collapsed, and would still take some off each shot, but they weren't a wall anymore.

"Hull damage," a display on my left helpfully informed me. The lack of blaring alarms or new flashing lights suggested it could wait.

Again came growing anxiety over one lucky engine hit leaving me crippled here, a sitting duck.

I set aside firing for the moment, shifting that power back to shields. Maybe evasion was the better tactic. But dodging and weaving, while it led to them hitting me less, cost me in speed. They closed again. I tried smaller movements, still trying not to be an easy target but without veering as much. It slowed their relentless closing, but didn't stop it.

60,000 km. The zone line waited dozens of times as far away. On the plus side, my shields had recovered about half just by giving them the power swiped from weapons. But the closer the fighters got, the more accurate they got, and the shield burn rate exceeded the recovery rate.

Shields were dwindling. They were closing. They'd reach me before I reached safety.

I gave both turrets just enough power to lock on. Still no jamming, the lock held. If only I had a macro to tie actions together! I threw all the power from engines into the two turrets, bringing them up to full in a flash. A tap to trigger them and red beams lanced out behind me. Both hit, carving the fighter into three exploding pieces.

+250 XP (10,850 total)

Level 9 gained!
+23 Health
+24 Stamina
+9 Mana
+17 Focus
+5 Primary Characteristic Points
+10 Skill Points

    I shunted the power back to thrusters as fast as I could while the remaining two fighters backed off. They fell back to 85,000 km before closing again. I'd rattled them, but they weren't breaking off. I'd leveled again, but my ship didn't recover all at once the way I would have. Darn. That would've helped! More skill points into Piloting or Gunnery both seemed a good idea, but I didn't dare take my attention from controls long enough to do it.

    With only two fighters my shields held better. They'd have to close more to get me, but they also had to know I could shunt power and vaporize another one. I locked onto one and it dodged like crazy. Now I had something, but for how long? I alternated targets and gained room, but each time they reacted less. Lull them into complacency and try again?

    The zone line drew closer, feeling in reach at last.

    "This is Jentassa Defense Force Destroyer Valiant to Dark Raptor. Power down weapons or you will be destroyed."

    What?

    I zoomed out the view. A larger dot off ahead and to the left, edging along the zone line and headed to intercept me. Oh, come on!

    I angled right, all I could do. The destroyer wasn't as fast as I was and still hung three times as far off as the fighters. 200,000 km. It fired at me. The shot went wide by a healthy margin, but showed I was in their range. Not fair.

    I cursed. I pounded the controls in front of me. The angles between my course and the destroyer's would mean the difference between reaching the zone line and escaping and, well, not. It fired again, missing by less.

    At least from this distance, and with the angle change, it was in my rear shield arc. I didn't have to power a second side. Small favors, right?

    A creeping, I-just-dropped-the-soap feeling sank into me.

    More shots reached out from the destroyer, intimidating and thick as they raked across my view. Each one came closer than the prior. As if I wasn't already worried enough, my shield struggled to hold 30%. That was about the level their shots leaked through. Not much protection against the kind of death that destroyer flung my way.

"Hull damage. Structural damage." A fighter hit. Why couldn't the ship have its own Health bar so I could tell how damaged it was? Space combat in this game was not fun!

And then it happened.

Chapter 19

"FTL Ready," the nav screen updated. I'd reached the zone line! I pressed the large ACTIVATE JUMP button and the universe around me streaked from existence. A shifting blue haze with occasional streaks of light replaced the star field outside the cockpit windows.

I'd made it. The sigh of relief brought the appropriate dramatic release of tension.

Now I had room to breathe, safely away and alone. Or could things attack in hyperspace or jump space or whatever this was? Whatever it was, the nav system estimated 34 hours to cross.

Now was time for leveling up. My character sheet warranted extra attention. Sometimes you can spend points without worrying too much or based on a character concept or personal preference. When you're playing a game, you can do that. Trust me, when your life is on the line it's more serious.

Name: Max McAlloy		Level: 9		XP: 10850		Skills
Primary Attributes		Secondary Attributes		Tertiary Attributes		
Strength	25	Health (CON)	359	Ranged Attack	139	Unarmed Combat 16
Agility	33	Stamina (CON/STR)	388	Melee Attack	129	Dodge 35
Constitution	23	Mana (WIL/Mag)	79	Evasion	149	Gunnery 3
						Pick Locks 17
Appearance	10	Focus (Will)	191	Toughness	10 (46)	Pick Pockets 20
Intellect	19			Resistance	10 (66)	Pilot 7
Magic	0			Melee Damage (STR)	25	Pistol 15
Willpower	17			Magic Damage (MAG)	0	Rifle 20
Charisma	17			Crit Chance	40	Sneak 35
				Crit Power	30	Demolitions 10
						Engineering 16
Boosted Jump	x4			Mitigation	0	Scavenge 1
Claws: +50% Melee Damage				Speed	53	Track 36
Nightvision	80					Bribery 5
						Haggle 2

Agility I was using a lot, but it was in good shape compared to the rest. Strength and Constitution both also mattered, considering the number of fights I'd been in lately. But I waffled between Intellect and Charisma. I'd been doing okay on intellectual challenges and skills, coming up with plans and handling engineering tasks.

Talking my way out of things was more of a weak point. Charisma it was.

Most of my newer skills progressed well. Gunnery seemed a weak area and Scavenge sat far too low for something with so much potential use. So, I split the ten skill points evenly between those two.

I'd even have time to sleep on the trip, so I scoped out the staterooms more. The forward two were larger. Personal effects in the starboard one marked it as the prior captain's. A basic wardrobe cabinet offered a coat and some common clothes. He was about my size, so those could come in handy.

More interesting, a weapon locker presented more proper loot: a stubby rifle, grenades, rifle and pistol energy packs and a portable recharger for them. The recharger mounted to a dedicated spot in the locker, plugged into a power socket. I set an empty charging right away, glad I hadn't discarded them.

Item acquired: Improved Bounty Hunter Blaster Carbine		
A powerful rifle for its compact size, firing short blaster bolts packing more punch than a more accurate beam. A scope on it allows for Sniper Shots. Weapon Link compatible.		
	Range	75m
	Accuracy	+25
	Damage	85
	Shots	40
	Durability	65/65

Talk about upgrade. For something supposedly less accurate than a beam it was still 5 points better than my beam rifle, for better than double the damage. The range reduction I could live with. Long range sniping opportunities weren't coming up often. But closer-in heavy punch I needed. You should've seen my smile when I spied a box of grenades:

Item acquired: Mk II Stun Grenade	
Stun grenades inflict stun damage that can incapacitate but not kill.	
Damage	85*

Finally, right? Stun versus lethal was fine, better even.

The soft bed called to me, but I also had damage to the ship to investigate. I moved to the rearward passageway.

First, to port, I found a cargo hold. Empty except for a few boxes of basic provisions. The space was about three times the size of the stateroom, including a section of floor marked out as an elevator platform that lowered for loading and unloading below the ship.

The corridor ended at a T with side passages leading to doors labeled port and starboard turret access. Another door led further aft to Engineering.

Consoles and displays and tool lockers filled a space not big enough to call an office. It reminded me of a tight galley kitchen, not room enough for two to work at once. Signs marked one console and locker pair DAMAGE CONTROL. This was an important find. The first screen showed a layout of the ship with markers for damage. Fuel storage sat opposite the cargo bay. The maneuver drive lived behind Engineering while the FTL drive and power reactor sat to either side.

A flashing red line marked a gash in the hull under the cargo bay, but since it hadn't depressurized the hold, it hadn't breached it. The hull and structure hit loomed over the FTL drive. Close one. Tapping the display let me zoom for more information, including a display of which access spaces had depressurized from the hull breaches.

The damage control locker included a vacuum suit along with an array of tools. First step: an up-close assessment of the damage.

I had to suit up and depressurize Engineering to open a ceiling hatch into an access space only just tall enough to crawl in. But from there I could see the damage, where charred, crisscrossing support beams bent away from each other at cut ends. Beyond that I saw the circular hole in the hull, and the flickering of shields just beyond. Dropping those shields in FTL seemed a disaster in the making. I wouldn't be able to access the hull breach from inside well enough to seal it. That had to wait until I was in regular space, or whatever the term was. I supposed if I'd been trained in piloting either someone would've told me the terms, or I'd just know it like I knew engineering things Sira hadn't told me, or which sides were port and starboard.

But the structural concern I could fix. Damage missed the FTL drive outer housing by less than half a meter. Yikes. That close to game-ending right there. Tools and spare materials from the locker, and some three hours, netted me two more points of Engineering and what looked like a solid repair job.

Hefting supplies and tools with me, I moved to scope out the damage under the cargo hold. As suspected, floor panels removed for access. Again, after depressurizing the cargo space. The gash ran most of a meter long, fore to aft. A grazing hit that cut in without any real penetration. The patch job took about an hour and netted me yet another Engineering increase. Every point of that was valuable.

With all that done, and twenty-nine hours of autopilot time, I crawled into bed. It was softer than I used to like, but that had been before prison and their alleged mattresses. Now, softer was just fine.

The night's dream fled when I woke up. Just like I'd fled someone in my dreams. A certain bounty hunter. I'd prefer the game reaching into my subconscious and affecting my dreams than the ship being haunted by its prior owner. I shook the thought away and rubbed my eye. The implant replacing the right one didn't need rubbing. The alloy hand felt so real, so natural. As if that prior life in prison with two fleshy hands were the dream I'd awaken from.

Rested up, I confirmed the supplies in the cargo hold. Foodstuffs for several weeks of just me. A solid week of feeding Silleste if I found her within about a week. None of it was amazing, but for the moment, food was food.

I familiarized myself more with the ship and its systems while the rest of the trip passed.

The view outside the cockpit windows shuddered to a stop, resolving into a black expanse decorated with a panoramic mural of stars. I pulled up the local navigation view, taking in a system with six planets. Hor'chan, the third planet, was also the only one with its own name and not just Hora I through VII. A circle blinked near me on the display and a beeping alarm sounded.

Two blips on scanners. They raced forward, no warning, no provocation. They'd been waiting at the zone line for someone to show up. It'd been a while since my last player ambush, and this had PVP written all over it. PVP can be a fun challenge in games where the AI isn't as clever as other players. But this game was challenging enough without it.

Fighters, larger and blockier looking than the Jentassan ones. Where the Jentassa Defense Force painted their fighters white with blue and green stripes and an emblem I'd seen on the planet, these were a dull gray with no markings except a black skull and crossbones on the nose.

Really? Space Pirates?

I wasn't supposed to be soloing these zones, was I?

Their weapons already locked on, they fired from long range. I kicked shields up high while dumping about half power into thrusters. Setting course for Hor'chan took little more than tapping on it and selecting it. Two fighters seemed more manageable, unless they were high level with upgrades up the wazoo. But my ship wasn't newbie grade either. Full shields should be tougher than theirs. I dragged one to the identification window, which just listed them as unidentified.

They missed several times before they scored a hit on me, speaking to their accuracy—not as good as the Jentassans. The shields dropped less than before, too. A second pair of fighters came into sensor range. Based on the spacing between them I'd have time to deal with the first pair before the second came into play.

My first kill came fairly quick, and his partner grew more defensive. As if they weren't counting on armed resistance.

> **+400 XP (11,250 total)**

I alternated between small maneuvers, to at least not be going in a straight line, and firing. Little gunner seats in the turret enclosures would have allowed individual gunners, but I didn't have people to man them. Altion could have picked up gunnery. But missing him was something I didn't have time for.

The second man bid his time until his friends drew into range. He stayed within range but skirted the edge of it. At this point my shields were doing fine, and I hadn't taken damage.

I took out another one as the remaining two tried swarming around me, forcing me to keep shields all around.

> **+400 XP (11,650 total)**

Without being able to concentrate them my shields took more abuse when hit. The fighters were much more maneuverable than I was, especially while I controlled turrets. Slaved together, the turrets packed a good wallop. It was just a matter of hitting.

My side shields dropped to half, and I still had one fighter on each side. These fighters hit harder than the last ones. Time to switch things up again. I turned and charged one. It veered up, which might have worked if I was a fighter with weapons pointing forward. But side-mounted turrets handle up and down just fine. I cut the thing in half and it exploded.

> **+400 XP (12,050 total)**

In retrospect, I should have asked myself where those fighters came from. If I had, I might have been more prepared for what came next.

A new blip appeared at the edge of my scanner. Six sub-blips launched from it. I brought them up on visual at full magnification. The main ship was at least ten times the size of mine. Big enough to carry ten fighters.

Four gave me a run for my money earlier. Six? No way. They were off to the side, so they'd have to at least angle to catch up.

The close by one broke off and kept his distance. He still followed, but he stayed out of weapons range. Waiting for his friends to join him. Seven to one. Nope. No thanks.

Power distribution was easy: thrusters to maximum, the rest to shields shifted all rear. During the downtime while jumping I'd found how to overpower the thrusters. Their normal operation from the cockpit maxed out at 85%. From Engineering I could push them higher, in theory up to 110. What I didn't have was the computer skill to patch together a way to do that from here. Engineering was not the place to be while being shot at.

I considered angling away from the carrier and the main fighter force. That would delay them getting into weapons range but take me off course from the planet. No, running for the planet was the priority.

These fighters weren't as fast as the Jentassan interceptors and weren't as maneuverable. Strike fighters, then, trading some of their speed for firepower. Their shields didn't do much against twin turrets.

The main pirate group closed to 400,000 km. The planet was so much further away that if I zoomed out enough to see it, I and the ships around me went from individual dots to one blob. Slower than interceptors or not, they still had more speed and maneuverability than I did. Their carrier lagged behind. It was still one fighter on my tail and six more coming. Those six weren't going to come in waves for me to take on one at a time.

I had a plan for dealing with the fighter behind me, but it was risky. Would the distance it cost me just kill me later? Only one way to find out. . . .

Full thruster power cut my speed with a lurch. The fighter behind me jumped into range. I fired the turrets, still locked on.

+400 XP (12,450 total)

Pilot Skill +1 (8)

Gunnery Skill +1 (9)

"Ha!" Six to go. And all in the same direction. That at least meant more options. I slammed the throttle back to forward.

With death now 300,000 km behind me, safety still sat two commas further away than that. Oh, for mines to drop behind me. . . .

Closing that distance would take them several minutes at least. A short window of safety. I hopped out of my chair and sprinted aft.

The thruster control console had quite a few controls, but I'd already taken time to scope it out. I tweaked the thruster output to 95%. Blowing out the drive redlining it would end up just as fatal as not going fast enough.

I ran back to the cockpit to see if it made enough difference.

They still closed, but nothing like before.

I'm good at math. I don't enjoy it, but I had to learn enough those two years of college before being arrested. Not like I was ever astrophysics-level good. I knew a straight line wouldn't really work in space, but the game designers kept things simpler. Good thing, too. If off-the-cuff figures were right, I'd just get to the planet before they got into range.

A warning gauge showed thruster heat climbing ever closer to the danger mark.

100,000 km between me and my pursuers. The planet still sat too far away. My initial math was off. I'd have six fighters pounding me for at least five minutes. Pushing the engines harder was more likely to break them than save me.

A much bigger blip showed up near the planet.

"Unidentified fighters, this is the battle cruiser Gestant. You are flying without transponders in violation of galactic law. Break off your pursuit or we will open fire." A woman's voice.

Was I saved, or doomed even worse? Was the woman an angel, or the angel of death?

The fighters hesitated, falling back. A minute passed before they regained the distance.

The sensor blip marking the Gestant flashed and spat out a swarm of smaller blips. Interceptors. Twenty in precise formation. Those people were not playing around.

"Unidentified fighters, this is your final warning. If you do not break off our fighters will attack as soon as they enter range. If that happens, we will pursue you to your base ship, which we can swat out of space with one volley."

The fighters turned and fled.

Train the enemy to the guards, a tactic almost as old as MMORPGs themselves.

"Thank you for the assist, Gestant. They jumped me as soon as I dropped out of jump." Give them something now and maybe they'd ask fewer questions.

"Dark Raptor," the woman on the Gestant announced, "I don't see your registration information in our system."

That was better than it being reported stolen, or belonging to a criminal, right?

"I, uh . . . I just bought it. I guess the paperwork hasn't gotten this far?" The long wedge of fighters advanced. I cut thruster throttle by half.

"There has been pirate activity reported in this region of space, Dark Raptor. I'd suggest you file your flight plans in advance and stick to designated vectors."

"Yeah. I see that. I'll definitely do that. Thank you."

The fighters banked off to return to their carrier.

The blue sphere of Hor'chan hung before me. As I drew closer, white lines resolved themselves into thin bands of horizontal clouds striping across the planet. I cut power more and slowed into orbit. The nav system received landing instructions and displayed them as a lane to a city on the planet's largest island. I guided the ship, keeping it between the offered lines.

Strong wing buffeted my little ship, which had glided through Jentassa IV's atmosphere as if it weren't there. The clouds streaking across the sphere made sense now. With so little land mass, the wind blew unimpeded. My path took me into the wind shadow of a large mountain dominating the island and the air fell calm. A glowing city lit the mountainside.

My course took me above the city sprawling to the shoreline beneath me. Just above the city top a huge cavern opened into the mountainside. I slowed more and maneuvered my way inside. Local traffic control greeted me and directed me down a side corridor lined with parking garages. I eased my way into one that opened for me, spun around, and set down.

Chapter 20

An exit sign over a rear door caught my eye. The door led to a corridor ending at an elevator. That took me to a market space where merchants and traders hawked wares from tables and kiosks. The whole feel said flea market more than mall.

If only I had a name for Mr. Skull Head the android. But I had the picture of him on my data pad, and he was distinctive looking. Where to ask around for him remained the next question. I stopped at a couple vendors, asking questions on where to get good local information in with other innocent ones.

The one that hit closest to pay dirt was, "What are the shady parts of town to avoid?" A bald human woman in a jumpsuit more pockets than not directed me to—or rather away from—the waterside docks.

> **Quest: Find the Hor'chan Rogues**
> The rough neighborhood around the waterside docks seems a likely place to find shady people

Think about this for a minute. I never said I was looking for rogues. Asking what part of town to *avoid* triggered a quest to find rogues? Counter-intuitive, to say the least. So, did it give me the quest because I'm a rogue and the game is leading me to more of my kind, and therefore more quests? Or was the game reading more into my mind than I thought? Was it giving me the quest having already figured out what I was really after?

Just how deep was the game reaching into my brain? How many ways could someone abuse that? So many questions I didn't want to delve into. I walked away from the spaceport.

The city itself sprawled in three tiers from the spaceport cave network to the shoreline. Wealth tiers seemed to correspond, and I passed from nice and futuristic looking to older and more weathered down to functional poverty. If the woman hadn't warned me about the area, I would've figured it out now.

On my way down, I saw actual ocean ships docked below. For a planet mostly water that made sense. Piers reached fingers out in a long line, a huge comb with several missing teeth. Where to from here, though?

I wandered, looking for unmarked, shadowed doors. I noted several taverns but wasn't ready to ask around yet. And let's face it, my track record at bars wasn't encouraging.

Then I spied someone following me. I used the occasional window clean enough to offer a reflection to scope out my tail. A rodent of a man in a long coat, way to avoid stereotypes there, dude. If this was a player hoping to catch me off guard it was a sorry attempt.

I'd seen well shadowed spots before, and nothing about this guy suggested night vision. I circled around to a block I'd walked before. Yep, he still followed. I stepped around a corner and leapt to reach cover faster, melting into the shadows. I hadn't used Sneak in a while and didn't get the increase I wanted.

It worked, though, his head darted back and forth as he looked around. He hurried down the alley, quiet for his speed. I stepped out and grabbed his shoulder with a hand ready to shove four blades into him. My right put the barrel of my new blaster pistol to his forehead.

"Who sent you?" What can I say, it seemed to be the question Rogues asked.

"I could ask you the same thing." See?

"I'm looking for people, and for information," I explained. "The kind of people and information you can't find higher up in the city." His eyes ran from the gun to my face. I offered him a cheerful smile quite at odds with his situation. His brows alternated between furrowed and raised, a good confusion. "And I think you know where I need to go."

Quest completed: Find the Hor'chan Rogues
Quest Rewards: Reputation increase with Hor'chan Rogues' Guild +100XP (Total 12,550)

"You're good," he said. "Quiet-like. We watch who comes close. If you aren't good enough to spot us, you don't get to find us. But I'm not the one you need to talk to." He patted my arm, hoping I'd lower the gun. I let him go and took a step back. I lowered the gun a little, but not so much I couldn't pull the trigger and still hit him.

"Then who *is* the one I need to talk to?"

"A bar off Pier 83. Dockers. Order a Dark Nebula and find Agfir. He'll be wearing a fish pin. Tell him Wren sent you."

> **Quest: Find the Hor'chan Rogues**
> Go to Dockers and introduce yourself to Agfir.

Getting quests for things I needed to do anyway was a handy bonus. Free XP is never something to turn away.

I passed one police patrol on the way. Full-face helmets hid their faces. Hard armor plates covered their torsos, but no other real armor added to their blue Federalist uniforms. Oversized pistols hung at their hips. Cops and Criminals were a common enough theme for opposing factions. And these were police, not soldiers. They strolled more than marched. Walking a beat more than patrolling. I kept my distance and they ignored me.

The bar sat a block removed from the docks, and only the name on the sign over the door distinguished it from the warehouses around it. It could've passed for a dockworkers' guild hall. For all I knew it was one, too.

Sultry lounge music filled the dark, smoky interior. Tiny white lights on the ceiling resembling a spiral galaxy lent discrete, dim illumination. Nightvision again came in handy and seeing the dark-clad figures in the shadows wasn't an issue. A rough-and-tumble looking crowd, most of them scowled at me if they made eye contact as I scanned the room. They'd all taken a uniform interest in me. Regulars eyeing the stranger with distrust.

I stood tall. I was a cyborg with tricks up my ... arm and I wasn't a newbie anymore. And this quest line felt like a newbie quest to get rogues right out of the tutorial started. As long as I didn't cause trouble they'd have no reason to start any. Right?

I slid onto a stool before a grimy bartender in a black leather vest and full biker beard.

"I'll have a Dark Nebula, please." He raised an eyebrow at my order but served it. It came in a wide clear mug showing off a dark liquid swirled with something gray. At 14 silver chips it was seriously overpriced. Pretty, but I was reluctant to drink it. The motor oil feel it left in my mouth reinforced that.

Three stools away a silver fish leapt out of waves on the lapel of a brutish Mordian. Of course, because they'd *so* been my favorite people so far. But if this was the guy I was here for. . . .

I shifted over next to him, bringing my drink. Even as it sloshed around the lighter and darker components refused to mix.

"Interesting choice of drink." The Mordian's voice was as pretty as his face, which wasn't saying much. Yet the fingers holding his red martini didn't match, too slender for the rest of him, as if transplanted from a more dexterous race.

"Wren said I should try it. Maybe it's an acquired taste like he is."

His laugh shook the bar and startled the man on the other side of him, who took his drink and wandered off.

"That's Wren alright. Any friend of his can't be all bad. What's your name friend?"

Chalk it up to the recent investment in Charisma, or just my natural coolness. Yeah, okay, gained Charisma pays off. "Max. Max McAlloy."

"Good to meet you, Max McAlloy. I'm Brek."

Quest completed: Rogue's Introduction
Quest Rewards:
Reputation increase with Hor'chan Rogues' Guild.
You already have the Rogue class.
+100XP (Total 12,650)

Level 10 gained!
+23 Health
+24 Stamina
+9 Mana
+17 Focus
+5 Primary Characteristic Points
+10 Skill Points
You are now eligible for tier 1 prestige classes.

Level ten, and prestige classes. This had to warrant exploring, but not mid-conversation.

"So, what can I do for you, friend?" He took a delicate sip of his drink. I made a mental note to stop stereotyping. Mordians can be rogues and weren't all thugs.

"I'm new here, and trying to find my way around. I'm also looking for this guy." I set the datapad with the picture on the bar in front of him.

Brek growled, hardening up the softer image I'd been developing of him. "Kraxxan. I hate pirates. They cause us nothing but trouble." Pirates. Aren't those everybody's favorite?

"Yeah, I got attacked when I arrived in system. They jumped me. I ran for orbit. I've never been happy to see government fighters before. Let's just say it's a good thing they didn't check me out too close." I was a rogue after all, it couldn't hurt to play the part. Schmooze. You never know when it'll save your life.

"They've been worse and worse every week. if somebody dealt with him it'd make things better for everyone."

Quest: Pirates' Bane
If somebody would just "deal with" pirate boss Kraxxan, the rogues would be grateful.

A quest directly related to my mission. Handy, or unsettling.

"He's got ... something I want. But I can't steal it back until I find him."

Did all Mordians have diamond-shaped irises, or just him? The look he gave me might have been suspicion or surprise. Or blend of both. Music paused between songs, stretching out while too many eyes judged me.

"He's on one of the islands, but we've never been able to track him to which one. But ... he goes to a strip club called Wet Fish over by pier 12. Scummy place. Not for the ... squeamish. Every now and then he takes one of the girls home. If anybody knows which island, it would be one of them." No new quest dialog popped up. A new song started, harsher and less sultry vocals.

I nodded and took another gulp of my drink. I guess I wasn't convincing keeping the distaste off my face.

"You don't have to finish it. I won't tell him."

"Thanks. I appreciate it. And the tip." I slid off my stool. A tall redheaded elf shook his hips creating a dance space. Time to go. If dancing were a skill in here it certainly wasn't one I had IRL.

Rain fell outside as I made my way down the quay. The narrower streets inland seemed more dangerous than better lit dock sides. Cargo shuttles flitted overhead while heavy cargo robots trudged crates and cases back and forth.

I never expected to see a fish in a bikini. Not mermaid, full on fish. One fin reached over the bikini bottom, a fish touching itself. If that wasn't the sign of a strip club called Wet Fish what was? A round door irised open under the glowing sign and I stepped inside.

Garish was the word; every light shone a different color. The floor shifted colors in a rippling pattern like lapping waves. If there was ever a place I never wanted to be too drunk in, this was it.

A huge bouncer rippling with fat rolls waited on a tree stump of a stool. I took a moment to shake rain off, pretense to linger at the door.

"Hey, maybe you can help me. I'm supposed to deliver a message for my boss, Kraxxan. I'm sure you've seen him here, he's kind of distinctive looking."

"Yeah, I've seen him." Didn't even need a description. When the bouncer knows people by name, play it careful.

"Good. Anyway, he wanted to invite one of the women back to the island. He said there were a couple he had before, and I should offer the invitation and see if any were interested. He wasn't too clear on which ones though. Yeah, I kind of messed up, but I was afraid to ask questions. You know how he is." I held out a ten-silver chip. "I don't want to have to ask them all. Any chance you can point out one's he's paid . . . extra attention to?"

He took the chip and palmed it.

Bribery Skill +1 (6)

"You want to talk to Yuelle," he jerked his chins towards a corner. "Silver hair, can't miss her."

I thanked the man and stepped inside a den of creepy perverts far worse than any of the clubs I'd been in before. My college years weren't without their entertainments. You know, other than committing currency fraud and manipulation.

Every stage was a different color. Women, men, and one who seemed to be a one of each spliced at the middle danced around poles or in cages. Men and the occasional woman leered and slotted money chips into railing posts topped with lights that blinked for every chip inserted. Two men stood opposite an orange-skinned elf literally bidding for her attention. Classy, right?

Bubba Bouncer wasn't wrong. Yuelle's silver hair stood out, and up, in the most outrageous chrome-shiny punk rock mohawk I'd ever seen. Silver tattoos sprinkled from her temples down her neck. She wiggled silver fingers as she danced—the only cyborg in the place other than yours truly.

Her song ended and the lone blue-skinned android watching her wandered off. The spotlight on her faded. Her eyes had an orange glow to them when they weren't overpowered by the spotlight.

"Hey," I said to get her attention. Yeah, I know, that last five points wasn't enough. I slid five chips in a row in the railing post. "I was hoping to talk to you about... a mutual acquaintance. Kraxxan. I understand you've been to his island."

She recoiled. "That creep? No, I'm not interested in going back. Not even for ten times what he paid before."

"Oh, I don't work for him. I... I've got a problem with him. But I can't confront him about it until I find him. And I think he'd enjoy the surprise more at home than he would here. Well, okay, enjoy isn't the right word...."

She leaned in, taking the bait.

"Okay, I'll be blunt." Let's face it, I didn't have the Charisma to mince words. "He kidnapped a woman I care about, and I want her back. Can you tell me how to get there?"

Orange eyes shifted to golden yellow.

"Wish I could. He flew me out there in a private shuttle. No windows. I couldn't tell you where we went."

I sighed, and she continued.

"But, when I went I was a little scared. Private island? So I talked to a friend of mine, Stavin. He works traffic control at the starport. I asked him to track the shuttle in case I didn't come back. But Kraxxan did bring me back, so I never thought about it again. But Stavin's a data rat. He never deletes anything. I'm sure he's still got it. Tell him... tell him I'd like to see him again, will you?"

"Sure. I can do that." I slotted five more chips and gained another point of Bribery. Along with the information, not a bad trade. "Thanks."

She gave me a quick description of Stavin, who she said was probably working now but I should catch him on his way out.

Now I had a minute to spare. I sat in a stool to allocate points. I should have done so right away. With all the talking I'd been doing, more Charisma wasn't a hard decision. As for skills, Bribery seemed all too useful. I dumped all ten points there, a respectable increase.

The prestige classes were of more interest. Unlocked Tier I prestige classes were Bounty Hunter, Pilot, Pirate, and Scout. Given the mission I was on, Bounty Hunter made sense. The decision all but made itself when I looked a little closer:

Prestige Class Gained: Bounty Hunter
+3 Agility, +3 Con
+20 Focus
+10 Evasion, +20 Crit Chance, +20 Crit Damage, +10 Melee Attack, +10 Ranged Attack
+10 Sneak, +10 Dodge, +20 Track, +20 Bribery
Special: Stunning Strike

I was right about Bribery. All of it was good stuff, and likely to be needed soon. Stunning Strike sounded promising, but lacked an "unlocked" notification.

I'd had a full day already, and the sun sank as I ascended towards the spaceport again. Deep, long shadows stretched over the city as the sun fell behind rugged mountains. Urban glow spread below me, lending a beauty to the city harder to find by daylight. A gray tower rose above the spaceport entrance with a clear view of the city and the sky above.

With no visible external entrance, I made my way inside and explored the sprawling underground complex. Shops and stores edged the open market. Offices ranged in corridors outside that. I gave a wide berth to a hallway marked Security by a large sign in several languages.

Administration proved more helpful, bringing me through office spaces and blocks of individual offices. Many offered service windows where I gained directions and offers of extensive paperwork. I mocked appropriate gratitude when I couldn't give something sincere.

Traffic Control sat behind a security door controlled by a badge scanner but lacking overt surveillance. The hallway extended both directions, but only a short distance to the left. In either case, someone could step around the corner with little notice. Past that door I'd be able to wait for Stavin. Out here I'd either have to stand at the door or risk him going a different direction. Too many routes led outside to reliably wait elsewhere.

I knelt with my tools and got to work.

Buzz, access denied. Not even a skill gain.

Buzz again. Would a third failure set off an alarm?

This time it beeped, and the door slid open. I pocketed the tools, rushed inside, and let it close behind me. One near-skeletal android woman looked up from a table at me, then went back to tapping away at a hand computer. Three other tables sat open in a break room. Snack and beverage dispensers lined a counter on a side wall. A console to clock in and out sat next to the door across the room.

Since the woman wasn't concerned with my arrival, or my presence, I sat at a table away from her to wait. Just another worker on break or waiting for my shift to start, right?

I waited an hour before he stepped out. Stavin was a lanky, red-headed man with a data interface at his temple. A boring gray uniform hung loose on him, a nametag on his shirt and a security badge on a lanyard. I stood.

"Stavin, my name is Max. Yuelle said I'd find you here."

"How do you know Yuelle?"

How to approach this? I'd mulled over a few approaches during the wait, but none had risen to the surface as best over the others. Time to put those new Charisma points to work.

"I met her at the club as part of an investigation. I'm investigating the pirate Kraxxan. She tells me she's been to his island, and that you might have tracking information about that trip."

"I'm sorry, I just work here. And any flight tracking data is secured and classified." He tried to edge around me.

"I'm sure it is," I said, stepping to stay between him and the door. "And as much as I'd like to come back with a warrant, time is an issue. Yuelle said she'd been worried about not coming back from his island, that that's why you tracked him. Well, now there's another girl involved. This one has been kidnapped. If I can find him, I can rescue her."

He shuddered, his imagination considering what might be happening. I hoped whatever he imagined was worse than anything actually happening. I almost had him, I just needed to nudge him over the line.

"Yuelle tells me you collect interesting data." I pulled out a chip I'd looted from Gelrick. "I have two video logs linking him to the kidnapping. How about a trade of information?"

"Let me see." He held out his hand expectantly. To trust him or not? If he took the chip and refused, I'd follow him home if I had to.

No, he wasn't leaving this room without giving me what I needed. I handed him the chip and he slotted it into his head.

"Oh, that is interesting. That could be worth money."

"Dangerous money, but yes."

"And if I tell you where the island is?" I had him now.

"Then I'm going there and taking him down." No room for doubts, pure confidence now. It worked.

He swapped the chip with another and concentrated a moment.

"Here, all the flight tracking data. Plug that into any nav system and it will take you right there."

I plugged the chip into my data tab and pulled up map views with overlaid trajectories leading from here to an island. Perfect.

"Excellent. Thank you, Stavin. You've helped save this girl's life and who knows how many others. And possibly bringing an end to piracy in this system."

He beamed at that. Let him feel like a hero, that didn't cost me anything. I kept my face official and strode away. If nothing else, better to get some distance before he asked questions I couldn't answer.

But now I knew where to go. This was the most solid lead I'd had yet. If Kraxxan went to so much effort to get her alive she'd still be that way. If he was behind taking her, he'd still have her. That seemed more likely than someone hiring him and him in turn hiring Gelrick who hired mercenaries to help him. Too many layers. But, if Kraxxan was working for someone else I'd follow that lead.

Much more likely, she was on that island. At each step I'd had a smaller area to search. The island didn't even look that big. Things were looking up.

They were until I got back to my ship that is. I didn't even get to it, just to the door for the garage it waited in. The door slid open to reveal two Inquisitors in their red power armor standing at the ramp to my ship. Waiting.

Were they waiting for me, or had someone tipped them off to the ship's original, criminal owner? Or its stolen status? None of those boded well for me. The main garage door stood open, I just needed to get to my ship. I needed a distraction again. Something better than stealing a car and crashing it. I had my new rifle with its better damage, but no.

Blank. Nothing. Except one fantastically stupid idea.

I had one stun grenade on me. Why I hadn't bagged the lot of them I don't know. For the armor they wore, I doubt they'd even flinch. But, I wasn't going to get anywhere waiting. Was it a stupid enough idea to work?

The Inquisitors weren't watching the rear entrance I came in but stood at the foot of the boarding ramp watching the open hangar exit. Boosters threw me upwards as I leapt onto the ship's sloped upper hull. Thankfully, my hunter's boots were soft enough and didn't clang as I landed. I needed my left hand for stability but kept the alloy right one off the hull.

"This better work," I muttered under my breath as I activated the stun grenade. I lobbed it high, and it exploded in the open doorway shy of hitting the floor. I prayed. I held my breath.

The Inquisitors strode forward brazenly, safe in their armor, to investigate. Both readied their rifles, big enough to warrant tripods if that armor wasn't powered. I didn't hear any communication between them, and no hand signals, but I expected helmet radios. They stepped past the front edge the ship and kept advancing.

I dropped behind them and dashed for the ramp, slapping the button to close it behind me. It closed too slow and too loud. They turned. One rifle rose faster than the other, faster than I could duck. The writhing orange shot hit hard, 197 damage, more than half my Health in one hit. The other gestured with his left and a ball of crackling blue electricity formed in his hand. He hurled the ball, which spattered against the ramp's edge. The inner door opened, and I bolted for the cockpit.

I shot the ship forward as hard as I dared enter the corridor, and nearly scraped a turret against the far wall. All it would take was one ship inbound for a parking spot. I edged the throttle up and lurched forward.

I careened out into the sky and something slammed into the ship from behind, knocking me back into my seat. Red damage indicators blinked, but I ignored them, banking and swerving like mad before pouring on more power and rocketing away.

I was away. Scanners weren't showing any signs of pursuit. I set course for the island. With a few minutes before arrival I scoped out the damage.

Two structure damage indicators, one for FTL off line, and one for power reduced to 25%. Ouch. But I couldn't repair while flying, so it would have to wait until I landed. I flew as low as I dared. Turbulence rocked and shoved the ship around. I gave myself a little more altitude. Crashing would be the last thing I needed. The wind on this planet was something else.

The island came into view through cockpit windows spattered with droplets. No wipers.

The ship shuddered, and I pulled at the controls to keep the starboard side dipping into the ocean. "Control system failing," a display told me in flashing red text. An alert beeped at me in case I hadn't noticed.

Wonderful.

But the island was close. I'd make it that far. Once I set down I'd have time to figure it out.

A new set of beeps added to the others. A pair of blips chasing me on sensors.

Fantastic.

The island offered a cluster of buildings—Kraxxan's island estate, no doubt—a big volcano, and some forest.

And the wreckage of a spaceship big enough to be a cruiser or small fighter carrier. Well, the front three quarters of a ship. The rear engine section must have snapped off, leaving ragged edges and a gaping interior.

It looked big enough, and desperate times call for desperate measures, right?

I waited until the last minute and cut speed hard. Thrusters only fired on one side and I entered the wreckage backwards and vertical instead of horizontal. We came to a stop at an angle and sections of bulkhead and equipment collapsed and blocked my view.

Chapter 21

I held my breath watching the screen as the blips closed. They slowed and spread, searching, and moved on. Hiding in the shipwreck worked.

An overhead panel sparked as dust settled. An array of damage indicators spread themselves across the cockpit, but I made for Engineering to get a better view of the situation.

The damage control console gave a much clearer picture. While not outright dire, things didn't look good.

Hull integrity was down a third, but no new breaches showed. Structural damage was widespread but in small amounts. It could wait. The ship would hold together, as long as I kept it from getting pounded.

Main maneuvering thrusters were out.

The FTL drive was out.

A main control circuit board was out.

Four separate shield generator modules showed offline.

Hefting repair tools, I started clockwise to assess and see what I could repair. What kind of rescue would it be if I couldn't get her off the island?

The port turret, another red indicator in Engineering, was gone. Not damaged, not out. Gone. Torn from the ship in the crash. The access hatch remained intact, sealed and air-tight. I crossed that one off as too big to repair on my own.

One shield module I reconnected. The others were trash. I'd have shields, but the upper aft field would be weak and unreliable. Perfect place for that, right?

The thrusters I made partial progress with. I'd be able to fly the ship and have it stable, but fancy maneuvering was off the table unless I found replacement actuator modules.

Identifying the fried control board was easy. Black and charred, it still smoked when I opened the access cover. No fixing that one, but it was part of relaying control to the missing turret. The remaining one would work just fine. I hoped.

The FTL drive? That turned out to be a bigger, and strange problem. Its outer casing looked fine. Removing an access cover showed machinery halfway to slag. Like butter half melted in a microwave. Burned away from the inside.

The strange impact as I got away—it had to be. They either fired some kind of weapon designed for this very effect, or the Inquisitors had a nasty spell to make sure ships didn't leave.

With some repairs the ship would fly off the island, but I wasn't leaving the planet in it. I'd noticed a couple of things on the nav screens on my way in, so there were options yet. If nothing else, if we made it off the island we'd hire a ship or buy passage off-world.

I gained three more points of Engineering, up to a respectable 22, but I needed spare parts. If the wreckage outside had them, I'd harvest what I found. Otherwise, I guessed I'd be stealing something on my way out with Silleste. Work with what you have.

I lowered the ramp, which stopped partway, blocked by a metal beam but open enough to slip through. I shone the beam of a repair kit flashlight around me.

Whatever compartment I'd ended up in had room for the ship with some to spare. The deck sloped the opposite direction from my ship. This thing hadn't made a much better landing than I had. The debris atop the ship didn't look major, and the budding engineer in me gauged I'd be able to fly out from under it.

I found a passageway and began my search.

The ship had to be a half kilometer long at least. One passageway brought me to a burned-through airlock to the forest outside. Armor plating sloped down eight meters to low underbrush, an easy enough scramble or slide down and an effortless, for me, jump back up.

I found areas where trees grew through cracks in the hull, surviving on what sunlight filtered through other cracks and the occasional missing hull sections. Vines spread through areas they should never have enough sunlight to survive in.

And I found bodies. I stopped counting after twenty, spread around multiple decks and sections. They'd been dead long enough to decay to bones in what remained of dark uniforms. Or nibbled to bones. Crew members that must have died in the crash.

I'd done a fair amount of exploring before I discovered my first intact consoles. Ten minutes gained me Two Scavenge points and a fair stock of control boards and circuit panels and modules. Some whole ship sections turned up nothing harvestable. Low skills fail more often.

I paused when I found half a body. This was not someone in a crash position, but one arm outstretched as if reaching for something. And it was just the upper half. Pelvis to boots was all missing, and nowhere in this area.

Something had killed this guy. And nasty, too.

I'd seen enough. It was time to head back and start repairing. At least Engineering was higher, so I hoped failures wouldn't destroy components I'd have to go hunt for all over again.

Something moved.

At least, I thought something moved. I saw it out of the corner of my eye. Not enough to catch what it was, but something had moved down a corridor to the left. Towards the ... which direction was aft?

Wandering in this wrecked tomb was messing with my head. I'd gotten turned around and nervous. The half corpse had me jumpy. But this place had been lifeless for ... years? Some forest critter curious about me poking around.

Better. That explanation made sense. Just a space raccoon or squirrel. Squirrel. Those were common enough in games, more so than raccoons. My hand rested on Gelrick's pistol at my hip, more useful in tight quarters than his carbine. Jumpy over a space squirrel. Some hero, right?

It happens so often in movies I should've expected it. You know what I'm talking about, right? Music gets tense, a cat jumps out. Scene continues, and we think we're past the scary part. Maybe the music creeps up again, maybe it doesn't. And then, bam. Axe to the face.

I fell flat on my face, my foot pulled out from under me.

In that instant I understood the pose of the half-man as I reached forward for something to grab onto while a gross, bluish tentacle dragged me backwards. I rolled to my back, still sliding right foot first toward an open doorway I'd ignored going past.

I saw it through the door. A mutant space squid from hell, bruise-blue with a body the size of an elephant's but without legs. Its hard shell scraped against the deck as it used other tentacles to pull itself towards me. A beaked mouth ringed with cone teeth opened side to side instead of up and down.

I swear the thing's tongue had eyes on it.

I managed to brace my free foot in the doorway, but this thing was strong. If I wanted to keep my leg, I needed to make this thing let go. Claws wouldn't reach, so I drew my pistol and emptied the power pack into the tentacle, praying I'd sever the thing before hitting my leg.

It let go. The bloody tentacle recoiled back to its body, hurt but still one long wriggling piece. Two others lashed out at me, and I scrambled backwards for dear life. One whipped my chest but didn't have enough length to grab. I triggered boosters to leap away as the beast slammed against the doorway, too big to fit through.

Twenty shots had only just pissed it off. Okay, fewer than half of those hit, but still. No, I couldn't put this monstrosity down with what I had on me.

I circled around, cautious of doorways, until I had my bearings. I found a cargo bay I'd crossed before, where vines hung from the ceiling and drums had rolled down the tilted deck to a pile. Now I wasn't far from the exit I'd found, which meant I also wasn't far from my ship.

A twig snapped. Except the twig was a vine about as thick as my wrist.

The mutant space squid hauled itself through underbrush that didn't belong. One bloody tentacle confirmed it was the same beast. I ran for the one of two doors I knew led to safety. I'm a quick hunter slash rogue slash bounty hunter, and I outran it and burst through the open doorway.

I'll be honest, I didn't stop running until I closed my ship's entry hatch behind me.

I checked the cockpit long enough to scan for any other ships in the area, but the sky remained clear. Just had to make sure.

I started on repairs, the control circuitry first. I hadn't been able to find an exact match, but between six others I'd pulled I cobbled together a combination that worked. An important first step.

I'd found two thruster actuator modules, which was a good thing. Yes, crafting and repairing skills in RiftWorlds Online can use up components on failures. I'd been raising Engineering at a steady rate since getting it, and the second failure didn't cost me the module. A third attempt worked.

I'd still have croissant-flaky upper rear shields, and I was still limited to this star system, but I had a ship to get me off the island. Plus, I'd happened upon a good place to leave it hidden while I went off on my rescue mission.

Stealing a bounty hunter's ship meant it came with his collection of bounty hunter gear. Binoculars I set aside with a chuckle; my own replaced eyes offered better magnification.

I grabbed the whole load of stun grenades. I plugged my empty power pack into the charger and loaded up with the full ones. Plenty of ammunition. Hopefully.

A comm set the size of a small lunch box meant I'd be able to scan comm frequencies, eavesdrop, and even jam them. No way I was leaving that behind.

A belt-mounted grappling hook line came with a compact launcher resembling a flare gun and came with four uses. Options.

And, to top it off, demolition charges and detonators with remotes!

No jetpack, though, and no hover bike in the cargo bay. Although even if I had one, I doubted the cargo elevator would open enough to get it out. So, hiking it was. That didn't bother me. I could cover ground at a good clip without getting tired. The nav screen suggested about four kilometers. An easy stroll through the forest.

About a kilometer out I froze as I heard voices ahead. A moment of quiet preceded the cracking and brushing noises of two men moving through the growth without even trying to be quiet. I waited, still, while their path led them across mine ten meters ahead.

Their green uniforms could've been any military or mercenary band, but a lack of insignia suggested otherwise. Simple cloth caps covered their heads instead of helmets, and basic looking communicators hung at their belts. No headsets, not even a shoulder mic. They did carry compact rifles at the ready.

I let them get some distance before I leapt. They heard my launch, and spun, rifles aimed where I'd been. They didn't register up enough though. I came down with an impressive hit.

> **Sneak Leap Power Attack Critical Hit! 401 Damage!**

> **+350 XP (13,000 total)**

Now that's what I'm talking about!

I'd already drawn the stun pistol. I blasted away at his partner until the sixth shot put him down. Each shot had added a cumulative effect, so hitting him the first time was critical, and after that he never stood a chance. Stun damage came with a debuff or stun effect. The inventory listing neglected to mention that.

+350 XP (13,350 total)

I stripped them of their communicators right away, and I used them to calibrate my comm scanner, telling it which frequencies to center on. These guys had been tough, all things considered. My level or higher. Good thing I had the jump on them—literally. If these represented what I'd find further on, this wasn't going to be easy.

Chapter 22

I prowled through the forest and reached the palace without other encounters. My comm scanner picked up guards checking in, giving me a partial inventory of my opposition. Each checked in about a minute after the group before.

"Rooftop One, all clear."

"Rooftop Two, good here." It was time to get closer.

"Grounds One, quiet."

"Grounds Two, rotating to the front."

This group came into view over a wall I climbed a tree to see over. Another pair, suggesting each group was a pair.

"Grounds Three, good here, too."

"Perimeter One, ready to rotate back."

Then came the pause I dreaded.

"Perimeter Two?"

I had to try, right? I keyed the mic on my looted communicator. "Perimeter Two, clear."

"Foyer, all quiet," the next group in line added. Nobody challenged me. My voice was either close enough or nobody was too attentive. Complacent? I could live with that.

Three more inside teams checked in before silence fell.

Assuming these were NPCs, they might spend their entire day, their entire existence, on their patrol area. But, RiftWorlds Online was proving itself more detailed than I expected. What if they rotated off in shifts like actual people would? I should have hidden the bodies of the ones I'd taken out, or at least moved them. Too late now.

From my tree branch vantage point I saw two sides of the palace. That was the word for it. Like a stereotype drug cartel boss's estate. Three separate small garages sat in a triangle formation from the main entrance where two huge doors might have withstood a ramming car if it made it up the steps and past pillars holding up a decorated overhang.

Two guards waited at the doors. Another pair, Grounds Two, wandered an expansive front yard with fountains and topiary. A holographic spaceship rotated on display, sleek with engine pods at the end of short wings.

A rooftop pair walked the edge of the roof behind a half wall. The sloped roof hid the other pair.

Another pair patrolled the side yard, close to the house out of view from the rooftop goons. A side door sat near the center of that wall. The pair stayed close to the door, not straying far. They were there as much to guard that door as much as watch the side yard.

Serious security. And nobody knew where this guy was? What did they think was going on here? It only took a short look to see criminal lair written all over the place.

I watched for five more minutes, shifting position closer to that side door, before the check-ins started again. Once more I passed myself off unchallenged. So perhaps not too serious. Or just not used to having to do their jobs. How many people just showed up here by accident? How often did someone try to break in?

Four pairs of eyes in the area watched for someone like me. No activating a magic hide ability and walking right up. I'd done okay so far with distractions, but saw fewer options for that here. But my tactical implant, good at tracking targets and trajectories, helped me notice something vital.

They patrolled with NPC regularity. For a seven-second window they all faced outward from the door, looking along the side of the house. The rooftop pair turned out first, walking a longer path than their grounded allies. As for the two blocking the door, the right one would turn first. The window came.

Leaping from a tree meant I got to start by jumping forward more than down. I tucked the landing and actually pulled off rolling to my feet. Two seconds of running got me behind Guard Right. Leap damage would have helped, but I'd take whatever I could get.

Sneak Power Attack Critical Hit! 321 Damage!

It didn't take him down without the added leap damage, but oh, so close. One shot from the stun pistol and he collapsed.

> **+350 XP (14,050 total)**

I spun and fired nine times to hit his partner six times and put him down.

I looted a security access card and looked at the door with a smile. No alarms sounded. No calls came through radios. I held the card up to a scanner by the door. Beep, the door slid open. Oh, yes. I had this.

The restaurant-grade kitchen I found inside sat empty this time of night. Good. Like I needed either some panicked staffer to sound an alarm or face off with an angry, knife-wielding cook. I could take a cook, but the fewer people I had to hurt the better. Even if none of them were real, every one meant the chance of an alarm sounded.

Few charges remained on the stun pistol, and its power pack wouldn't interchange with anything else. But it was quieter than the blasters, and as long as I had the element of surprise that mattered.

One door led to a pantry, easy to ignore and move on. But two more guards entered the far side of the dining room as I stepped into it.

With no sneak attack on my side a fire fight ensued. I ducked in the doorway for cover, and they did the same. I was more accurate, but they needed it less. Intense red laser beams sliced through wall and armor and flesh alike, hitting hard and claiming about a fifth of my Health before the first one went down to a run of carbine fire.

> **+350 XP (14,400 total)**

"Intruder in the dining room, taking fire," the second said through his radio. It echoed in mine. His focus on his radio rather than fighting cost him his life. But the element of surprise was gone.

> **+350 XP (14,750 total)**

Level 11 gained!
+26 Health
+26 Stamina
+9 Mana
+17 Focus
+5 Primary Characteristic Points
+10 Skill Points

With leveling up came full healing, and not bad timing. Still, I'd trade it back for him not getting that radio call off. An alarm sounded. I shook my head and sighed. Time to move. I snatched up the stun pistol I'd dropped for the carbine. Empty or not, I wanted to keep it for recharging back at the ship.

A short hallway brought me to a great hall lined with art and statues on posts. Doors led off in six directions. There was a day when loot in games didn't take up space in bags. A bag or backpack would hold a set number of items, or up to a maximum weight. I've played some of those retro games. Fun, but nowhere near as immersive. Stashing statues or paintings in a bag without worrying about how they'd fit would've been nice. The loot value in the room had to be considerable.

One statue distracted me for a moment, a detailed carving of a woman with a rifle. Her pose suggested leading a charge.

Her head exploded in a shower of dust as a laser beam sliced through it, too close to my own head.

Four guards had come in across the room. I lobbed a stun grenade at them and ran down a hallway. Two at once had worked as much through luck as anything else, and only with surprise. Four? No way.

This was not good.

Two more found me at an intersection. I took cover behind the corner long enough to wound both. I got away without taking damage, but worried they were herding me.

Rounding another corner brought me into a long hallway with doors on both sides. I needed time to think and come up with a plan. 'Sneak in and rescue the girl' was off the table now.

I ducked into a far room and shot the door controls behind me once the door closed. If they checked each door, at least they'd have to check a few before this one, and then they'd still have to get in. Perhaps only a couple minutes, but time to consider my options.

A conversation in the room stopped. I turned around, taking in the room and the eyes watching me.

Chapter 23

The room stretched out, big verging on cavernous, with a towering vaulted ceiling. To my left a practically naked elf with green hair in a ropy ponytail paused her dance on a peninsula stage reaching out from the wall. Past her, a gold and silver android bartender looked at me with emotionless orange eyes from behind a bar at the corner.

Taking in the room clockwise, two alcoves recessed into the left wall with shadowed booth seating. Massive murals of shifting artwork sat to either side of large double doors on the wall across from me.

If the room had started square, the wall to my right had been the start of converting it to a hexagon. Alcoves, similar to those on the opposite wall, lined it, one on each angled wall and a third in the corner. In that middle alcove an elven woman in a white gown stared at me with bewildered eyes, a stark contrast to the expressions on every other face. A chain ran from her neck to a bracket on the wall. Silleste, the only person in the room alone. The only one chained.

I mentioned other faces. Aside from figures in the alcoves, perhaps a dozen party-goers gathered near the middle of the room around a taller central figure. A central figure with an all too recognizable, gunmetal blue skull. Red eyes glared at me. The men and women around him dispersed to corners and alcoves as far out of the way as they could.

Nobody told me Kraxxan had four arms.

A red coat hung open to his knees, decorated in gold and screaming old-school pirate. All he lacked was the hat. An eye patch would've looked out of place on an android. Both legs ended in claw-toed feet. No peg legs here.

"You must be our intruder," his grating voice pointed out. One hand rested on a pistol, another on a sword hilt, the upper two arms he crossed in front of his chest.

"Nothing misses you, huh?" Damn, I needed more points in Charisma. Or was that charisma at work? Hey banter's cool, right?

Faces in the small crowd, the woman I was here for, and the android space pirate captain, all looked at me with variations on expecting.

"I'm here for the girl." No point in beating around the bush, right?

"Girl!" she protested. And there's the first impression I made on her.

"For Silleste," I corrected.

"No." He shook his head. "I don't think you'll be leaving here alive. But this could be fun. Who's ready for the entertainment?"

Cheers rose up around me. And they weren't cheering me on. Why didn't I refuse this whole thing? I could be in prison talking my way out of butt-stuff. Just then that seemed safer.

Kraxxan drew a pistol, quite the hand cannon, and his basket-hilted sword. I swapped for a fresh power pack in my rifle.

A hush fell like a curtain before the clicks and clacks and clangs—and a whine—of weapons being drawn throughout the room.

"No, he's mine," the pirate captain said with a dismissing wave of his sword. "Clear the room."

Feet shuffled as people who hadn't yet risen from booths joined others to inch their way around the room's circumference to the big doors. Kraxxan was big. Contours on his face suggested armor more than any attempt at a realistic appearance.

Buff: Nolora's Blessing of Valor
Divine blessings wash through you, lending you bravery and guiding your melee attacks. +66 Willpower, Toughness, Melee Attack, and Crit Power.

That was unexpected, but where it came from hardly confused me. If anyone else in the improvised arena had access to divine magic and had any reason to help me out, I sure didn't see them.

He fired first, an orange bolt of plasma, and I dodged towards the stage. The angry, hot blob of energized gas probably thousands of degrees passed so close I felt the heat on my cheek. I crouched along the stage edge for any cover I could get.

He avoided the shots I fired over the stage with an agility I didn't expect. Not a slow, cumbersome robot. The dancer shrieked and hopped off the stage, ducking down to put it between her and me. I didn't blame her, although why she hadn't already I don't know.

People closest to the double doors on the far wall filed out. They seemed calm about it but not wasting time. Not running away or evacuating, just deciding they had better places to be.

Kraxxan ran up and hopped onto the stage, doing away with any cover. Metal talons dug into the hard wood surface. I fired and fired, shots ripping into the tops of alcoves beyond the stage. The crowd dispersed through the doors faster, newfound motivation urging them on.

In the exchange we each hit the other. His health nudged down maybe 5%, I took 78 damage, almost all to my red Health bar. Plasma seared flesh more than it harmed the artificial parts of me. I guess that made sense for a pirate. Burning through bulkheads and hulls during a boarding attack wasn't the best move.

I leapt at him, throwing a claw power attack on the way up. He wasn't expecting that!

Sneak Leap Power Attack! 299 Damage!

It wasn't a critical hit, but still some serious damage. It took him to about 60%; I'd really hoped for more.

I continued past him, but before I'd even landed he grabbed me from behind and threw me. I hit the ceiling for a hard-hitting 140. Pain flashed as my red Health had fallen now to 36%, silver to 60%.

Buff: Nolora's Blessing of Protection
Divine blessings wash through you, hardening and protecting you.
+66 Toughness, Resistance, Mitigation, and Evasion.

Praise be to clerics, right? At least she was taking my side.

Another pistol plasma shot hit me as I regained my feet. It only hit for 15 after Resistance, but still knocked me down to just 28%.

He ran at me, and I got a shot off as he closed. And missed. I dove right, just avoiding his sword. It whistled as it sliced the air.

I spun and fired while he turned. Even that close he sidestepped and avoided my shot. His sword flashed, and the carbine sailed across the room out of my grip. My eyes followed it as it skittered toward a corner. I should have been paying attention to him, and my punishment was a plasma blast punching my stomach.

Just 20% of my red Health left. This was not going well. I was outclassed.

> **Holy light suffuses your body from within, healing you for 25 Health.**

That brought me back to 35%, not touching the silver bar at all.

With a snarl he turned and shot Silleste, knocking her down a solid third and scorching her white gown.

I had to get his attention off her! I drew my pistol and blasted away, hitting him three times . . . and not doing any damage at all. He had more Toughness than I did. How much more I couldn't guess. He had to be closer to mid-level content, intended for higher level players or small raiding groups.

He half turned and fired twice, barely looking where he was aiming, but still hit me once before I dove out of the way of the second. With the protection buff the pistol hit with a lot less oomph, but was still enough to knock me down to 30%. My silver bar still hovered above half.

He drew a dagger with one of his free hands, pairing it with his sword as he stalked towards Silleste, ignoring the pistol at his back that couldn't harm him. At some point she'd gotten free of her chains. She backed into the booth seat behind her and fell into it.

Oh, but turn your back on a Rogue, do you! I risked precious seconds for aim, needing every benefit I could get. I squeezed the trigger. Come on Sniper Shot.

> **Sneak Attack Critical hit! 347 damage!**

> **Pistol Skill +1 (16)**

The blast took him square in the back of the head. For all that damage, it didn't move him. But now he was the one down to just a quarter. He whirled as Silleste became a secondary threat. The look on his face, the blend of surprise and rage, . . . oh, that was priceless.

"Now I'm done playing around, boy." The anger faded into a cold, murderous intent.

I think I actually gulped.

I still had the gun lined up on him, and I fired away, but it just wasn't enough to hurt him. He charged, sword cocked back.

I still had claws. I wasn't out of this fight yet.

At the last second I leapt. He stepped around it easily, seeing it coming. You can't just use the same trick over and over. His swing caught me in the back as I sailed past him to crash into an alcove table, crushing the wood underneath me. At least that didn't do damage. As it was, Silleste's protection buff did more than my armor to stop it.

"Is that how you want to play it?" I taunted him, giving Silleste time to get another heal on me. Red bumped up to 40%. Perhaps I had a chance at this yet.

"Maybe." His fourth hand pulled a grenade from behind his back.

Really? Come on! Have I mentioned how much I hate grenades?

It seemed to sail through the air forever, a silver orb with blue and red stripes. The Leap cooldown timer taunted me, counting down much too slowly to save me. I dove forward out of the alcove, trading places with the grenade that ripped the booth behind me to splinters and threw me forward.

Stacking Toughness buffs, and some distance, meant I didn't take damage.

Until the kick I sailed into. I'm pretty sure it would have taken the wind out of me if I were human. As it was, I found myself spinning to land on my butt, useless pistol still in hand, in the middle of the room. Silver bar 32%, red 16.

Another 25 point heal made it 32 and 28%.

"Don't stretch this out, whoever you are," Silleste warned. How much mana did she have to trade for my ever-draining Health? This guy was too much for me to handle alone, no question. With a dedicated healer? Maybe.

Special Move: Backup Redundancy (Android special heal)

His Health bar shot back to 75%.

Not fair!

I got back to my feet, sorely in need of a plan. I backed toward the stage.

He ran at me again and I prayed he'd fall for it. After all, you can only use the same move so many times before they figure it out, and he already had.

He dodged to my right to avoid my claw strike, but I started my leap in that direction too, hoping for that feint bonus.

> **Leap Power Attack! 299 Damage!**

His sword came around in a fast back swing, but still didn't have enough force behind it to cause damage, just enough to mess up my landing. I tumbled and made it back to one knee.

He'd fallen to 40%, better but not enough.

Now it was his turn to be sailing through the air, coming down with a broadcasted power attack, his sword in a two-handed grip.

I still had my pistol out. I rolled and fired, not expecting it to do anything.

> **Critical hit! 173 damage!**

His sword dug into the floor, wedged deep. The critical hit took him to 20%, but it wasn't slowing him. He grabbed me once more and threw me. I landed on the bar, smashing through it and taking 10 damage. A heal fixed that and then some almost right away.

I had to get up. There was no backing down from this. He'd kill me if I didn't kill him first.

His pistol blasted hunks of plasma at me and the trashed bar. None of it hit me, but one blob ignited the spilled alcohol all around me. Flames spread across the floor, up the wall, and into more bottles stored under the bar. I leapt out and a bottle exploded beneath me.

Kraxxan disappeared through the big double doors. He'd ran away? Tactical withdrawal, I guess. No way he was afraid of fire, right? With 20% of his health, he had a decent amount left. There had to be another reason. Now wasn't the time to worry about it, though. Damn, that was close. too close.

"You're welcome. One more heal and then we should get going. I'm Silleste."

She finished her spell and pushed me up to 62% red, silver still hung unhealed at 29%. Repairs would take time I couldn't afford yet.

"I'm Max. I'm here to rescue you."

"The way that fight went, I'm not sure it wasn't me rescuing you."

"Thank you. Can we hash that out somewhere else?"

Flames spread along both walls from the corner bar and began their trip across the ceiling. Yes, staying and repairing here was not an option. Plus, I couldn't afford the chance Kraxxan had run for help instead of just running.

I grabbed my fallen rifle and we bolted to the hallway I'd come from, both to avoid the Space Pirate as to head back to the kitchen exit and freedom. Four guards blocked the way. Rifles came up. Silleste didn't need convincing. We ran deeper into the palace, away from kitchens or any parts I'd explored yet.

An explosion rumbled behind us as we ran. What might the expanding fire have found? Now was not really the time to question that. If one thing could explode, others could, too.

I spared a peek back before rounding a corner. The explosion hadn't affected the guards, who had grown in number from four to six. Sheesh.

I fired behind me blindly, not expecting to hit but hoping to slow them down.

A short hallway with a door on each side and another intersection beyond. Time to take a chance. 'Chase me,' I dared them in my head.

Footsteps pounded. I slapped a door control and tossed a stun grenade around the corner. As soon as I shoved Silleste through the door, I spun to close it behind us. I drew the stun pistol and pointed both guns at the door, hoping it wouldn't open and they'd keep running.

It had to turn out better than last time, right?

Chapter 24

Nothing moved in the dark. The room was dim even to my enhanced vision. No windows, no light sources. The thin line of dim gray at the bottom of the door offered the only hint of light.

Light blinked on; she'd found the switch. We took in a storeroom stacked with boxes and crates. Her eyes lit up spotting a spear leaning against one crate set aside from the rest. It stuck out.

She caught my attention more than haphazardly stacked boxes. Now I wasn't in immediate danger I studied the woman I'd been searching for. Gold highlights shone in brown hair in a classic pixie cut, just right for letting pointed ears poke out.

The greenest eyes I'd ever seen stared from a heart-shaped face with soft features, rounded off slopes. Her smile added a delightful warmth to skin leaning towards pale. Prettier in real life than her picture. Well, in person.

She opened the crate, popping latches and removing the cover. She squeaked. I'm not kidding. It was adorable, but don't tell her I said that.

"This'll help a lot," she announced. "My gear. And now this god-awful dress can go."

I didn't think it was that bad. The neckline was more conservative than I'd have suggested for her figure. Compared to what I'd seen so far, it was down-right modest.

Then again, this was also the President's eighteen-year-old daughter. Plunging cleavage wasn't what either of us needed right now.

She pulled at the laces down the front. "Do you mind?" She cleared her throat for punctuation.

"Sorry," I said as I turned.

"Too bad I can't simply insta-equip. Right now I wouldn't mind a little less realism. Give me a couple minutes here. Armor, you know."

"Armor's a good thing." I started on self-repair first aid while she was busy. I'd taken quite the pounding.

"So, you came to rescue me?" Chain mail rustled.

"It took some tracking down, but yes."

What to tell her? I hadn't taken the time to think that one out yet.

"There were some side quests on the way. I tracked down the bounty hunter who nabbed you. Did he do that himself, or was it the thugs he hired?"

"Oh, I know which one you're talking about. No, I only saw him. I'm dressed."

I turned.

If I hadn't known how old she was, I would've guessed older. She stood with a confident maturity, all woman and no helpless girl needing rescue. Hell, she was probably higher level than I was.

A white tabard hung to her knees draped over a chain hauberk neck to mid-thigh, slit up the front and back for riding. Steel pauldrons covered her shoulders and upper arms while sturdy gauntlets reached well past her wrists and encased most of her forearms. Polished greaves covered her knees and ran down over the front of brown boots. No ridiculous "boob armor," but the practical armor of a crusader. Yet it clung to her just enough to retain her femininity.

A brown leather pack hung at her back, a more Medieval version of mine. She held the double-ended spear in one hand while a large, round metal shield covered the left; a full-on Spartan warrior kit she hefted like someone well trained in their use. A curved scimitar hung at her hip. She looked more like a knight than Altion had.

"That looks more cleric."

"Thank you. I feel a lot better now."

"Good. I'm not sure how much chain mail works against lasers, though." Had it helped Altion? I honestly couldn't say.

"Energy weapons and spells go against Resistance, not Toughness. I have some advantages there. Besides, it looked like you needed more plain old physical armor against that android, Krakken or something like that."

"Kraxxan." Like I needed her to explain the difference between Resistance and Toughness. Even if the tutorial hadn't spelled it out, it wasn't hard to figure out. This wasn't the first game to separate the two.

"So, what got you started going after the bounty hunter . . . Grellick?"

"Gelrick, close. I think that's a story for a little later. I've got his ship a few clicks away at the beach. Let's get off this island, huh?"

"Fair enough.

I'd healed a good amount of biological Health, and repaired the artificial half past two thirds. Best I was going to get just now.

I put a fresh power pack in my rifle. Just one more after this.

"Let's go."

The hallway was clear. We moved out cautiously. Any minute I expected hordes of guard to round every corner. Or they had moved past and spread further away by the minute. We could follow behind their moving wave. That would be nice.

Which meant it couldn't happen.

The third corner we rounded brought us before another pair. Rifles came up, mine and theirs, and I hopped back for cover behind the corner. Silleste stayed cool, moving back and giving me room, heals at the ready. At least, I assumed she stood ready to heal me if I needed it.

I took a hit before downing one, but a grazing hit, nothing too bad. The man's partner broke and bolted. I checked the fallen rifle, the power pack was interchangeable with mine, but my rifle was better. These were not weapon link compatible. I took the pack from the rifle and two more off the dead man.

A large, formal living room expanded behind an open doorway. Three different conversation spaces with couches surrounding low tables with hologram projectors. One offered a 3-D model of the island. While nobody else was in the room with us I spared enough time to find out the model didn't show me much I didn't already know.

From there we pushed on through a pair of double doors into what proved to be the front entry atrium. Model ships lined the wall, showing a history of ships of sea and space. The Jolly Roger flew on each of the sail ones. A progression of pirate ships leading up to space piracy?

An explosion rocked the palace floor beneath our feet. Time to move. I signaled at the door and she readied her spear. I yanked a door open and we stormed through, an unlikely looking pair of commandos.

No guards stood on the patio, their posts deserted. Explosions boomed through the night one after the other and we ran for the wall.

"Hang on," I warned as I grabbed her and jumped over the wall. A final explosion tore leaves off tree branches above us. If we'd been seconds slower, we'd still be on the other side of the wall, the wall that sheltered us from the blast.

"Wow," was all Silleste had to say.

"I'm going to guess we won't be seeing more guards coming out of there." Another chance to breathe. A short hike to the ship and we'd be home free.

Chapter 25

"We've got a bit of a hike, but not too bad. Like I said, I've got a ship stashed and then we're out of here." I led the way through the forest.

The tree canopy shadowed the undergrowth and the brown and green forest floor and lent us both a sense of security. Silleste breathed easier. My breathing stayed just as steady as ever. The air cooled and a soft musk hung in the evening air. To my enhanced vision, it might as well have been noon. Her footing came sure and easy with elven night vision, not the careful steps of someone unsure of their footing in the dimness.

"So, who's Nolora?" I asked over my shoulder. Steel rings rubbed against each other as she walked. Not a lot of noise, but more than I made. Prowling through forests was becoming second nature for me.

"She's the goddess of Magic and Knowledge. You can be Clerics here, but I haven't heard anyone refer to her since leaving the Fantasy world. She's about knowledge being light, and sharing that light to push back the darkness of ignorance. Shining light to expose secrets. Stuff like that."

A simple and concise answer, I appreciated that. I'd realized as she started the risk of getting a complete sermon. Not all clerics are priests or priestesses.

"I take it you started here?" Her turn for questions, only fair.

"Well, not this planet, but this World, yeah. I'd—" I still didn't have a good explanation other than the awkward truth.

"It seemed like a good place to start," I covered. Hey, it was even honest. Starting a relationship lying wasn't a good start. With no way to know how long we'd be trapped here I wanted her a willing companion, even a friend. That meant being honest with her. Well, as honest as I could be.

How would she react if I told her everything? Would she appreciate the risk I'd taken coming in here? Would she ask what I'd been doing beforehand? She'd gotten out of the chains on her own. For all I knew she didn't need much actual rescuing. Or protecting, for that matter.

Whether she needed protecting, or how much, didn't matter. If she died, I was never leaving the room my body waited in. So, I had a vested interest regardless. That vested interest would become harder if she didn't want me around. I needed to be useful and non-offensive.

Yeah, non-offensive hasn't been a strong suit of mine so far.

"How'd you find out about me, anyway? I didn't get the impression I'd been kidnapped to create a quest for someone else. At the same time, nobody's struck me as another player. Not since the last planet I was on."

"Sir Altion?"

"You know him?"

"I ran into him on Relkit III." Now I knew how to explain things. "That's the planet I started on. We met at a bar, chatted over drinks, figured we quest together a bit." Hey, it was basically true. "When I asked how he'd gotten here, he told me about you and how you ended up here together. Then he talked about you guys being attacked, and him holding them off, and him seeing you get on a ship and getting away.

"He'd been watching for other signs of anyone following you. But he was worried. So I convinced him we should go track you down. We got jumped not long after getting here. That turned out to be Gelrick's men."

How close had she gotten with Altion? He'd never talked about how well they knew each other. Not enough to know who she was outside, but close enough for a friendship at least.

"There's something you're trying not to say, isn't there?"

I stopped and turned. This wasn't something to just say over my shoulder.

"He died in that attack. Saved me with a healing potion, but he got gunned down before he could drink his own."

"That sounds like him."

The happy glow I'd seen early faded from her face.

"I'm sorry."

"I've heard rumors," she started. "Rumor's that if we die here, we die outside. Do you think that's true?"

"I don't think there's a way to find out for sure. But we can't log out. Something's going on. I wouldn't be surprised if it's true, and I'm going on the assumption it is. I'd rather think that and be wrong than the other way around."

She shuddered. It had been an idea to her before, a possibility. One I'd made more real, more concrete. Way to go, right?

"So we stay careful," I suggested. "We assume it's true and we avoid unnecessary risks. We stay alive, no matter what."

"Yeah." The somber in her voice hurt to hear. Her footsteps came heavier, weighted down by a heart that lost its lightness.

"Good thing we've got a cleric with us," I teased. Her chuckle lifted things a little, but not to where things had been before.

I hadn't meant it to be prophetic.

Red beams of death carved through branches from above trying to reach us. I spun and brought up my rifle while she ran to the nearest tree for cover. A pair of aerial drones maneuvered among the branches where they had partial cover. My vision was still more than enough to spot them even if their laser fire didn't give away their position so thoroughly.

I aimed a shot, which hit and took the thing down by a solid two thirds. Their fire came in long, continuing beams that burned through thin branches as it chased me. I took 33 damage by the time I'd gotten a second hit to kill the first one.

+100 XP (14,850 total)

With only one I could avoid its fire a little easier. The two had coordinated their attacks, coming from either side and herding me so I had nowhere to dodge to. I rolled to another tree and blasted away until I knocked the second down.

+100 XP (14,950 total)

Not as much XP as the guards, or several recent encounters for that matter, but also easier to take down. We got moving again, not bothering with conversation and focusing more on speed.

More came, and we ran harder until Silleste's panting came in heaves. My Stamina bar shortened a little, but I'd make it to the ship before it ran out.

I was also faster than she was. Rogue versus cleric in armor.

"Keep running," I told her as I stopped and blasted another one out of the sky.

Four sliced at me with their lasers, and I avoided them long enough to take a second before I had to run. An added droning buzz meant more closing.

I fired behind me as I ran, now and then rounding a tree for enough cover for an aimed shot. One critical hit or two regular hits—that's what it took.

I nailed six before I gave up firing and focused on ducking and weaving and trying to never move in a straight line but also not move in any predictable pattern. She healed me as we ran, keeping up with the damage to my bio-Health.

"Fifty percent mana," she warned me when my silver bar had 10% left.

But we'd reached the hulk. The drones peeled off, replaced by a transport swooping out of the sky.

I pointed out the entrance as ten black-clad commando slash space ninjas jumped out of the transport behind us. We raced inside under a hail of plasma rifle fire.

Four cybernetic hit points remained. If the plasma fire had been laser or blaster fire, I would've died in the doorway.

"I've got a plan. It might be a really stupid one, but it's a plan." I led her down the corridor. Space Ninjas. Sheesh.

"Better than I've got," she said as she followed. "I wish I could heal and run at the same time. I'm down to 40% Health, and mana's getting low."

"Save it. If this goes wrong you're going to need all of it."

I all but pushed her around a corner and out of the straightaway as plasma bolts flew behind us. They were inside and close behind. And quiet, too. Stupid Space Ninjas.

Through an open space, yes, I'd found it. I led her into the large bay. Foliage spread across the angled deck. Vines draping from the ceiling provided minor visual obstruction. But there were a few things large enough to hide behind. I led her past them, urging her to move as quietly as she could.

She didn't pull off silent, but quieter than she'd walked before, and a lot quieter than running. Her tortured breathing came loudest of all.

A blast hit her backpack, scorching but not destroying it. But we'd reached the far door, the important one.

"Move down the corridor and wait. Throw a heal, I need to slow them down."

I took cover in the doorway while laying down fire to slow their advance. Black ninjas spread throughout the open space. Sword hilts rose above each right shoulder. I'm serious: Space Ninjas. With plasma rifles.

But I had a weapon of my own. I just needed them forward enough to spring the trap. I tossed a stun grenade. It didn't get close enough to any of them to affect them, but the noise and flash in the enclosed space drew attention. I emptied another power pack with delaying fire.

A black form fell to the deck, and the screaming began.

Ha! Deal with that, jerks.

"Come on, time to go. If they make it through that at all it'll at least buy us enough time to get off this island."

"Get through what?"

"Something they weren't expecting. Something I found when I got here." The tentacle monster.

Chapter 26

Screams echoed behind us. Tortured, blood-curdling ones. The ship had never looked so welcoming, so inviting. I escorted her in and closed the ramp behind us.

"I don't think they're going to bother us again."

"Do I want to know what's back there?"

"You ever heard of Cthulhu?"

"Cth-what?"

"No, then. Never mind. Creepy monster with long tentacles. The kind that rip people apart. So, I don't think we're going to see those guys again." What do eighteen-year-olds read these days, anyway?

She shuddered and followed me to the cockpit and parceled out mana, healing me while I rushed through pre-flight checks. "Mana comes back faster than Health." Healing didn't seem crucial, but I saw no reason to complain.

Damage to the artificial parts still worried me, and that wasn't going to come back on its own fast enough to matter while I was working on other things. I spared a minute for some quick repairs while the reactor warmed up. At the same time, if something took out the ship it wouldn't matter how many hit points I had.

"Clever hiding your ship in here." She took the empty seat, looking at navigational displays. They bewildered her. "You can read this?"

I chuckled, changing power distribution to ready the thrusters. "Yes. Between starting off here to begin with and some points in the Pilot skill it mostly makes sense so far."

"It's just gibberish to me. Might as well be Egyptian hieroglyphs."

"Do you have any classes other than Cleric?"

"Not so far, no."

"Then I guess reading starship controls isn't really in a fantasy Cleric skillset," I suggested. "I probably have as much chance of reading a magic scroll."

"What about you?" she asked.

"Hang on." I nudged the throttle and metal groaned as the ship pushed against debris on top of it. More throttle brought scraping, and we broke free, lurching out over the waves. I pulled us up and angled for the sky.

"So, classes?" she asked again, not giving up.

Orbit would take about a minute, I could spare a little time for conversation. "I started out a Hunter. Basically the space safari type, I guess. Then I came across a group of rogues, and picked that up. Once I hit level ten, and after dealing with the bounty hunter, I got to add that one, too."

A quick lean over to check the screens at her station gave me the chance to notice she smelled good. A nice floral aroma like a really nice shampoo. Must be an elf thing, although I hadn't noticed other elves having any scent to them. Then again, I hadn't spent much time that close to any.

But I wasn't leaning close to her to check her out. Instruments. Navigation and short-range scanners first. I pointed them out as I checked them. If there was any pursuit, it would show up right . . . crap.

One blip coming out from behind the mountain and closing fast. I shoved the throttle forward to put on speed, but it still closed. I tapped on it and dragged to the identification software as a laser bolt lanced overhead.

I pointed at the screen, all the time I could spare, before banking hard left.

"What does that say?"

"I can't read it, remember?"

Right. So she was going to be completely useless for the moment. Fine. More lasers came after me and I kept dodging, but each dodge let whoever it was close even faster.

"You are not getting off this planet alive," Kraxxan's voice warned over communications. I think I actually growled out loud.

"Bite me," I replied without triggering the transmitter. Swerving and weaving and setting up targeting took enough attention as it was.

An insistent beeping I hadn't heard before stole some of that attention.

"MISSILE LOCK," a display warned. Two new blips raced from Kraxxan's ship. My evasion turned me around completely, enough to see his ship, a heavy fighter all black except the white skull and crossbones prominent on tail fins. I dove at the last minute, hoping my ship was more maneuverable than the missiles.

Two proximity blasts shook the ship and rattled my teeth. Damage indicators sprang up all around the cockpit. I pulled up away from the water; the ship reacting sluggishly.

Shields! That's what I'd forgotten. I threw their power into the one turret and fired. The fireball brought a wave of relief.

+500 XP (15,450 total)

Five hundred, huh? I'd expected more, considering how outclassed I was for my level.

Red lights spread across the controls as if a disease epidemic were being mapped out. New beeping added to an already unpleasant out-of-tune chorus of them.

"Are we okay?"

I pulled up more. Once I reached orbit I could assess the damage and see what I could fix while we cruised to jump distance.

The ship shuddered as one thruster struggled to work at all. We weren't gaining altitude. I increased throttle more, almost leveling off. No, still descending, just slower.

"No, we're not okay. Not unless. . . ."

I changed the navigation display to local. I needed a place to set down, but I'd be damned if I was going back to that island.

Ocean in every direction. No other land in view. I zoomed out one step. Still no land, but one unlabeled blue marker I'd noticed on the way in. I steered for it, not seeing any other choice.

"There's something ahead. Maybe an ocean ship or something. If we can reach that maybe we can get help."

The ship's nose angled up, blocking me from seeing how close the waves lapped below us. But an altitude display counted down with alarming speed. 450 . . . meters?

Another thruster failed, and the ship leaned to the right. Artificial gravity went next, and my left hand grabbed a handle on the bulkhead so I wouldn't fall into Silleste. Flying the ship one-handed didn't help. The altitude display winked out at 385. Now even flight instruments were failing.

Some rescue. I'd come all this way to find her and get her just to crash into the ocean.

"That's a Rift." Silleste pointed forward, identifying the blue dot for me.

"That's where we're headed," I explained as if I'd known the whole time. "We'll get through there, which also gets us away from this World and any other friends Kraxxan might have left. Then we'll see about repairing the ship."

"Any idea where it goes?"

The rift hung in the air before us, an oval shaped hole torn in reality. Uneven, jagged edges shifted. I didn't want to think about what touching that edge would do. The most impenetrable blackness I'd ever imagined didn't even show a true surface. I had no idea what to expect when we hit it, but diving through it was our only escape.

"We're about to find out."

Blackness expanded before us, growing larger to accommodate the ship. Touching the edge wasn't a concern, then. We reached the blackness, diving into it. She'd been though one before and knew what it was. So we weren't falling into a black hole or oblivion. We'd come out the other side to an entirely different game world.

Somewhere safe.

Somewhere we could start fresh while we waited for techs outside to fix things so we could log off.

I'd rescued her after all.

Entering Fantasa'an. . . .

~~~

Thank you for reading! I hope you enjoyed it! If you did, please leave a review at Amazon or Goodreads or your favorite book site. Reviews and word-of-mouth are some of the best ways to help other people find me and my books. It helps a ton and I really appreciate it.

Be among the first to find out about my newest releases by signing up at my website NOW:
            www.BrianDHowardAuthor.wordpress.com/preferred

If you're on Facebook, check out my discussion group for all things LitRPG and for inside scoops on RiftWorlds:
            RiftWorlds Online and Other LitRPG

ALSO AVAILABLE FROM BRIAN HOWARD

Simon Rising

A telekinetic on the run. An FBI Agent determined to stop him. A mob boss with a secret plan. A hitman with too much on the line.

Steven Ambrose wakes up paralyzed in the hospital with no memory, only to be told he's a serial bank robber shot in the head while being arrested. Everything changes when he discovers he has telekinetic powers.

Now on the run, hunted by FBI Special Agent Rachel Moore, and with unknown enemies around every corner, can he change who he is, or is the dark criminal everyone accuses him of being too deeply a part of his nature to escape?

Rectifier - The Electric Man

Oliver Stewart just wanted to be left alone after his life fell apart. He never expected to be kidnapped by a secret lab and dumped in a mass grave, left for dead as a failed experiment.

Except it didn't fail.

Now he can control electricity.

When the people he feels most responsible for, some only teenagers, are abducted by the same men in their van, the clock ticks down before they end up dead—or worse.

To save them he'll have to confront his most shameful mistakes, find the lab to mount an impossible rescue, and pick sides in a vicious gang war with far-reaching implications.

This gritty, must-read adventure is the second book in the After the Crash superhero series but stands alone as a complete story.

ABOUT BRIAN D HOWARD

I have been creating and writing stories since my early childhood. I am driven by "what if" questions, and often those lead to story or book ideas. I have lived in a motorhome seeing much of the United States and plan international travel later.

My favorite genres to write are:
- Superhero (After the Crash series: what if an alien ship crashed to Earth and gave people powers?)
- LitRPG (what if virtual MMOs let us upload ourselves into them...but we can't log out?)
- Post-Apocalypse (After the Fall series: what if we defeated an alien invasion, but civilization collapsed in the process?)
- Military Sci-Fi (Series to be named: What if aliens found us and gave us the chance to explore the galaxy?)
- Urban Fantasy (What if aliens . . . sorry. What if magic *was* real?)

Want to know more? I post progress updates and insights into my writing process at my blog at:
www.BrianDHowardAuthor.wordpress.com

Made in the USA
Columbia, SC
10 March 2019